THE MUSHROOM JUNGLE

A HISTORY OF POSTWAR PAPERBACK PUBLISHING

Steve Holland

ZEON BOOKS, ENGLAND

First published 1993

by ZEON Books, an associate company of Zardoz Books

20 Whitecroft, Dilton Marsh, Westbury, Wiltshire BA13 4DJ

copyright 1993 Steve Holland

Illustrations provided by Maurice Flanagan, Steve Chibnall &
Roland Gigg. Illustration notes - M Flanagan. Manuscript
editing by Steve Chibnall

Printed by Hobbs the Printers of Southampton

STEVE HOLLAND, the author of THE MUSHROOM
JUNGLE, is the editor of the national monthly magazine Comic
World (winner of the 1993 CCG Special Award) and author of
two earlier popular histories of British publishing, THE
TRIALS OF HANK JANSON and VULTURES OF THE
VOID (the latter with Philip Harbottle). Regarded by many as
the authority on British paperback publishing, he has written
over 250 articles on a variety of topics, published in Britain,
America, Holland, Germany, Sweden and Italy. He has
appeared on BBC and local radio, BBC1 and Channel 4
television, and written everything from childrens comic strips to
entries for encyclopaedias.

Dedication

**This is for Phil Harbottle who started me off on this crazy
road. But, thankfully, provided me with a map**

British Library Cataloguing in Publication Data

Holland, Steve

The Mushroom Jungle - A history of Postwar Paperback
Publishing

ISBN 1-874113-01-7

THE

MUSHROOM

JUNGLE

A HISTORY OF POSTWAR PAPERBACK PUBLISHING

The modern paperback book is familiar to us all, and is regarded as a disposable form of literature by many. When asked about paperbacks, we immediately think of "blockbuster" authors who may be regarded with some degree of literary contempt by the "cognisati". This picture has changed little since the 50s when the novels of "Hank Janson" may have sold in hundreds of thousands but were regarded with even more contempt by the then establishment.

The 50s may have been a so-called period of austerity, with rationing still in place and few of todays luxuries, but in publishing this impression couldn't have been further from the truth. The postwar years brought new blood, and fresh ideas into publishing that would revolutionize the industry and leave its legacy to this day.

A new generation of publishers, authors and artists burst out from the war year restrictions and capitalised on the lack of, particularly US, competition to produce a "mushrooming" of paperback publishing.

The paperbacks sported "lurid" covers, most unlike their immediate forbears and contemporaries, such as Penguin, Albatross and Cherry Tree. They covered every possible genre from Crime to Romance, and Science Fiction to Westerns. Whilst the larger paperback houses of Penguin and Pan produced popular reprints of mainstream authors, the "mushroom" publishers" produced many original fast moving adventure stories, and even invented a few "genres" of their own.

HERE FOR THE FIRST TIME IS THEIR STORY

CONTENTS

ACKNOWLEDGMENTS

A work of this length cannot be written without help, and the following people have provided so much insight into the workings of the mushroom publishers that I am forever in their debt. I hope this brief telling of a piece of British publishing history justifies all the hard work they put in.

A special thanks must be made to Phil Harbottle, Mike Ashley and Bill Lofts who first set me on this rocky road, and to Vic Berch for his detective work in the USA tracking down copyright records. Steve Chibnall, enthusiast, researcher, and all-round expert on the mushroom publishers, acted as my editor on this volume, and his advice and valiant efforts to keep me on track (and concise) cannot be over praised.

My thanks are due also to Derek J. Adley, John Clark, Henry Assael, Brian Babani, W. Howard Baker, Christine Barnes, John Boothe, Syd J. Bounds, David and Rita Boyce, Geoff Bradley, Victor Briggs, John Brunner, Ken Bulmer, John F. Burke, Mrs. Arthur Catherall, Vince Clarke, Tony Crouch, Ron S. Embleton, Doug Enefer, Gerald Evans, Lionel and Patricia Fanthorpe, Ralph L. Finn, Graham and Heather Fisher, Maurice Flanagan, Stephen and Theresa Frances, Denis Gifford, Tony Glynn, Barrington Gray, Leonard Gribble, John T. Griffin, Peter Haining, John Hammond, Vic J. Hanson, Peter Hawkins, George Hay, Richard Hoggart, Geraldine Hossent, Doris Howe, Allen J. Hubin, Robert Hugill, Mrs Irene Ingham, Matthew Japp, Hector Kelly, Arthur Kent, John Knight, Gordon Landsborough, Norman Lazenby, Cliff and Judy Lewis, Chris Lowder, Patrick McCormick, Phillipa Macleish of the Society of Authors, Thomas Martin, William Newton, Victor and Elizabeth Norwood, Frank S. Pepper, Stephen Reiter, John Reynolds, Patricia Robins, Derrick Rowles, Geoff Sadler, Patrick Selby, Dick Sharples, Charles Skilton, Oswald F. Snelling, Brian Stableford, Derek Thompson, Ted Tubb, Eve Turvey, Jon Tuska, Gray Usher, Dave Ward, Mrs. Mavis Ward, John Watson, David Whitehead, Richard Williams, Lisle Willis, Bevis Winter, Mrs. Joan Whitford, the staff of the British Library, Chelmsford Library, and the various other libraries up and down the country who responded to enquiries. If I have missed anyone out, I apologise in advance.

Quotes used throughout come from personal correspondence unless otherwise stated. A number of quotes are extracted from articles originally commissioned by Philip Harbottle and are used by permission. The extract from *The Uses of Literacy* by Richard Hoggert is used by permission of Richard Hoggert and Chatto & Windus.

FOREWORD

by Brian Stableford

It is traditional for books like this one to begin, guardedly, by quoting their enemies. Steve Holland begins his own introduction by quoting Queenie Leavis, the Literary Establishment's answer to Red Sonja, so - for the sake of being different - I shall start with a more subtle but no less destructive litcrit Robocop: C. S. Lewis.

Lewis attempts in *An Experiment in Criticism* to reach an understanding of the differences between good and bad books by means of a study of the behaviour patterns of their readers. He begins by pointing out that not all acts of reading are alike, and that such acts extend over a spectrum so wide as to call into question the use of a single term of description, and wonders whether certain kinds of book-use should be considered as "reading" at all. Not unnaturally, Lewis's inclination is to think of his manner of book-use as the "correct" one, while the different kinds of use which some other people make of texts - texts of the kind which form the subject-matter of *The Mushroom Jungle* - seem to him both alien and perverse. He is somewhat alarmed, if not frankly horrified, by the realization that the majority of people not only fail to appreciate the books which he considers to be worth reading, but actually finds them inadequate to their own purposes.

Lewis sums up this observation as follows: "Offer an unliterary twelve-year-old.... *Treasure Island* instead of the Boys' Bloods about pirates which are his usual fare, or offer Wells's *First Men in the Moon* to a reader of the infimal sorts of science fiction. You will often be disappointed. You give them, it would seem, just the sort of matter they want, but all far better done; descriptions that really describe, dialogue that can produce some illusion, characters one can distinctly imagine. They peck about at it and presently lay the book aside. There is something about it that has put them off."

The word "infimal" is not in Chambers, but the Latin phrase

infima species is; this is defined as "the lowest species included in a genus or class". Unlike C.S. Lewis, I am a biologist by training, and I am thus conscious of the fact that the term *infima species* is a hangover from an obsolete way of thinking. People do still speak of natural organisms as "higher" or "lower" (not unnaturally, our inclination is to think of our own species as the highest of all) but in the post-Darwinian era such terms cannot have the literal implications which they had in the days when people believed in a devinely-ordained Great Chain of Being in which every species had its allotted status. We know well enough how nonsensical it would be for a modern biologist to proclaim that the invertebrates were unworthy of scientific study because they were "lower" than the vertebrates, or that biological research in the universities ought to concentrate entirely on birds, because birds were intrinsically more beautiful than lesser species. We are however, well used to hearing literary critics speak in that sort of way about their own field and it is not entirely surprising that Lewis should find the biologically-obsolete term "infimal" convenient for the purposes of his argument.

****

It is no surprise, given the nature of his initial assumptions, that Lewis's experiment in criticism does not produce the goods. He fails to reach any real understanding of why it is that the majority of people like to read books that he deplores. It does not help him, in the end, to reverse the direction of the argument that bad taste is a preference for bad books, because the reversal only permits him to say that bad books are produced in order to serve bad taste. The word "bad" and all it implies is built into his argument at the axiomatic level, and although he tries hard to build a competent description of what "bad reading" is, in order to complement his convictions about what "bad books" are, the only result is that he is led to express abhorrence for the people who read the books he deplores as well as the texts themselves.

Lewis is not alone in this; hatred and revulsion for what the majority of readers enjoy reading lie at the heart of the great tradition of English literary criticism, amply exemplified in the vituperations of Dr. and Dr. Leavis. All members of this remarkable and not-yet-extinct species takes it for granted that readers who read the wrong books in the wrong way do so because they are less worthy people than themselves, and that readers who like "the infimal sorts of science fiction" (or, of course, any of the others kinds of fiction which flourished in "the mushroom jungle") are part of the *infima species* of mankind.

Lewis goes on to draw up a list of attributes of "unliterary reading". Such reading, he points out, is frequently reserved for time which might otherwise be difficult to fill - people read on journeys, or while sunbathing, in order to relieve boredom. There is, he notes, a practice called "reading oneself to sleep" whereby unliterary readers who begin a book with no memory of having read it before will instantly stop and discard it when they realise they *have* read it, even though they can remember almost nothing about it. Lewis is unable to understand any of this; it seems to him to be at best unintelligent and at worst perverse - so much so that it almost makes his flesh creep.

****

A more constructive attempt to understand these phenomena has been undertaken by the sociologist of literature Robert Escarpit, who draws a useful distinction between "connoisseur reading" and "consumer reading". Broadly speaking, connoisseur reading involves close attention, intelligent interest and some sense of educative purpose; it is an active kind of reading whereby the attentive reader brings to bear upon the text various kinds of knowledge he already has, without whose recruitment much of the meaning of the text would evade him. Consumer reading is a more relaxed business which can be accomplished far more passively; it is much less like hard work. In consumer reading the text is only important while it is being consumed - it does not require careful attention from the reader or leave much of a lasting impression. It is more akin to daydreaming than it is to constructive thought.

Escarpit notes that we sometimes talk about books using metaphors borrowed from the vocabulary of nutrition, and suggests that literary critics are like dieticians in that they generally approve of books which are full of meaty food for thought and generally disapprove of books which are, metaphorically speaking, sugary literary confections. Unlike Lewis, Escarpit does not think that there are two distict tribes of readers, but rather that we all do both kinds of reading. He suggests that just as all food has some nutritional value and some taste, so all books have some potential for connoisseur reading and some potential for consumer reading. Just as there are some foods which are valued almost entirely for their nutritional qualities and some almost entirely for their sweet taste, though, so there are some books which may be valued almost entirely for their usefulness in connoisseur reading and some which may be valued almost entirely for their appeal in consumer reading.

In this way of thinking, the mere fact that "consumer reading" is not "connoisseur reading" should not be held against it, and the fact that consumer fiction does not suit the purposes of consumer reading is no justification for condemnation. Rather than simply writing consumer fiction off as something horrid and hateful, which is not only undeserving of study but should be conscientiously excluded from study, one ought actually to try to understand how such fiction comes into being and what functions it actually performs. The Lewises and Leavises of this world are as ill-fitted to this task as arachnophobes are to the study of spiders, but this does not mean that the work should remain undone. In time, no doubt, it will be done - but before it can even be started, the bibliographical groundwork must be laid. Before the phenomenon of consumer fiction can be understood, it must first be described, and that is why *The Mushroom Jungle* is a very valuable book, in spite of being the kind of book that the Lewises and Leavises of this world hate and despise.

The work which Steve Holland has done in order to research this book has been undertaken as a labour of love, out of interest's sake alone, but its readers ought to recognise that this authentic scholarship of a kind that is all the more valuable by virtue of the fact that it deals with a subject-matter of which many people are proud - ludicrously, insanely, stupidly *proud* - to be utterly ignorant. *The Mushroom Jungle* is a precious resource for anyone interested in the evolution of consumer fiction in Britain, complementing the work which has recently been done on Victoria "penny dreadfuls" by such writers as Louis James. If the Ivory Towers of Literary Academe are ever to be penetrated by the revolutionary idea that the work of authentic scholars is to study what exists, and to study all that exists, rather than campaigning on behalf of those things which somehow seem more *deserving* of existence than the rest, *The Mushroom Jungle* - or, more likely, a semi-sanitised semi-plagiarism by some academic hack who specialises in repackaging the research of better men - will take its place on university reading lists,

Fiction - including the kinds which are dignified by the title of Literature - is a product, and it is shaped by its marketplaces. It is not a crudely utilitarian product like wheat, or copper, or paper, whose economics can fairly easily be described in with the aid of simple instruments like the "law" of supply and demand. It is more like patent medicines, women's clothing and soft furnishings - products which are vulnerable to such economically-problematic phenomena as the placebo effect, fashion and comfort. Like the marketplace of patent medicines, the marketplace of fiction is an arena of wild hype, blatant dishonesty and absurd mysticism; like the marketplace of soft furnishings, the marketplace of fiction is much concerned with the things people lie on when they are or are not asleep, and with the curtaining of the transparent boundaries which separate the public and private worlds, through which people peep in both directions.

Because of its nature, the fiction market is very vulnerable to such buffetings as the cartel-inspired price-fixing it suffered in the 19th. century, when Mudie's Circulating Library took such a high percentage of the print run of new novels that Mudie was able to dictate - purely in his own economic interest - that upmarket novels (i.e., textual patent medicines, fashion garments and lace curtains specialising in the existential angsts of the rich) must be three volumes long and must retail at an absurdly high price per volume. It is to Mudie, and not to the genius of its authors, that we owe the absurdly overblown character of the 19th century English novel; and - because the Invisible Hand of the marketplace becomes prey to idiosyncrasy whenever corners are created - it is to Mudie's horror of prurience that we owe the 19th century English's novel's absurdly extreme prissiness.

Had it not been for railways and America, Mudie's descendants might still be controlling the form of English fiction to the present day, but railways begat long, boring journeys which even the aspirin-adoring lower middle-classes could afford, and hence begat railway bookstalls whose franchise was awarded to the old firm of W.H. Smith, and thus begat cheap single-volume reprints which made Lord Lytton a rich man even before he inherited the family estate from the censorious parent who had earlier cut him off without a penny, and... well, the rest is history.

The point of all this is that species of fiction emerge from specific sets of economic circumstances, not from some magical wellhead of genius which struggles to spurt forth from the pens of those appointed by Destiny to be Authors. As Steve Holland explains herein, the buffeting which the British fiction market received between 1940 and 1947 as a result of paper rationing was Adolf Hitler's gift to the British paperback book, which had previously struggled to get a toehold in a marketplace which was as firmly stitched-up as any Mafia-operated scam; as well as making the fortune of John Lane's Penguin books (which would otherwise have been swiftly driven into bankruptcy), the Panzer divisions begat Paul Renin and Hank Janson and Vargo Statten and.... well, the rest is history, although the history is as yet largely untold.

The Mushroom Jungle is an important pioneering work in this telling, and it boldly sets forth along paths which few human feet have ever trod. For the moment, it's most enthusiastic audience will be composed of collectors of old paperback books, who are becoming steadily more numerous and more avid as the books themselves become scarcer, that being the logic of all esoteric marketplaces - but history teaches us that where eccentric antiquarians lead, methodical archeologists eventually follow.

The collecting of old paperbacks may appear to blinkered onlookers to be a proto-neurotic manifestation of Asperger's syndrome (in whose full-blown form sufferers take such assiduous refuge from complex reality in cultivating special fields of expertise that they gradually lose contact with the reality) but the people who are doing it are building up treasure troves which will one day enlighten and enrich their eventual finders. The assistance which Steve Holland's book can render to such collectors now will be a valuable asset - and the legacy of that assistance will, in the longer term, be a significant contribution to a proper understanding of why people like to read the things they like to read and not (for the most part) the things literary critics insist they ought to like to read.

INTRODUCTION

In her study of popular writing, *Fiction and the Reading Public*
Q.D. Leavis made a lengthy examination of the most popular
authors of her day. Penned in the early 1930s, the book was
something of a detective novel itself, with Mrs. Leavis playing
at different times the tough, cynical shamus, the coroner and the
judge.

The book opens, like many a good crime novel, with a body, in
this case the body of fiction known as Great Literature.

Great Literature is dead. Mrs. Leavis launches into her forensic
examination. Expert witnesses are called: Edgar Wallace, Edgar
Rice Burroughs, Philip Gibbs, Maud Diver and twenty or so
other highly popular authors of the 1920s give evidence from
which the character of popular fiction is determined. Who were
the people associated with "best-sellers"? Sworn testimony
points to the reading public who not only knew them, but
actively sought them out at every opportunity. Where did they
meet? At circulating libraries, at newsagents and bookshops.
Mrs. Leavis reaches her first conclusion: best-sellers are so
popular that Great Literature has been smothered.

The corpse is tagged and left in the morgue as Mrs. Leavis sets
out to find the murderer in the second part of her study. She
pulls in history for questioning and cross-examines the
development of journalism and book publishing. What events
led up to the ghastly suffocation of Literature? Mrs. Leavis
discovers that the advent of cheap editions around 1850 meant
that "the fiction habit, therefore, had been acquired by the
general public long before the Education Act of 1870, the only
effect of which on the book market was to swell the ranks of
the half-educated half a generation later (until then educated
taste had managed to hold its own)."

Already dizzy from the grim realization that educated taste was
being threatened by the man on the street, Mrs. Leavis rounds
up her suspects, but makes the unfortunate mistake of revealing
the murderer half-way through the book instead of holding out
for a gripping drawing room showdown: her accusing finger

points at Lord Lytton (author of such works as Paul Clifford (1830) and *The Last Days of Pompeii* (1834)) of whom she says "to make a useful generalisation, bestsellers before Lytton are at worst dull, but ever since they have almost always been vulgar...the direction Lytton gave to popular fiction caused it to set its face away from literature".

Thereon, the downfall of Literature is charted with breathless speed: "Nothing can better illustrate the immense drop from the highly critical and intelligent society led by Charles Fox to later Victorian taste than the nature of Marie Corelli," says Mrs L. "If one considers successively a few pages of Mrs. Radcliffe or Scott, of George Eliot, of Mrs. Humphrey Ward, and finally of Hugh Walpole or Wells or Galsworthy (to restrict the test to the reading of the educated), one is impressed both with the sudden atrophy of the attention in the reader and his reduced reading capacity...apply the same test to the reading of the uneducated - Dickens, Marie Corelli, Edgar Wallace..."

The whodunnit is solved: it was the public, in the circulating library, with the best-seller. Mrs. Leavis dons her black cap and solemnly intones her judgement: "Working from the findings of this essay a censorship of fiction would find it necessary to suppress most of the bestsellers of the last fifty years and some before them - Charles Kingsley for instance...If this essay has given evidence only to this effect, it will in the writer's opinion have amply justified itself."

If Mrs Leavis wanted to suppress the works of Charles Dickens in the 1930s it makes you wonder what she would have made of *Hot Dames on Cold Slabs* or *Virgin's Die Lonely,* not to mention *Blondie Beg Your Bullet,* or any one of the paperback books read in their hundreds of thousands two decades later.

* * * * * * *

This is the story of a publishing phenomenon, the story of the mushroom publishers of the post-War decade. I use the term "mushroom" throughout to describe the many small publishers who sprang up in the days of paper rationing to slake the public's thirst for reading matter, usually with cheaply produced paperback novels. The term was used by contemporary writers to describe the fly-by-night antics of some of these publishers, whom one writer described as the "here today, gone tomorrow variety".

This book was never intended as a deep psychological or sociological study of fiction, but perhaps it will provide a skeleton of history for any analysts who care to follow. The history of the British mass market paperback has been conspicuously absent in studies of the Great British Novel, and no doubt much could be made of the Americanisation of British fiction appearing in paperback in comparison to the work of Orwell, Koestler, Priestley, or Evelyn Waugh which was appearing at the same time in hardcover. The novels of Hank Janson and Ben Sarto outsold these authors by tens of thousands, but neither have appeared in any study of British fiction: when history is written, the tastes of the reading public count for nothing. I very much doubt if any of the novels quoted in this book were written with any intention other than to put food on the table of the author, but, like so much that is thought by the literary establishment to be ephemeral or unworthy, they stick in the memory of the reading public and tug at those parts of the mind dedicated to backward-glances and feelings of nostalgia.

Here then is the story of the mushroom publishers, a story that spans the ten years of post-War Britain when rationing and regulation dictated our lives in a way that can barely be conceived by those who did not live through it. It is also the story of some of the people who created the paperback· boom, the authors and publishers who produced the best-sellers of the day, and the very substantial effect they had on the publishing scene. Finally, it is the story of the government and press backlash that that eventually led to the collapse of the mushroom publishers, many in bitter court battles, the legacy of which is still with us even though the books themselves are long gone.

-**Steve Holland**, Colchester, August 1993

1

GROWING PAINS

"A class of literature has grown up around us...playing no inconsiderable part in moulding the minds and forming the habits and tates of its generation; and doing so principally, we had almost said exclusively, by 'preaching on the nerves'... Excitement, and excitement alone, seems to be the great end at which they aim"

The Quarterly, 1863,

quoted in "Snobbery With Violence" by Colin Watson

The simplest analogy for historical research is to compare it to putting a jigsaw together. You have a selection of pieces which somehow fit together to form a picture. If we continue the analogy, the problem with researching the extraordinary history of British publishing in the post-war decade, despite the fact that the events were within living memory, was that many of the pieces lay face down, some were missing, and, at first, the historians and collectors who came upon these books had little idea what the picture on the puzzle would eventually show.

That the history of the mushroom publishers was extraordinary is not in question: the second world war left Britain in a turbulent storm of political, economic and social chaos that can only now be imagined. On V.E. Day, the war may have been over, but the battle between publishers was still to be fought. The paperback boom was played out against a background of turmoil, and the history of the mushroom publishers is as stormy as any that could be written about that period.

Like all pictures, the history of popular fiction is a broad canvas, of which some parts have been seen and studied for many years.

Periodicals had first appeared in Britain in the 17th century, although in retrospect these look more like catalogues than the journals we are used to today, desribing themselves as repository's for information on literature, science, politics and theology. The word magazine was established in 1731 by *Gentleman's Magazine,* published by Edward Cave, a monthly collation from various newspapers alongside original articles and verse, his most famous contributor being Samuel Johnson.

Magazines, reviews and journals thrived in the 19th century, although they were invariably couched in elevated tones and aimed at the upper- and middle-to-upper classes. A scandalous broadsheet, however, could sell a million copies. By the 1870s, three quarters of the adult population could read, and the Education Act of 1870 put elementary education within the reach of all.

The popular press of the time consisted of the scandal sheets, and satirical magazines with their caricature engravings; books were not intended for the working classes but were seen as one of the benefits granted to the higher classes - a snob attitude that was to remain for many many years. Things were, however, changing.

The Gothic novel is generally considered to have originated with the publication of *The Castle of Otranto* by Horace Walpole in 1765, followed by many other sensational novels, notably the works of Mrs. Radcliffe, the Brontes, and Mary Shelley who produced the classic Gothic in *Frankenstein* (1818). Charles Dickens was a best-seller from his very first book, *Sketches by Boz* (1836), his popularity increasing with every subsequent book, which were usually originally serialised in monthly parts; priced at a shilling they would have been out of reach of some pockets, but they were clearly aimed at the man on the street.

At the other extreme were the Penny Dreadful's (also known as Penny Bloods, or Blood and Thunders) which emerged in the 1830s. The Bloods were priced at a penny per weekly part which was within the reach of most. The publications of Edward Lloyd and others popularised the horror stories of the nineteenth century, with bloodthirsty tales of skulduggery, highwaymen and footpads. Titles included *The Maniac Father, The Death Grasp,* and the highly popular *Varney the Vampire.* The Penny Dreadfuls made heroes of Dick Turpin, Sweeney Todd and Spring-Heeled Jack, and were eagerly sought after by the working classes who could buy them from news-vendors on street corners.

The birth of mass market distribution could be dated from 1848 when W.H. Smith secured the rights to sell books and newspapers at railway stations; until then it was rare to find bookshops outside of the university towns or large cities. Smiths put Bulwer Lytton and Captain Marryatt at the head of their best-seller lists, and the traditional three-volume Victorian novel was replaced by one-volume editions in yellow covers. These one-shilling "yellow backs" attracted competition from other publishers, and soon all manner of fiction was in the hands of the general public.

At the same time, the more literary magazines were adjusting to the audiences: *Cornhill Magazine* reached a readership of 100,000, before competition reduced the figure. Amongst the most popular were *The Strand,* one of the first magazines of light literature which owed much to the success of new printing techniques which allowed publisher Geroge Newnes to print a picture on every page, a gamble which proved successful, although much of the success can also be laid at the feet of Arthur Conan Doyle who submitted two stories in the Spring of 1891 featuring a new character, Sherlock Holmes. These stories, and those that followed, guaranteed the success of the magazine, and by the two hundredth issue *The Strand* could boast total sales of 80,000,000 copies.

Two developments in popular fiction in America in the late 1800's were to have an influence on British fiction: the dime novels and the pulps. The former - almost wholly aimed at boys and usually only costing a nickel - found their way to Britain in the days before copyright, amongst the most popular being the reprints of the *Frank Reade Library,* the creation of publisher Frank Tousey and writer Harold Cohen, although based on the earlier work of Edward S. Ellis. The high-speed adventures of Reade were fuelled by the imagination of his most prolific writer, Luis Senarens, who helped Reade invent aircraft, submarines and sent him on countless adventures in exotic, if occasionally lost, lands.

In Britain his stories were published by Aldine Publishing Co. of Crown Court, London, founded by Charles Perry Brown in the late 1880s, a company responsible for a great many boys' papers and an equal number of generic paperbacks appearing in the UK for thirty years, supplying countless tales of war, horse racing, soccer and detection for a predominantly youthful male audience. Amongst the most popular were the countless colourful tales of British folk hero Dick Turpin written by Charlton Lea and Stephen Agnew, the adventures of French cavalier, Claude Duval, and an endless stream of frontier conflicts for Buffalo Bill. Surprisingly, the Crown Court offices were tiny, and consisted of two dingy rooms occupied by editor Walter H. Light, his assistant and an office boy. The frenetic action of the juvenile papers were the entertainment of a new generation who had missed the thrills and gaudy horror of the penny dreadfuls.

The late 1890s saw another development in America: the pulp magazine. With hundreds of titles published, the pulp boom was really at its height in the 1920's and 1930s. Named after the cheap wood-pulp paper they were printed on, the pulp formula was developed by Frank Munsey, whose *Argosy* became an all-fiction magazine in 1896. The name of the game was action.

Single genre titles arrived in 1915 with Street & Smith's *Detective Stories,* and once the seed was sown others quickly followed; before long there were hundreds of magazines each devoted to the thrills or heartaches of their respective subjects: detective, war and aviation, science fiction, western, love and romance, and sport were the most popular subjects. In Britain the pulps were a natural progression from the likes of *The Strand* and proved highly popular when they arrived on our shores, often as ballast in the holds of ships returning from America with low cargoes, to be sold at 2d (later 3d) by F.W. Woolworth's chain of stores, an American owned company founded here in the 1920s. The pulps introduced many readers to the the gangster tales of *Black Mask,* the cowboy yarns of *Western Magazine,* the science fiction thrills of *Astounding,* and many, many others. A number of British pulps were developed, notably *Hutchinson's Adventure Story Magazine* which began in 1922 and the Master Thriller series published by World's Work (Kingswood) Ltd., itself a subsidiary of Hutchinsons, from 1933. George Newnes produced a number of genre titles in the 1930s under the editorship of T. Stanhope Sprigg, starting with **Air Stories** in 1935, based on the popular American aviation pulps and often featuring the excellent cover work of Russian born artist Serge Drigin.

The standard of living for most of the population was rising and with it the number of printing houses and the books they produced was growing to match the demand of increased leisure time. During the twenties, despite the depression, there were at least between seven to ten thousand books published each year (compared to over seventy thousand nowadays). This figure increased steadily during the thirties until it peaked in 1937 when over seventeen thousand titles appeared. Of these some 5,100 were fiction, 3,000 of which were reprints of stories previously available and somewhat over 2,000 were stories appearing in Britain for the first time.

These figures, published by Whitaker's Cumulative Book List - the standard reference for the book trade - do not, unfortunately, include the increasing number of publishers who were issuing paperback originals over this period, since many were published at a price below 6d, the cut-off price for inclusion.

The paperback was still suffering from class prejudice: it was not great literature. This, at first glance a rather sweeping generalisation, was a bias born of the Victorian publishing industry whose decorative cloth covered, gilt-embossed books are now highly sought after by collectors. A single book could require up to seven volumes to tell its story. The paperback was a decidedly inferior looking specimen, reducing great works to a single volume, the text printed far smaller to reduce the page count, and perhaps abridged to fit. The paperback was instantly disposable after reading, literature for the masses.

Amongst the largest publishers of paperbound fiction were those companies who produced 'Colonial Editions' which were highly popular in the early years of the century before the Great War, and it is interesting to note some of the most popular authors appearing at the time on their lists. Particularly popular were the romance novels of Alice and Claude Askew, Madame Albanesi, Mrs. Coulson Kernahan, L.T. Meade and Katherine Tynan, followed closely by the adventure and crime novels of Sir Arthur Conan Doyle, H. Rider Haggard, William Le Queux and Fergus Hume; these were the best-sellers of their day. On the other hand there were still the more *risque* publications appearing, paperbound editions of *The Awful Disclosures of Maria Monk, as Exhibited in a Narrative of Her Sufferings* which closeted the paperback novel into the same class as the Penny Dreadful, a hangover of Victorian sensationalism.

The thirties were the days of the great detective stories by Agatha Christie and Dorothy L. Sayers, of thrillers such as Graham Greene's *Brighton Rock*, of classic novels by Aldous Huxley, Evelyn Waugh, J.B. Priestley and Robert Graves. Readers were well served with the increasing number of libraries around the country: for a small fee of between a penny and sixpence you could borrow books from many other sources for up to a fortnight. Boots the Chemists had their own library, the Boot's Booklover's Library, founded in 1899, which by the mid-thirties could be found in over 450 branches. Mudie's and W.H. Smith's also had lending libraries in many of their branches, and even the smallest villages were visited by the travelling libraries which toured constantly. The most popular author of all was Edgar Wallace who wrote some 180 books in 14 years, achieving sales of over 20 million copies. During his peak, Wallace was only outsold by the Bible.

In 1935 Allen Lane, whose career in publishing had begun at he Bodley Head at the age of 16, founded Penguin Books and the paperback gained some measure of respectability. Perhaps the most revealing remarks about the prejudice surrounding paperbacks were spoken when, in 1960, Penguin Books were taken to court for publishing *Lady Chatterley's Lover*. In his opening address the defending council, Mr. Griffith-Jones, said that Lane:

> thought it would be a good thing if the ordinary people were able to afford to buy good books. The ordinary book was expensive then, as it is expensive now. He himself had not had the advantage of a university. He had a passion for books. He left school at the age of sixteen...there were those who thought he was mad. They said it's no good giving the working classes any good books, they wouldn't understand them if they read them.

The next year he formed this company, Penguin Books Limited, to publish books at the price of ten cigarettes. It was 6d.

The measure of Lane's success was that by the time of the court case, Penguin's 3,500 books had sold 250 million copies between them and sales were increasing that number at a rate of 13 million a year. But this was 25 years in the future...

Whilst many of the major publishers already had paperback lines, (amongst the most popular being the famous Hodder & Stoughton Yellow Jackets which had first appeared in the mid-twenties), it was Penguin who galvanised the industry: other publishers followed Lane's lead, and soon Penguin and their Pelican line jostled in the market with many other imprints.

The Hutchinson's Pocket Library first appeared in 1935, with their coloured, designed covers, and Collins White Circle Books followed in 1936, their first title being *Murder on the Orient Express* by Agatha Christie; other new series included Cherry Tree Books (published by Kemsley Newspapers), Chevron Books (published by Queensway Press), Sampson Low's Sixpennies, Methuen's Sixpennies, etc. These were followed in the early days of the War by Evergreen Books, Vintage Books and many others, not least the many publications of George Newnes and C. Arthur Pearson who had for many years also covered the more popular markets.

Below: Hutchinson's Pocket Library add a touch more excitement to prewar crime cover design than their Penguin competitors

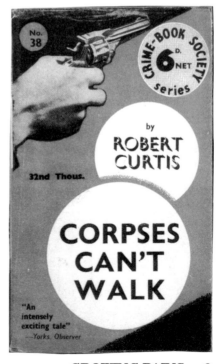

At the lower end of the market were the 2d Mill-girl novelettes published in the romance libraries of Amalgamated Press, John Leng, and D.C. Thomson. All three companies had grown out of successful magazine and newspaper lines, the first founded by Alfred Harmsworth (Lord Northcliffe) after the success of the *Daily Mail.* David C. Thomson had founded his publishing company in 1886, becoming proprietor of the *Dundee Courier,* later taking over the firm of John Leng during the General Strike after many years of rivalry to form Thomson-Leng. Between them, Thomsons and Amalgamated Press, alongside Newnes and Pearsons, dominated the field of cheap genre fiction, outstripping any other rivals to the point of totally overwhelming them. By the 1930's the news-stands were awash with countless booklets filling every niche of the market.

* * * * * * *

The new flood of publications was soon stemmed: Great Britain went to War, with all the hardships and problems that implied. Germany invaded Poland on September 1st 1939, and British reaction was swift: over a period of four days evacuation schemes were put in motion which relocated 1,200,000 people, and compulsory military service was introduced for all males aged between 18 and 41. The first enemy air-raid on Britain arrived on the 6th.

The rationing of all essentials, clothing and food became a necessity. British industry battled the crippling cuts forced upon it. The Ministry of Supply discussed paper rationing on February 1st 1940, and the Control of Paper order came into effect on April 13th 1940 (only days after Germany invaded Denmark and Norway and the "Phoney War" ended): supplies plummeted, and paper became a commodity that suffered as much as any other. Publishers were allocated only 60% of the paper they had consumed in the year ending in August 1939, a figure later dropped to 40%. Paper supplies from Canada and America were still getting through the Atlantic blockade but European supplies quickly vanished; gradually all overseas imports were stopped, either by the ever present U-Boats of the enemy or the economic collapse that was overtaking the country. Britain became self-supporting, imports an increasing luxury the economy could barely sustain, even with the lend-lease agreement with America which allowed Britain deposit-free food imports.

It is vital to remember that the repercussions from rationing and restricted importation would still be felt for many years after the war ended. Announced at 7.30pm on May 7th 1945, the war officially ended at one minute past midnight on May 8th, although a "state of war" still existed between Britain and Germany until July 1951.

Rationing, however, was still in force for many years, and in some cases became more strict when American President Harry S. Truman put an end to the lend-lease agreement in August 1945. In February 1946 the government announced further food ration cuts in response to world shortage; bread rationing was introduced for the first time in May. Further chaos was caused by the winter of 1946/47, with meat rationing cut again in January (and again in January 1951). The roads and rail were at a standstill, blocked by ice, which made fuel impossible to transport during the coldest weather on record since 1880/81. By the end of February, 4 million workers were idle because of power cuts. As the snow and ice began to thaw in March, many towns were hit by floods.

Over the next few years, the rationing began to ease: clothes rationing was finally lifted in 1949, having been introduced in 1941, and the points system of rationing, also introduced in 1941, was lifted in 1950. Throughout 1950 more restrictions were lifted. It is almost impossible to imagine in these days when everything is readily available that restrictions were in force for even that great British institution, tea, only deregulated in 1952, and if you took sugar that was only freely available from the autumn of 1953, after nearly 14 years of rationing. Food rationing was officially ended on July 4th 1954.

Trade was strictly controlled in the post-War years, and import controls only slowly dismantled, the last as late as 1959, allowing British imitations to proliferate without opposition or comparison. A War Loan approved by the American House of Representatives in 1946 was not fully paid off until 1957. The British economy was struggling desperately, and harsh tactics were forced upon the government. In September 1949 the pound was devalued by 30%, the exchange rate dropping from $4.03 to a new figure of $2.80. The cost of living went up by 5%.

****

Rationing was only part of the socio-economic background against which the mushroom publishers played out their part in the history of British publishing. In the June 1945 General Election, the Labour party had won a landslide victory, but only just clung to power in February 1950; a third election in October 1952 saw Winston Churchill returned to Downing Street.

The Ministry of Supply's decision to restrict paper supplies meant that from April 1940 publishers would only be allowed a strict quota. Further controls came into force on May 27th 1940, prohibiting the publication of new magazines and periodicals, and it was here that many publishers sustained their most crippling blow: in the early days of the War it was hoped that a solution would be quickly found, but as time passed the struggle continued unabated. No new periodicals were allowed during the time rationing was in force, devastating to an industry that relied on its ability to change and reflect everyday life as the climate changed. Periodicals that had previously flourished became shadows of their former glory: newspapers were down to a whispy four or six pages, and hardcover books were a luxury. Publishers tried to overcome the problems by printing their books without margins, without fly-leaves, in fact any way they could to comply with the War Economy Standards. But the valuable cloth was in short supply, and the paperback book became an increasingly more important economic necessity to publishers if they were to survive the war.

The paperback had a number of advantages: they were generally smaller books, the print smaller which reduced the page count. Being smaller had advantages other than the saving in paper: being lighter it was easier to ship to servicemen overseas or displaced civilians. Some publishers issued a Service Edition, the best known being that of the Penguin Forces Book Club which printed ten titles a month from October 1942, each with a print run of 75,000 copies. The forces were seen as a very important market (Penguin budgeted £200,000 for this series alone) and certainly the Government considered reading matter highly as a moral booster for the troops, even allocating an additional sixty tons of paper per month to Penguin to keep the series going. It has been pointed out that the knee pocket in the average battledress worn by the British soldiers, although intended to contain an entrenching tool, was just the right size to carry a paperback book.

In the War years no publisher could be said to have flourished, but the paperback market held its own and became a workable replacement for the hardcover. The number of books published slumped, and *The Bookseller,* although their monthly listings were not wholly accurate, show the trend in their annual summary:

1939: 14,904 (total number) 4,222 (fiction titles)

1940: 11,053	” ”	3,791 ” ”
1941: 7,581	” ”	2,342 ” ”
1942: 7,205	” ”	1,559 ” ”
1943: 6,705	” ”	1,408 ” ”
1944: 6,781	” ”	1,255 ” ”
1945: 6,747	” ”	1,246 ” ”

In only two years it can be seen that British publishing was forced to drastically cut its output until the 1943 figure was only a little over a third of the 1937 peak. Whilst this trend covered the overall publishing figures, it is also interesting to compare the trend followed by fiction publishing shown in the right hand column of the above table. From these figures it can be seen that the number of fiction titles dropped to around a third of their 1939 figure at their lowest slump, whilst the total book issue was down to just under half. These figures can, however, be amended if we take into account the number of reprints issued, for example, in 1939 the percentage of reprints counted in the total overall figure of books published was 30%, whilst for fiction it was 55%. By 1945 these figures became roughly 14% and 11%, a dramatic fall in the number of reprints. Only a fifth of fiction titles were reprints, and the number of fiction titles being made available for the first time was actually on the increase, partly attributable to the number of paperback novels that were being published.

The popularity of the paperback was increased to a fantastic degree. The artificial conditions bought about by rationing meant that reading matter was desperately sought after by a book-starved public. The average print run for a pre-War book was 1,000 copies for a first edition hardback, and many books never surpassed that figure. The popularity of certain authors coupled with the increase in the library lending services meant that this figure rose to 2,500 and even as high 5,000 for the most popular titles. But during the War anything that appeared on the market would sell in phenomenal quantities, as many as the publishers could produce. It was economically more sound therefore to produce larger print runs of one title than shorter

Below: Cheap "Girlie" magazines proliferated in the '50s, featuring gags and gals.

runs of two titles which would also mean paying money to a second author and to the printers for setting up two books - if you could get the paper. Thus the figures above also hide a number of other factors which made the production of paperbacks more profitable. That they were profitable is illustrated by one 16 page booklet which featured a number of film stills of Rita Heyworth in various poses: at a shilling a copy it was fairly expensive, the price no doubt dictated by its contents, and yet it still managed to sell over 200,000 copies.

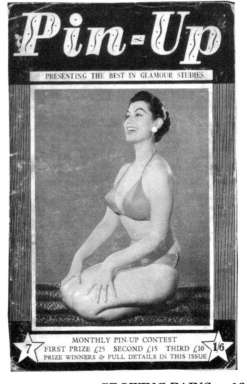

These small booklets proliferated during the War, selling many thousands of copies to displaced civilians, soldiers on leave, or American servicemen transferred to Britain; some of the more racy titles with provocative covers were being sold for five shillings (the price of a hardcover book) in sealed bags by some of the less salubrious booksellers off Charing Cross Road. Some of the biggest circulation titles were little more than short stories, printed on something that looked suspiciously like toilet paper; the paper sometimes so thin and the print so microscopic that the stories were almost illegible. One childrens' publisher, Clifford Lewis, recalled one lucky break, saying "a wholesale grocer sold me a large quantity of paper in which he had intended to wrap margerine. But his margerine quota hiccoughed and he was glad to sell the paper to me. Then a transfer manufacturer sold me his warehouse full of Duplex Backing Paper - the sheet that was discarded after the printing of the transfer. Some of the paper bore some floral design or other design and was not suitable for hardbacks, so I began publishing 6d fiction."

The paperback market expanded, especially for original fiction. Paperback originals were not new, and had long been popular with readers of cheap genre fiction. Amongst the most prolific exploiters of this market during the 1930s were Irish publishers, Mellifont Press, whose list covered every aspect of fiction publishing from fairy stories to adult fiction. They had a lengthy list of 3d and 2d crime and romance titles, some of them reprints dating back to before the Great War, but an equal number of them original novels and novelettes. Such was their success as both publisher and printer (as Cahill & Co. Ltd. of Dublin, later known as Parkgate Printing Works) that Mellifont quickly set up offices in London and South Africa. The company continued to publish original novels and novelettes for many years, and continued to publish fiction (notably the racing novels of Nat Gould) into the 1960s although their heyday was the thirties and forties.

Another publisher to exploit the original market was Fiction House who produced the long running Piccadilly Novels series, publishing the early works of a number of popular authors, notably John Creasey, still recognised as one of the most prolific writers ever. His early work appeared under a variety of names: Rodney Mathieson, M.E. Cooke, Margaret Cooke and Elise Fecamps from Piccadilly, as well as his own name. For Mellifont he worked under M.E. and Margaret Cooke, and became Patrick Gill, Peter Manton and James Marsden at various times. Gramol Publications, directed by Arthur Gray and Fred M. Mowl, were a third company to make use of his ubiquitous talents as part of their Mystery Novels series which also included many tales by prolific crime writers L.C. Douthwaite and John Hunter.

The paperback was a profitable and lucrative business. Printing and packaging costs were kept as low as possible and the profits could be enormous. Authors new and old found that many of their markets had folded or were struggling under the grip of rationing and publishers who could get hold of paper were in a commanding position. British rates of pay for stories were low compared to many countries, and whilst many of the pre-War publishers may have paid their authors on acceptance of a story

CREASEY *Mystery* MAGAZINE 2/-

FEBRUARY, 1957   VOLUME 1 No. 6

JOHN CREASEY •   PETER CHEYNEY
AGATHA CHRISTIE   BRUCE GRAEM

R.W.S

Above: John Creasey's popularity led to his own crime magazine, here published by Dalrow of Bolton

the wartime publishers would usually only pay on publication; with many companies still located in London there was a constant threat of bombing raids by the German Luftwaffe and few publishers would risk paying for contributions that might be blown out of existence or tie their money up in stories when their printers were too busy printing emergency leaflets or booklets for the War Office - wartime government printing was consuming some 100,000 tons of paper a year, 25,000 tons of that by the War Office alone. Payment was usually made when the book or magazine was safely printed and distributed.

Another problem faced by the freelance writer during the years of wartime rationing was that many of the larger combines already had authors under contract who were quite able to fill their reduced publishing schedules, little room remaining for the freelancer or newcomer. Many publishers were offering as little as ten shillings per thousand words for stories, and articles often received less, yet publishers easily managed to fill their magazines. Many writers found on their return from service that their regular pre-war markets had folded or were struggling to

GROWING PAINS   15

survive the restrictions of rationing, and the only markets open to them were the new breed, prolific when paper fell into their hands, quick to exploit an opening, but often hamstrung by poor distribution and cash flow.

While many brave publishers tried their hands at respectable magazines they found that most of their efforts were in vain. The terrible restrictions were still in force despite the close of action and as more and more authors were demobbed the competition amongst free-lance writers became more intense. Bevis Winter, a freelance writer who had contributed to many top publications over many years, was one of the new breed publishers, having established W.B. Press in 1947, publishing and editing one of the first men's magazines in Britain, *Stag;* he knew his field well, and summed up the gloomy prospects for many a post-war publishing venture in his book *The Naked Truth About Free-Lance Writing* (1948):

> During the few months immediately following V.E. Day, controls were removed from new publications in a slight degree, enabling any new periodical to be started provided not more that eight hundredweight of paper was consumed in any four months. Three times a year a new paper could get 8 cwts. of paper, providing the paper was available.

> This, in blunt figures calculating so many pages per issue, meant that a weekly or monthly was an impossible proposition. The result was that a few enterprising people gambled their chance on quarterlies. The meagre amount of paper allowed to these concerns meant that such new periodicals could only reach a pegged circulation, and that more pages used in an issue, the less copies could be printed and published. Small circulation meant little advertising, and consequently low advertising rates...national advertisers are more responsible for the payments you get for your free-lance material than the publishing houses themselves. They feed the coffers of ninety percent of the publishing trade...This vicious circle caused more trouble for those new ventures than anyone could possibly imagine...

The vicious circle described by Winter killed off most of the new ventures that small periodical publishers tried in the years immediately after the war, quarterly - and very occasionally monthly - magazines like *Galaxy, Cosmopolitan, Male Mag and Modern Miss.* Paper restrictions on newspapers and periodicals were lifted on March 1st 1950, easing the situation but not solving it. Paper rationing was not fully lifted until June 1953. For ten years periodical publishing limped along, and in the immediate post-War period it looked fearfully bleak, prompting Winter to predict that "our newspapers will probably never get back to their pre-War size of sixteen and twenty-four daily pages in our lifetime"; thankfully this prediction did not come true, and newspapers recovered their size admirably in the fifties.

Many publishers did fail. It was not only the paper shortages that caused problems, but the whole set-up of some companies: some were one-man operations, poorly financed and poorly managed. Most publishers had terrible distribution problems and a great deal of money was tied up in unsold and undistributed stock. Many experiments collapsed before they came to fruition, and backruptcies amongst the small publishers were commonplace. Other problems beset them: power cuts and adverse weather, especially in the early months of 1947, were wreaking havoc on the industry, affecting everyone from small publishers like Pendulum Publications in the South to such major companies like D.C. Thomson located in Dundee, Scotland. The larger companies were able to ride the storm, but the small companies suffering from cash-flow problems were not so lucky and folded.

Many of the publishing companies were set up by servicemen returning from War, using their Severance Pay to finance their enterprises. One such was Barrington Gray, who recalled that it was not such a difficult proposition. Established in 1946 he used his home address in Leigh-on-Sea, Essex as an office and shared an office in London with Popular Fiction (London) Ltd. and Phoenix Press where he kept his stocks. He then applied for a paper quota ("This as far as I remember was one and a third tons every four months") and produced a number of children's painting books which included his own *How To Draw Comics and Draw My Way* by cartoonist Jack Greenall (better known as the creator of Useless Eustace for the *Daily Mirror*). Barrington Gray was later incorporated as a limited company and published fiction during the early fifties, and although never a particularly prolific company, Gray managed to keep afloat until 1961 when debts to printers forced him out of business.

Many companies did not have even this limited success and whilst the successful publishers found themselves a lucrative market, some of the poorly financed back-street enterprises soon found themselves out of business. Whilst it is an easy matter to work out the potential profits in publishing, it was just as easy to overlook the problems that existed between setting up the company and distributing the finished product. Some publishers found financial backing, and these were the cornerstones on which the paperback boom was founded.

* * * * * * *

Whilst the boom did not begin to gather strength until 1946, the momentum from which it sprung had already been sown during the War. Many new publishers were appearing, usually small enterprises, and usually producing paperback novels or novelettes. Amongst those publishers who turned to fiction to salvage their company from the ravages of paper shortage was Lloyd Cole, a technical book publisher based in London. Cole, himself the writer of a number of books (mostly religious tracts and books on economy), hired Benson Herbert to edit a new line, most of them small booklets such as the 48 page "Lighthouse Books" series. Herbert was already an established writer and had published stories in American and British science fiction magazines during the 1930s, as well as the novel *Crisis: 1999AD* (1936); he also had a good knowledge of literature and poetry, and had written a book of verse some years before. For Lloyd Cole he produced a series of booklets, often writing them himself, with titles such as *Hand of Glory* (1943) and *Time, Gentlemen, Please* (1942). A mixture of mysteries and juvenile stories appeared, but Herbert was quick to find that the most popular stories had titles like *They Don't Always Hang Murderers, Bedtime, The Red-Haired Girl* and *Strange Romance* (the latter is pure space-opera science fiction), all of which Herbert wrote and published between 1942 and 1944.

In 1944 Herbert left Lloyd Cole to set up his own company, Utopian Publications, with a long-time friend, Walter Gillings as co-director. Gillings had recently been released from war service and, as he said, had "only myself to direct, for it was Herbert who, when he was free of other allegiances, found the finance and managed the actual business of printing and publishing the company's modest productions."

But Gillings was about to have an education in what the average paperback was, as recalled in an article in 1970:

> Did I say modest? With few exceptions, the shiny covers consisted of genuine art studies of full-breasted ladies in provocative poses, and bore such titles as *The Sex Serum, Lady In Danger* and *Love In Time*. They were modest booklets of thirty-six pages priced at "one shilling net", though only a few of the cover girls wore flimsy draperies that left precious little concealed. One story generally sufficed, but in a few cases a filler or two completed the closely set pages which, compared to some of the airy productions available, certainly gave value for money. The authors, too, were hardly small in stature or maturity, at least to those who knew science fiction.

American fans caught in the draft and wafted to London, exploring the more intriguing bookstores off Charing Cross Road, must have halted goggle-eyed on seeing the names Jack Williamson, Edmond Hamilton, Stanton A. Coblentz, Robert Bloch and Raymond A. Palmer. Or any one or two of them, because a round dozen of these booklets appeared between September 1944 and February 1946, when we were able to produce more ambitious titles without relying on sex appeal to catch the eye of the prospective reader. Indeed, by that time busts had come under the ban. Legs, arms and shoulders were still permissible, but "adequate light clothing" was necessary if we wished to get our publications displayed in the more genteel shops. So Herbert advised me, and experience had taught him that to be guided by our wholesalers was the only way to stay in business.

Not all the publishers were producing quite such immodest material, but Utopian were quite a success at the time, particularly after Gillings' departure when Herbert turned to the racy magazines market.

Many other companies started at about the same time, mostly in the paperback market. Mitre Press began producing fiction booklets in 1943, particularly 32 page crime novelettes by F.W. Gumley and Michael Hervey for sale at 9d or 1/-, but had virtually ceased publishing by 1946, turning back to hardcover non-fiction, and acting as distributors under the umbrella name of Fudge & Co.

Another was Everybody's Books whose managing director was Hector Kelly; many of the books he published were written by his brother, Harold Kelly, who was better known as Darcy Glinto, having established the name with a series of gangster novels published by Wells Gardner, Darton. Everybody's went out of business in 1948; Hilary Book Co. suffered the same fate in 1948, and many other small companies - amongst them Pocket Editions, Beverley Publishing Co. and Gnome Publications - did not out-live the war. Many more were to fold soon after - Pictorial Art Ltd., Pan Press Publications, Libra Publications, Western Book Distributors to name but a few. Amongst the companies to set up immediately after the War were Diamond Books (Abbey Publications), who were to fold within two years.

Above: Wells, Gardner, Darton were very active in the late 1940s, mainly with their western series. It was with them that prolific cover and comic artist Denis McLoughlin was to get his first break before his long association with TV Boardman

The pattern of collapse was not followed by all and some new companies had a very healthy life-span; it was these survivors who brought about the paperback boom once they had settled the early teething troubles they encountered with finance and distribution.

Amongst these must be counted Fiction House, who, as mentioned earlier, had launched the Piccadilly Novels series in 1934 and had, therefore, become established by the time war broke out. In fact they had met with some success, and had published some 225 titles in the series by the time the War ended, but even they were forced to reprint earlier titles at times of financial crisis. The series mixed both crime and romance in nearly equal proportions, branching out to include westerns in 1948 as the market for the latter expanded. The Piccadilly Novels are a good example of the immediate post-War paperback original, their 96 page novels priced at 9d, brightly colourful cover artwork wrapped around easily readable stories by such prolific authors as W.R. Hutton and Eileen Wilmot.

Fiction House was allied to the printers, Blackfriars Press of Leicester, whose Blackfriar Books series began in 1944, publishing full-length original novels at 2/-.

Perhaps the greatest success of all the paperback publishers to be launched during the War was Pan Books Ltd. who were established in September 1944. Pan had the great advantage over the mushroom publishers of backing from the Book Society, which director Alan Bott had founded in 1929. Bott controlled the company until 1952, when Aubrey Forshaw became managing director, a position he held until 1970, succeeded by Ralph Vernon-Hunt, who had been sales director at Pan since 1950. Pan began publishing in 1945, although it was in 1947 that they made their first great impact, having reached an agreement with the Board of Trade to print their books abroad in batches of 250,000 on the promise that half of this number would be exported. Pan bought an ex-Royal Navy launch to ship their books from the printers in France, and the first titles under this agreement appeared in June 1947. Their success was immediate, and two million Pan Books were sold in the first year. Pan's initial titles included Rudyard Kipling,

Below: Pan #22 published in 1947 shows the trend towards artwork covers

James Hilton's *Paradise Lost*, an Agatha Christie, a collection of J.B. Priestley's plays, and novels by Margaret Sharp and Leo Walmsley. This mixture of popular titles was helped by striking pictorial covers (much to the derision of Allen Lane, who saw it as a cheap American gimmick). Yet the success of Pan was proof that paperbacks could sell, and in great numbers, and they quickly rose to second only in sales terms to Penguin.

Another aspect of publishing that distinguishes Pan and Penguin from the mushroom publishers was the backlist. Both companies would reprint books when they sold out; initial print-runs of 25,000 to 40,000 were soon dwarfed by multiple editions which could raise sales figures into their hundreds of thousands. The mushroom publishers could also produce 40,000 of a book, if the paper was available, but only a few titles would ever see a second edition.

Across: Its not too difficult to see how the
artwork of artists like
Reginald Heade helped
boost the "mushroom"
publishers sales when
compared with pre war
paperback covers. Af-
ter his long association
with the Hank Janson
line, Heade painted
many covers for Pan
under his Cy Webb
pseudonymn.

2

RISE OF THE MUSHROOM PUBLISHERS

"The ten year period from 1945 was, from a publishing point of view, so bizarre that what is written here might be dismissed as a writer's fantasy. It is not."

Gordon Landsborough, "The Crazy World" (1971)

It was around 1944 that a number of companies who were to play a large part in the history of the mushroom pubishers began to carve themselves a place in the publishing and distribution networks. And with the wartime growth of paperback fiction came certain trends that were to be followed over the next fifteen years.

The first of these were the racy titles given to novels; although this had been common for many years as a method of selling books that were otherwise innocuous, the mushroom publishers took it to a new degree, as they did the covers. Walter Gillings, amazed at the immodest covers, was no less amazed by the title his otherwise innocent collections hid behind: John Beynon Harris' "The Wanderers of Time" became *Love in Time* (1945), whilst Jack Williamson's "Wizard's Isle" became *Lady in Danger* (1945). The smut content of these 1930s science fiction yarns was zero, but the titles - plus naked models on the covers - no doubt took science fiction to otherwise untapped markets.

As far back as the 1920s British publishers had produced romances with a 'French' flavour. In France the laws of obscenity were nowhere as strict as they were in England and there were many books of French literature that, although now considered classics, could not be translated in English without attracting the attentions of the vice squad, notable amongst them Paul de Kock, whose work was translated extensively in the nineteenth century, and Emile Zola. Many British authors had their novels printed in France and imported to avoid problems, only to have their stories seized by custom's officials; two classic cases were the barring of *Ulysses* by James Joyce (1922) and *Lady Chatterley's Lover* by D.H. Lawrence (1929).

The feeling, prevalent during the thirties and exploited during the fifties, was that the French-flavour of a novel would guarantee sales, and to this end Britain enjoyed the works of a number of French authors such as Maurice Dekobra (Ernest Maurice Tessier), the highly popular author of *The Madonna of the Sleeping Cars* and *The Street of Painted Lips*, and Louis Charles Royer. But it was more likely that the works were by British authors such as Richard Goyne, the author behind the highly popular Paul Renin, or Frank Dubrez Fawcett, who used the pen-name Henri Dupres. Particularly prolific at the time were the presses of Gramol Publications whose sexy novels series' first appeared in the late 1920s, publishing the works of pseudonymous British writers under the names Roland Vane, Paul Reville, Jean Du Crois, Henri Lamonte and Jeanette Revere.

Below: Prewar Gramol books were the precursors of the postwar gangster book. Pseudo-French sexy romance also proved popular, Perl rivalling Heade as the premiere postwar good girl artist

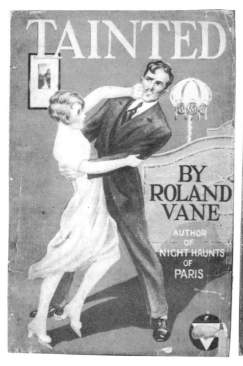

The idea that a magazine written by continental writers was somehow automatically more erotic continued throughout the 1940s and 1950s, as was discovered by one young newcomer, now a respected television and screen writer, who was asked to produce "a raunchy magazine of sex and titillation":

I wrote (this might make you smile) an eight-story magazine for Archie Carmichael under eight different names ‐ from 'Ricardo Milano' to 'Richard Mille'. The reason was simple. According to Archie, if one wanted to produce a (for the time) raunchy magazine of sex and titilation, one had to use continental writers. And Archie wanted to produce *Gay-etty Magazine* (his title) and I wanted to earn a guinea a thousand words. Hence, eight short stories by eight continental-sounding gentlemen in one magazine.

As I was merely a lad and my experience of *La Dolche Vita*/Sex/Titillation was what I managed to learn behind the school bicycle shed, the erotica (if that's what it was) was pure fiction and a lot of wishful thinking. But in order to learn one's trade, one was happy to write anything. At least I was, until *Gay-etty* was judged obscene by Salford Magistrate's Court and all copies were confiscated. Upset, I apologised to Archie, who simply smiled and gave me a £20 bonus. It would appear that since the court case, Archie had received inquiries from all over the country and was promptly printing another 100,000 copies.

Such were (and are) the laws of obscenity in Britain that a local magistrate may ban a book or magazine in one area, but it may remain on open sale elsewhere.

Many of the books that appeared with the legend "translated from the French" were nothing of the sort, and the standard of 'erotica' so low that many of the books were prosecuted as being obscene. Most concerned Paris street girls or club girls - usually naive young English roses attracted to the continent by romance who are cruelly spurned and forced onto the streets to earn a meagre, sordid living (at least, that was the implication). Little care was taken to make them authentic - in fact one author rarely bothered to change the name of his heroine.

One of the first publishers to discover the sales power of such romances was Gerald G. Swan Ltd. who had offices in Marylebone, London. Gerald George Swan (1902-1980) had started his business as a bookseller in the busy Church Street Market place at the age of nineteen, having borrowed thirty shillings from his mother to finance the venture. From his barrow Swan sold all sorts of second-hand books and magazines, but specialised in juvenile fiction, at the time dominated by the Amalgamated Press. He sold all his comics and papers at half-price and his books, some of which were new, for a price just under that of his competitors. His business,

not surprisingly, flourished, and in the late thirties Swan decided to go into publishing himself, at first simply allowing his products to build up before he started to distribute them.

This was a move of remarkable foresight since it meant that when war broke out in 1939 Swan had three warehouses stacked with books and magazines which he gradually distributed throughout the early years of the war. Even the destruction of one warehouse - destroyed by fire in 1940 - was not enough to ruin him, and much of that success can be put down to the rush of titles he put on the market at the start of his career. Although best remembered amongst collectors for his many comics and juvenile papers, Swan's early output included over sixty novels by Paul Renin and a number of novels written in similar style by Ruy Du Montesse and by Swan's most prolific writer, ex-actor William James Elliott, whose first Swan book was the non-fiction *Life Long Sex Harmony* which went through a number of editions after its first appearance in 1939.

Renin, as mentioned above, was the pen-name of Richard Goyne, the son of a schoolteacher who later became a vicar. Goyne studied at the Royal College of Music, winning awards for his playing, and later became a journalist with the Hornsey

Journal before turning freelance, writing hundreds of stories for D.C. Thomson, particularly for their romance magazine *Red Letter*. He also wrote for Amalgamated Press, his biggest market being the girls' fiction magazines. This familiarity with romance made him one of the most prolific writers for those publishers whose output included rather more sensational novels, and as Renin he produced about a hundred novels in the 1920s and 1930s, with such eye-catching titles as *Compromised, Dishonoured, Enticed* and *Sex*. Although the content was in no way as explicit as the titles implied, the books sold in their thousands. Publishers such as Federation Press and Gramol Publications had extensive lines of these racy romances, all similarly titled, often tales of white slavery (a favourite subject of twenties silent pornographic films) and "lost women". Sex education at the time was non-existant, particularly for young girls, and these 'snappy' novels probably attracted more female readers than male, whose reading matter at the time was otherwise dominated by tales of mill girls who want to become film stars and marry princes.

Gerald Swan was not the only publisher to exploit the potential of these racy titles. In 1945, Phoenix Press began to publish reprints of Paul Renin from their address at 10 Elephant Road in London, also the address of Popular Fiction (London) Ltd. to whom the company was allied. In 1946 more novels appeared, mostly distributed by R & L Locker, and these companies were to reprint novels by Renin and his contemporaries, Henri Lamartine and Paul Reville, for many years - Renin reprints were still appearing in the 1960s.

The husband and wife team of Raymond and Lilian Locker based their publishing and distributing company at 11 Hope Street in Hanley, a village near Stoke on Trent in the midlands. In 1944 they were publishing a number of children's comics, turning to the hardback romance market in the period immediately following V.E. Day. They bought the rights for the books from Gerald Swan, as well as many of Swan's original novels by Ruy Du Montesse, William Elliott and Pierre Flammeche. It is likely that Phoenix acted as publishers for a number of the Renin novels simply because the Lockers were unable to get the paper supplies they needed for saturation reprinting. In 1948 they took over Harborough Publishing Co., Ltd., and founded Archer Press: Harborough took over the publishing of Renin novels alongside the Locker editions, many featuring beautiful cover paintings by artist Reginald Heade, and continued to issue Renin books until January 1954 when the three companies suddenly ceased trading.

They were not the only companies to produce this type of novel: Clifford Lewis, at one-time a prolific romance writer for D.C. Thomson and Amalgamated Press, began publishing paperbacks from 2 High Street, Stone, in 1945, issuing the novels of Andre Lamour, Henri Duval and Paul Lestrange, all house names invented by Lewis to hide the identities of a number of authors, notably Norman Firth, boys' writer Reginald G. Thomas, and romance writer Norah Burke. As well as the usual love-in-the-desert stories such as *Desert Passion* and *Harem Captive* (a type of story made tremendously popular by E.M. Hull, whose *The Sheik* was first published in 1919), Lewis mixed sex and violence in a series of small booklets under the "Crime and Passion" banner, some with emphatically sadistic titles like *Marked Woman* by Gaston Lamond and *The Lady Got Burnt* by Andre Lamour. A number of these raunchy titles hid pre-War tales from the pages of women's magazines such as *Secrets, Miracle, Oracle,* and *Silver Star.*

Although the trend was to disguise the work of British authors behind foreign pseudonyms, a number of publishers did use the genuine article, with Maurice Dekobra, Albert Londres, Louis Charles Royer and Jean Bruce appearing at various times. The spicy novel was not the sole province of French writers, and a similar expansion in the 'racy-romance' field had developed in America in the thirties, spearheaded by the likes of Erolie Pearl Dern and James Noble Gifford. A number of these American novels were reprinted in the late forties by New York based publishers Exotic Books, Venus Books and Quarter Books, with whom World Distributors Ltd. of Manchester struck a deal in 1950, publishing a number of titles for the British market; these included such tastefully titled romances as *Respectable Harlot, Thrill Girl* and *Naughty Virgin.*

Whilst these novels were highly popular, it was the gangster novel that the mushroom publishers are best remembered for. These were written in a pseudo-American style which had become popular during the war. Their popularity was proved by one publisher who changed from producing westerns to publishing the new gangster novels, his turnover jumping from £1,200 per annum to £70,000 in only ten years. The style and settings were developed in the American pulp magazines such as *Detective Fiction Weekly, Dime Detective, Spicy Detective* and above all *Black Mask* in the 1920s and 1930s. It was in the latter that author Carroll John Daly introduced the first tough private-eye in the form of Three Gun Mack and the first popular series featuring Race Williams. Taking his cue from Daly, Dashiell Hammett wrote the Continental Op stories, and achieved great success with the adventures of Sam Spade (of *The Maltese Falcon* fame). The pages of *Black Mask* also played host to the remarkable Raymond Chandler whose early tales often featured on the covers. Chandler, born in Chicago but raised in England, wrote poetry in the days before the Great War and did not turn to writing pulp detective stories until the 1930's. His greatest creation, the tough, cynical Philip Marlowe, did not appear until the publication of *The Big Sleep* in 1939, by which time Chandler was already 51 years old.

Between them, these three authors and their followers developed a style that caught the imaginations of the pulp readers, the action removed from the Hollywood bright-lights portrayed in movies, taking their characters into the dark alleyways of New York, the ganglands of Chicago and the sleazy sidewalks and Los Angeles. These stories were slowly filtering across to England through the pulps and British editions of novels. Cassell & Co. had published Hammett's classics, *The Dain Curse, Red Harvest, The Maltese Falcon* and *The Glass Key* in 1929-31; W.R. Burnett's *Little Caeser* appeared courtesy of Jonathan Cape in 1929, a year before the film of the same name made a star of Edward G. Robinson, and the same author's *The Asphalt Jungle* some years later, by which time Burnett had already made a tremendous impact on the cinema with such original screenplays as *The Finger Points (1931), The Beast of the City (1932) and Scarface (1932)*. The *film noir* was to bring other Hollywood classics to the screens, including *The Maltese Falcon (1941)* and Chandler's *The Big Sleep (1946)*.

A number of British authors began to write in the American style, one of the most influential being James Hadley Chase (Rene Raymond) whose uncompromising *No Orchids For Miss Blandish* (1939) sold over a million copies in five years and was the start of a prolific and highly successful career, despite the intense criticism the book received, notably in George Orwell's article "Raffles and Miss Blandish" (1944). A host of imitators followed, including Darcy Glinto (Harold Kelly) whose *Lady - Don't Turn Over* appeared in 1940. These two authors can claim the distinction of being the first two gangster novelists to have their work declared obscene in 1942; they were certainly not the last.

The gangster market was proving to be lucrative, so much so that distributors began advising publishers to produce more of the same. Amongst the most popular of the early authors were Hank Janson and Ben Sarto. The former will be dealt with at length in a later chapter, but chronologically he was amongst the earliest of the new-style gangster writers to appear with *When Dames Get Tough* (1946). Sarto also appeared in 1946 with *Miss Otis Comes to Picadilly*, written by Frank Dubrez Fawcett who had been a prolific writer for many years. During the forties and fifties he claimed he was "writing a book every fortnight, straight onto the typewriter without even a read-through till I got the printer's proofs. So though very big sales resulted the quality was not high from a literary point of view." He achieved this prolific output by writing every day, even when on holiday, and preferred to write between 4 a.m. until noon, during which time he would neither eat nor drink (not even water).

Fawcett continued to write the adventures of Miss Otis and other hard-boiled characters for seven years, securing his

Below: Interest in american style crime led to the popularity of magazines like Detective Monthly and the Corgi editions of tough crime writer WR Burnett's novels, as in the 1956 book "Vanity Row " (Mortelmans art).

 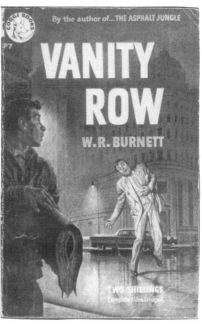

The early 50s also proved popular for crime author Darcy Glinto and Norman Lazenby (under the Gaston Lamond byline, overprinted in this case). The Modern Fiction bylines of "Griff" and "Ben Sarto" ventured into the areas of sex, sadism and drug peddling as below

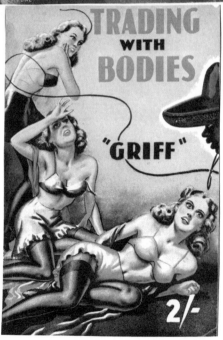

pen-names popularity and achieving sales of a million copies in one and a half years. By that time his publisher had begun to use other authors under the Sarto name which resulted in court action against them by Fawcett who maintained that he had invented the name and it was therefore owned by him, also that he was known to the publishers only as Sarto and receipts and cheques were made out to him in that name. Fawcett won the case, but an arrangement was made with Modern Fiction whereby they could use the name as well. Certainly many different authors were hidden behind the name during Sarto's twelve year lifespan.

Modern Fiction Ltd., the publishers of Ben Sarto, were made a limited company in 1943, directed by E.H. and I.L. Turvey, who also owned Bernado Amalgamated Industries. The company had previously been importers of magazines, operating in 1941 from 3 Northview Parade, Holloway in North London, but later moving to Tufnell Park Road. Once established as publishers they operated out of a large warehouse at 6 Morwell Street off Tottenham Court Road in London, but retained links with Craig Mitchell & Co., a printing works in Liverpool Road, Holloway, which was later to become E.H.T. (Printers) Ltd. Frank Dubrez Fawcett was their most prolific writer, using the pen-names Eugene Glen, H. Dupres and Ben Sarto. George Stanley was another early writer, with two novels featuring the character The Black Pilgrim, and others soon followed. Modern Fiction soon developed a group of house names, with Ramon Lacroix producing romances and 'Griff' producing gangster novels. The early tales under both were the work of Ernest McKeag, an editor with the Amalgamated Press since 1923 best known as a writer of boys' and girls' fiction, who had been writing romances under the name Roland Vane since the 1920s. As with many of the early publishers Modern Fiction acted as distributors for a number of books which were 'published' by the printers, a handy way of getting around paper supply shortages.

Paper supply was all important and was the making or breaking of most companies. To run a company was to enter into a world of endless searching for that one commodity, and the situation is summed up by Stephen Frances, who launched Pendulum Publications in 1945. The following account describes how he came into the world of publishing, aided by his colleague, Harry Whitby:

> It was a good time, and a bad time, to start publishing.
> Due to paper rationing and shortage the bookstalls had little reading matter on display and eagerly snapped up anything on offer. Sales were assured, but it was difficult to obtain paper. I spent almost all my time running around to find printers who had paper to spare and rarely having success. Most printers hadn't any paper to spare and those

that did have gave quotations that not only included their printer's profit, but a publishing profit too. Take it or leave it. I left it...

However there were a few small printers who had spare paper and who's quotations were not too outrageously high. So slowly, Pendulum Publications Ltd. began to publish and while visiting printers and book distributors I kept my ears open, asked questions and learned the rudiments of the publishing business...

All this took place during the last months of the war and into the uneasy peace. The problems and frustrations of publishing were enormous. Everything was in short supply and delay was a way of life. Bombs fell, disrupted deliveries and destroyed premises. Day-long electricity cuts during one of the worst winters on record *[1946-47]* stopped printers working and had us sitting at our desks in overcoats, trying to correct galley-proofs with numbed fingers. We were a staunch group of companions all trying to put Pendulum on the map...

Because of paper rationing printing costs were very high and profit margins extremely slender. Then, when Harry wanted to occupy his Lincoln's Inn Chambers, Pendulum Publications had to move its offices to a shop in Chancery Lane and rent a stockroom in Southampton Row. This increased our overheads, but our staff liked their work and accepted low wages while editors worked on a royalty basis. If it had been overwise we couldn't have stayed in business. My first task on Monday was to consult the list of distributors owing us money and chase after them until I'd brought in enough cash to pay next Friday's wage bill. I often failed and had to rely upon Harry for a temporary loan. We both drew for ourselves the same pay as one of our typists, but Harry never received his and it figured in the books as owing to him.

As a "Capitalist" employing some twenty people and running a business with a sizeable turnover, I found myself working for less wages than I could have earned as a costings clerk. In practise it was always touch and go if the business could pay the overheads and wages. It was the "incidentals" that provided a little economic reserve against rainy days. Some people didn't use their paper quota and instead sold it for a profit. On occasions I was offered Bible paper, or thick paper I couldn't use, while I knew a publisher who had need of it. I bought and resold the paper by telephone, making a considerable profit for a few minutes work. This "profit" went into the business.

On one occasion I went to a railway bookstall distributor with the mock-up of a lithographic picture-book of film stars. The printer had insisted I use all his paper that he had available. This meant that I would have an edition of 60,000. It was hard to judge the market. I couldn't be sure I'd sell even half this quantity, so I costed very carefully, bringing the selling price down as low as possible to attract buyers. At one and sixpence I confidently expected the buyer to give me a substantial order.

"How many will you take?" I asked.

"None."

I couldn't believe it. "What's wrong with it?" I asked.

"The price."

This was a blow. Any further reduction in selling price would yield only a nominal profit even if I sold out completely.

"How many are you printing?" asked the buyer.

"Sixty thousand."

"I can't take any at that price. It's not worth my while to handle them. But if you increase the price to two shillings I'll take the lot."

I walked away with an order that yielded sixty thousand sixpences more than I'd hoped for.

Pendulum were one of the many publishers who mixed non-fiction and fiction on their list. Film books were highly popular and amongst Pendulum's regular magazines was *Film Quarterly*, edited by Peter Noble and published by Pendulum's subsidiary, Ward & Hitchon, as well as film quiz books and other related items.

Another company launched in the War years was Bernards Publishers Ltd., established in 1942. The directors came from two families who were to have a strong grip on the original paperback field for many years: Bernard and Sadie Babani, and Albert and Judith Assael. Bernards still exists today, publishing mainly technical manuals on electronics and radio, much as they did in the early years. The importance of the company was as the launching pad from which some of the most prolific mushroom companies were founded, including three of the few to outlast the paperback boom.

Two companies were launched in 1943: Bear Hudson Ltd., directed by Ellie and Albert Assael and based at 63 Goldhawk Road, London W12, and Hamilton & Co. (Stafford) Ltd., who had premises close by at two adjoining shops, 1 & 2 Melville Court, directed by Henry Assael and Joseph Pacey. Bear Hudson were first off the mark with the publication of a variety of non-fiction and fiction novels from 1944; these were variously sized depending on what paper was available, and amongst the output were a number of crime novels by Frank

Dubrez Fawcett (as Coolidge McCann and Elmer Elliot Saks) and Norman Firth (under his own name and the pen-names Jackson Evans and Leslie Halward). Hamilton's began publishing in 1945, and again used a great many stories by Norman Firth in a programme which included romance, western and gangster novels.

Norman Firth is one of a group of writers who were closely associated with the mushroom publishers in the late 1940s and is worthy of a study in his own right. Born in 1920, he was the son of Henry Wesley Firth, a theatrical producer, and Mary E. Firth, little is known about his early life, although a strong theatrical flavour is introduced in many of his stories, probably the influence of his father. Certainly his father influenced his choice of the name under which he wrote: the majority of his stories appeared as by N. Wesley Firth, although birth records show that he had no middle name. The family lived in Birkenhead, Liverpool, where Firth worked during the War as an assembler in an aircraft factory. He married Olga Hendry in October 1944, which would appear to have been the launching point of his writing career, for in 1945 he suddenly burst upon the publishing world with a spate of stories.

Firth sold his first story to Gerald G. Swan, a short tale entitled "Professional Killer" which appeared in *Crime Shorts No.1* (1946). The story introduced Merrick Lawrence, as 'hard-boiled' a character as one could hope to meet, but unlike his contemporaries Lawrence was not a private eye, but (as the title implied), a professional killer; the twist to the character was that he would only kill those who deserved it ‑ a killer with morals. Lawrence appeared in numerous short stories and novels, and proved to be Firth's most enduring character. By the time the story was published, Firth had already seen a number of stories in print, quite a few of them in various Swan publications, as well as his first book, a collection of short stories entitled *This Is Murder, Lady!*, published in August 1945 by Bear Hudson, which introduced two other Firth characters, Al M'cfee and "Red" Benton who were also to appear elsewhere.

Lawrence had a touch of 'The Saint' about him, and Firth's stories often had elements of humour which were lacking in so many of his rivals. Hasty writing, and some repetitive story-lines (particularly in his westerns) are criticisms that could be levelled against him, but Firth's popularity was not diminished through cardboard characterisation: action was the call of the day, and his 'novels' (some of them lasting only 24 or 32 pages) did not allow the space for development unless a series ensued. Regular readers did not need to be told that their hero was tough and as ruthless as the crooks he fought ‑ it was expected of them, and Firth was so adept at this style of writing that he produced two million words of material in two years, and was easily capable of turning out 6,000 words at a sitting.

Not all his work was in the gangster field. With equal ease he turned his hand to detective stories, westerns, romances, science fiction, stories for schoolboys and even fairy tales. Firth's strength was in taking an already established formula and turning it to his own advantage. Thus his schoolboy stories in the 'Porky' and 'Harcourt' series were very closely based on Frank Richards' Greyfriars stories. The 'Harcourt' series introduced Eustace Green, Dave Montrose, Jimmy Wild, and Harry West, otherwise known as the Ferocious Four of the Remove... any reader of *The Magnet* will immediately recognise the influences! Richards (Charles Hamilton), almost certainly the most influencial boys' magazine writer of the century, was himself tapping the same market, as by now his regular school story markets, *The Magnet* and *The Gem*, had folded, and he was producing the 'Sparshott', 'Headland House' and 'Topham' series' for publishers William Merrett and John Matthew.

Firth's 'Harcourt' stories were comparative best-sellers and prompted a follow-up, the 'Castleton' stories published as by Olga Hendry. Formula plagiarism did not stop at the juvenile stories: the novel *Desire At Midnight* (Curzon, 1946) introduced Talbot Sinner, a gentleman-crook known as The Phantom, and written in the Raffles mould, and the science fiction adventure *Terror Strikes* (Hamiltons, 1946) was strongly based on H.G. Wells' *The Invisible Man*. Direct plagiarism was unnecessary: Firth had a fertile enough imagination to create his own situations, stifled by the demands of his publishers. Stories flowed from his typewriter at such a tremendous rate, and he was capable of filling a whole magazine with a variety of stories by himself. The well known habit of using pen-names (implying some kind of selectivness on the part of the often non-existent editor) was prevalent at the time, thus Net Anson, Jackson Haines and Mac Raine who filled the pages of *Paget's 1/- Western No.2* were all Firth in various guises. It is doubtful whether all of his pen-names will ever be discovered, as he used at least 100, many of them only once, as well as publishing stories anonymously. Amongst the more prolific of his pen-names were Joel Johnson, Rice Ackman and Leslie Halward; his most regular guise, Earl Ellison, was later used as a house name by John Spencer & Co.

Firth wrote much of the fiction published by Utopian Publications, and moved from Liverpool with his wife and newly born daughter (Sheila A. Firth, which he also used as a pen-name), to London, living at Benson Herbert's home in Roland Gardens. Whilst in London Firth became increasingly ill with Tuberculosis, eventually returning to Birkenhead where he died on December 13th 1949 at the tragically young age of 29. In only five years he produced some five million words of fiction and articles, as productive as many of the American pulp writers, and in England he rejoiced under the name "The Prince of the Pulp Pedlars". It cannot be said that any of his vast output could be seen as classic, or even worth reprinting, but his work retained a standard of action and adventure and humour over and above the requirements of most of the mushroom publishers. Even during his last months after contracting TB Firth was as compulsive a writer as ever, writing a complete 30,000 word racy magazine every month for Utopian, with titles such as *Harlem Hotspots, Cowgirl Capers* and *Hula Hotcha!* His last novel was published posthumously in hardcover: entitled *When Shall I Sleep Again?* it was dedicated to his wife, Olga, to whom he left nearly £1,500 earned from his writing in his will, a tidy sum in those days.

If he had lived it is impossible to predict what Firth might have achieved as a writer. In 1947 he was reported as saying he hoped to turn his pen to the creation of something a little more enduring. Critic and publisher Bevis Winter said "undoubtedly his vast store of knowledge and this grinding experience of the designing and delivery of plots and characters will enable him to attack his more serious subjects with considerable confidence. Who knows what literary achievements are possible."

What Firth's story illustrates, apart from the fact that a great deal of money could be made from high-speed writing, was the habit of using one author alone for all types of story. Most of the writers who filled the lists of the mushroom publishers were adept at turning out anything from light romances to the most shockingly violent gangster fiction, and it was this very versatility that attracted publishers. The rates of pay (generally between 10/- and £1 per thousand words) were relatively low (even at 1 cent a word, the pulps in America were paying the equivalent of £3/12/- a thousand), and the rule for writers was that if you wanted to survive in the field you had to write fast, and write for any publisher who required your work; if one writer fell by the wayside there were many others looking for a break, and there were more and more publishers arriving to grant them the opportunity of seeing their work in print. However, for those who could stand the pace of the tread-mill, the rewards could be great: Firth was earning up to £6 in one sitting at a time when the average wage was £7 a week!

As mentioned above, 1943 had seen the arrival of Bear Hudson and Hamiltons, and a third arrival from the same stable was Brown Watson Ltd. who had premises at Shop 1, The Grampions, Western Gate, London W6. The directors were husband and wife Bernard and Sadie Babani, who were also directors of the allied company Instructive Arts Ltd. The company was taken over by Bernard's younger brothers, Albert and Solomon, when they began publishing fiction in 1945, producing a number of 32 page pulp-sized anthology titles between 1946 and 1949. These were generally filled by one author alone, and whilst generally in the usual fields of western and confessions, they included such diverse titles as *Tales of the Turf.* One of their writers in the early days was Aida Reubens (Ada Rawkins) an ex-cinema pianist who had turned to writing sentimental verses for greetings cards with the arrival of 'talkies', and to crime novels when her first efforts at fiction were rejected with the note: "I like your style. Could you write thrillers?" Under the imprint Bush Publications Brown Watson published their first full-length novel, *Palm Beach Girl* by Vicki Rosa (1948) after which they became prolific publishers in all fields.

The Assael family (of Bear Hudson and Hamilton & Co.) had connections with yet another company when Sol Assael, along with Michael Nahum, launched John Spencer & Co. in 1946 with a number of crime anthologies, *Crime Confessions, Phantom Detective Cases*, and *Mystery Crime Cases* amongst them. The stories were the work of Norman Firth and another prolific writer of romances and westerns, John F. Watt, a Scotsman who had worked freelance since 1933 except for a spell in the R.A.F. during the War. Watt is later believed to have turned to science fiction stories, writing the majority of yarns that appeared in Spencer's four science fiction magazines which first appeared in April 1950. These four, *Futuristic Science Stories, Worlds of Fantasy, Tales of Tomorrow* and *Wonders of the Spaceways*, have the dubious honour of being widely regarded as the worst SF magazines to ever appear!

Many of these minor publishers were also publishing in another growth area, that of children's comics. In the same way as adult fiction and newspapers had been devastated by the wartime restrictions of paper, so had the major publishers of juvenile fiction. Amalgamated Press, the leading publisher of boys' and girls' fiction for many years, had folded over thirty magazines almost overnight in 1940, and their largest rival, D.C. Thomson, had laid off many of their staff earlier that same year.

A number of small publishers grew up in the provinces, and new comics appeared in Liverpool, Manchester, and in particular in Glasgow where many of the ex-Thomson artists were to find work. Amongst the first was Gerald Swan in 1940 whose American style comic books appeared at irregular intervals throughout the War. Swan was one of a number of publishers who discovered the popularity of American comic-books and magazines, and amongst other distributors who also imported from America were A. Soloway, Leonard Miller and the Anglo-American Magazine Co. Modern Fiction were importing material as early as 1941, but imports were soon stifled, and most of these distributors were forced to either publish their own material, or produce British editions of

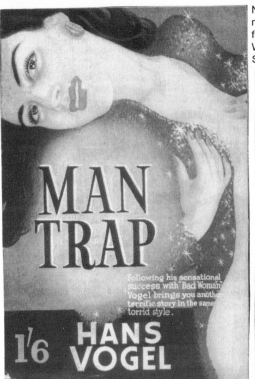

Norman Lazenby's career shows the versatility required by an author, producing tough romance for Modern Fiction (as Lacroix, 1952) and Muir Watson (as Vogel, 1950) as well as SF for Spencers and Gannet (as Bengo Mistral, 1953)

American magazines. These were recalled by Gordon Landsborough, an editor for Hamiltons at the time, who commented:

> After World War II periodicals were not permitted to be imported from America because of the dollar balance of payments problem. That is, except for newspapers, and one very astute Midlands company spotted a loophole in the Act.

> They shipped over vast numbers - tens of millions - of newspapers from Canada and the U.S. The papers were those with coloured comic supplements. When they reached England, the Midlands company solemnly threw away the newspaper and sold the comic supplements. All perfectly legal. And in that time of shortage the comics enjoyed enormous sales. In time, of course, the loophole was sealed, and comics were not permitted for import in this manner, and this set the Midlands company a problem.

> A big following had been made for American comic book heroes. The Midlands firm weren't going to lose this support, so they began to fly in matrices moulded from American comic books metal, from which they made there own plates and printed them in Britain. Because of this we became accustomed to the American comic book and those cartooned heroes "Superman", "Captain Marvel" and others.

R & L Locker had first produced comics before turning to their Paul Renin reprints, their first title, *Reel Comic*, appearing in 1944. Similarly, Modern Fiction were also producing such titles as *Comical Cuts* (1947) alongside sensational romances like *Informal Love* and *Slaves of Passion* by Ramon Lacroix. In 1949 they began a steady production of comics under the guiding hand of editor and packager Denis Gifford, although all were short lived. The best of these was *Ray Regan*, drawn by Ron S. Embleton, a sixteen-page comicbook printed in two-tone photogravure and modelled on the comics then being produced by T.V. Boardman & Co. Boardmans, who had been founded in the 1930's importing American comics, turned to British reprints in 1940, setting up a deal with Quality Comics which allowed them to reprint two 64 page American comicbooks as four 32 pagers. They also launched their own series of photogravure comics, reprinting the adventures of "Blackhawk", drawn by Reed Crandell and "The Spirit", drawn by another great American artist, Will Eisner. These were supplemented by original comics, "Swift Morgan" and "Roy Carson", both the work of Denis McLoughlin who was to take over another reprint line featuring "Buffalo Bill"; McLoughlin, whose work has in recent years come in for much critical appraisal, is now probably best known for his acclaimed work on Boardman's hardcover dust-jackets and paperback covers which he drew and painted for over twenty years, having gained a contract with

Boardmans in 1948.

Most of the comics produced during this period were, however, usually thin affairs of 8 or 12 pages, printed in two colours and sold for 3d. Historian and collector Denis Gifford noted in his *British Comic Catalogue* that they "were also printed on whatever paper was available, ranging from coloured paper and beige cardboard to one-sided silver paper! Available paper also dictated size and shape, from tiny folders in vest-pocket size to oblongs both upright and landscape."

One of the more prolific producers of comics were Martin & Reid Ltd. who issued many titles between 1944 and 1950. Amongst the editors of these comics were Louis Diamond, Mick Anglo and Bob Monkhouse (later a noted radio scriptwriter and TV celebrity, today hosting many popular games shows). During his time at Martin & Reid, Mick Anglo was also writing a number of novels, including westerns, and gangster novels under the name Johnny Dekker. Martin & Reid were also producing confessions magazines, as well as the Arrow and Mascot series' of novels which included stories of all types.

A number of other publishers produced both comics and short novels. Paget Publications launched many different titles in an effort to conform to the ruling that no new periodical was allowed, periodical being the key word here. A Christmas tradition in Britain was the Annual, a yearly, usually hardcover, edition of a children's magazines or comic, or featuring popular radio or newspaper characters. The word annual could not be used for any new venture, since it implied a regular schedule, so Gerald Swan called his annuals Albums, and even the giant Amalgamated Press produced the yearly *Knockout Fun Book* to avoid any potential problems. Paget distinguished their comics by their titles which, to give a sense of continuity, all began *The Paget....* These were essentially all one-offs, but even the *Paget's Tupney* which ran to ten issues was forced to insert a new word into the title when issued, leading to such titles as *Paget's Dazzle Tupney, Paget's Dandy Tupney* and *Paget's Daddle Tupney*. Around 1949 Paget cut down on their comic output in order to concentrate on short novels and, increasingly, racy magazines with titles like *Slick Bedtime Stories.*

Another prolific producer of comics was Scion Ltd. The driving force behind Scion was Binyimin Zeev Immanuel, a Latvian student born in Riga in 1907, who had come to Britain in 1933 when Hitler rose to power, arriving with only £3 to his name. He had studied economics at University College, London, and was encouraged to stay in Britain rather than return to his native land (which was soon to disappear as an independent country anyway). When war broke out he tried unsuccessfully to join the army, instead finding work as a milkman; after that he took a job teaching Hebrew at a private school in Brighton,

Artist Denis McLoughlin painted hundreds of covers for TV Boardman from the late '40s to late 50's in his unique style. Like many artists of the period he also drew comics (as he does to this day).

Many children of the '50s will be familiar with his "Buffalo Bill Annuals", put together almost singlehandedly or with the help of his brother Colin.

Boardman hardbacks with McLoughlin dustjackets were a familiar sight on Library shelves in the 50s.

and married Esther Benjamin in 1941. His teachers pay would not support his new family so he took a job selling advertising space, and after a year he had made enough money to buy the lease on 37a Kensington High Street, London, and set up Apex Publicity Service. From another room his wife launched an employment agency, the Court Agency, and within the year the Immanuels launched a small publishing venture under the name C.A.S. Ltd.

Their success was immediate: in 1947 they issued a small photo-book featuring Rita Heyworth in various film-still poses and, because of the unsettled publishing climate which guaranteed sales to anything appearing, the one-shilling, 16 page booklet sold two hundred thousand copies. Under C.A.S. Ltd. and Apex Publicity Services they issued children's comics, and the success of these early publications led them to set up Scion Ltd. in 1948, publishing a number of comics in the *Big...* series. This was a similar ploy as that used by Paget, with titles including *Big-Time Comic* (1947), *Big Chuckle Comic* (1948) and *Big Shot Comic* (1949). Their two best artists were Ron Embleton and Ron Turner, both of whom were appearing in comics for the first time. Another fine artist, James Holdaway (later to become the artist of "Modesty Blaise" in the *Evening Standard)* was a staff artist with Scion for some time. Scion's comics were a small but constant part of their output, but they turned to fiction publishing in 1948 producing a series of 32 and 40 page romance novelettes, expanding quickly to 112 and 128 page full-length novels and assembling a popular line of gangster and western novel writers.

Whilst many other publishers tried their hand at the occasional comic (including Bear Hudson, Grant Hughes, Hamilton & Co., Kangaroo Books and Bernard Kaye), it never formed as great a market for most as the novels, especially as the market was dominated by two companies with many years experience behind them. That experience has shown over the years, and even today the two companies - Dundee based D.C. Thomson and London based Amalgamated Press, now known as Fleetway Editions - still dominate the juvenile market.

Scion's success was due partly to the business acumen of the Immanuels, partly to the editorship of Maurice Read and his successors Julian Franklyn and Alistair Paterson. It should be mentioned that many of the publishers seemed to lack any sort of editorial control, and novels seemed to be accepted by some on being the right length rather than for any sort of quality. One author, a journalist who wrote thrillers and foreign legion novels briefly, noted that his publishers "had no literary or cultural gloss at all. They could quite easily have been mass producing stockings of doubtful quality for the barrow trade." They were in the publishing business solely for profit, and cut costs wherever possible; the author of one novel noted: "When I went to collect the dough [the publisher] dealt with me. They paid £1 a thousand and although the contract stipulated 47,000 words [he] had counted them - he claimed - and said there were only 45,000, so caught me for a couple of quid." Another cost-cutting publisher found an easier way than counting wordage: he simply removed the middle of the manuscript, with no thought to the continuity of the story, and paid for what remained!

Those who operated without the help of experienced editors were prone to all sorts of problems, not least of all the occasional author who pulled a fast one. In one case an author approached a publisher with a thriller whilst the editor was out; the publisher liked it immediately and paid for it on the spot, proudly showing the thriller to his editor when he returned. The editor took one look and announced "Great, you've just bought Raymond Chandler's *The Big Sleep!*"

The publishers who had the fortune to employ even half-decent editors, many of whom had as little previous experience at editing as the publishers had at publishing, were very lucky indeed.

One such publisher was Hamilton & Co. Editors in the early days included Dennis H. Pratt, and Edwin Self. The latter had some twenty years of experience in the publishing field, and was quick to spot the potentials of the western and gangster in the days of paper shortage. Early novels by Norman Firth and Michael Hervey exploited the crime and even the science fiction market, but Hamiltons quickly turned to westerns and gangsters as their mainstays. Self moved on to set up two new companies with Hamilton's co-director, Joe Pacey, and Hamiltons found themselves an excellent editor in Gordon Landsborough, who recalls the events thus:

> I came into this curious world of publishing in 1949 for the simple reason that I was flat broke. As a writer and journalist (among other things, I had launched *Reveille* for its first owner in 1940), I was just one of thousands who came through the war to find there were few jobs going in publishing, whether it was in newspapers, periodicals or books. One day I saw an advertisement in *Advertisers' Weekly:* "Wanted, Production Manager". I decided I was a production manager, and went after the job.

> The advertiser was Hamilton & Co. (Stafford) Ltd., who operated from two adjacent shops in Goldhawk Road, Shepherds Bush, London. I learned that the production manager was required for paperback book production, of which I had no experience. The inadequacies of salary ˉ £8.10s.0d a week ˉ matching my inadequacies in this field, I got the job. But I was married, had three children, and couldn't live on that money. So I stipulated that

Scion are most re-
membered for the se-
ries of "Scientific"
novels under the
bylines of Vargo Stat-
ten and Volsted Grid-
ban. The former being
the prolific author
John Russell Fearn
and the latter either
Fearn or EC (Ted)
Tubb. It was the suc-
cess of these that
prompted the "mush-
room" publishers to
flood out a multitude
of often inferior SF
novels.

Hamiltons rapid development under the guidance of Gordon Landsborough can be seen in the difference between the early Strange Adventures magazine (with Perl at his worst painting a monster cover) through the acclaimed Science Fiction Fortnightly/Authentic Series to the still familiar Panther books.

Hamilton's must contract to buy one book a month from me, to supplement my salary to the tune of some £18 a month ‑ and I needed the "lolly".

Before accepting the job at that low rate of pay, I took home some of the firm's products. I read them and I was appalled. Until that moment I had never known of the existence of this type of publishing. I'd been brought up on Penguins, and those *were* books. These weren't worthy of the description.

I was shocked by the deplorably low standard of story-telling. At no other time in history, I am confident, could such wretched examples of craftsmanship have had money invested in them. So bad were they that my first reaction was to turn down the job, with its poor rate of pay. Then came the realisation that here was a golden opportunity. With such dreadful story-telling, I could see ways of improving the situation and getting more for myself into the bargain...

My job as production manager proved to be something of a euphemism. For £8.10s.0d a week I was everything ‑ editor, sub-editor, blurb writer and, for a time, proof-reader, *and I had to commission and handle twelve to fourteen original manuscripts a month.* Manuscripts rolled in unsolicited, and these I had to read because from the start I was looking for talent ‑ except for two writers there was none on Hamilton's list in those days...

Each day I spent reading, punctuating, correcting spelling, "subbing" manuscript after manuscript as I went along. The MSS were a little more presentable when I'd finished with them, but they were still terrible. It was murderous work, and I do not know how I coped with handling over a dozen MSS a month, each night forcing myself to write 3,000 words of a western. I think the quality of product I was handling was so much against my instincts, and the pace at which I had to work so intense, that I developed a headache which remained with me for years...

My publisher, for all my critical feelings of him, had many likeable qualities. We battled, but we got on well together. He listened to my blasphemous comments on the quality of his products and there were signs that he could see ahead and might agree to a change in policy.

Six weeks after I had started with Hamilton's he said I was doing an excellent job and he was going to raise my pay to £16 a week. This was quite big money in those days. He recognised that I could not work at that pace and also write a book a month and keep sane. He asked me not to write any more books for him: we compromised and I continued writing, but at a more leisurely pace...

I advertised for writers in various journals ⁻ for westerns, American gangster stories and for science fiction. I was able to increase the rate of pay to 15/- a thousand words for the westerns, but up to £1 a thousand for the other two. We were on our way to better things. I began to visualise a list of quality in a few years' time, confident that better pay would bring better authors and a bigger readership...I was very innocent!

The adverts did attract authors of some quality, and Hamiltons began to develop a far better line of books than many of their contemporaries, with writers like Leonard T. Barnard, Richard Conroy, Graham Fisher, James McCormick, William Maconachie and Norman Robson all capable of producing readable gangster and western stories. Harry Hossent was attracted by an advert, saying later: "It was October, I needed some money for Christmas and saw an advertisement asking for 50,000 word thrillers. So I locked myself in the kitchen and I typed the words 'The blonde was very dead'. After that it all seemed to work." The finished novel was sold to Hamiltons where it appeared as *Book A Hearse Now* by Jeff Bogar (1951).

Landsborough instigated a series of science fiction novels which he linked by the banner *Authentic Science Fiction*. This series attracted the talents of H.J. (Bert) Campbell, a research chemist and member of the Royal Horticultural Society, who wrote a number of excellent tales under his own name and the pen-name Roy Sheldon. Campbell was later to become editor of the series, by which time it was firmly established as a magazine and included a number of departments and later short stories in its pages.

The success of Hamiltons had earlier led to the launch of two more companies. D.A. Fletcher and Joseph Pacey, the co-director of Hamiltons, launched Grant Hughes from 131 Brackenbury Road, London W6 in 1946. They produced a mixture of westerns, romance, crime and non-fiction. In the latter category came children's books on soccer, boxing and cricket, and a series of *Boys Book of Famous...* hardcovers which included *Aeroplanes, Liners* and *Railway Engines* (all 1948). The fiction was written in the main by Norman Firth, Frank Griffin, James A. Jordan and Dennis T. Hughes, all of whom were capable of churning out short novels on any subject as required.

A third company, Curtis Warren, was formed in 1948, and with all three producing almost identical product and a great deal of swapping around went on: Norman Lazenby sold one novel to Hamiltons and it appeared from Grant Hughes, Curtis reused old Grant Hughes artwork, and company co-director and editor Edwin Self had a habit of writing to his authors on whatever headed notepaper first came to hand. The new company, whose original offices were given at 42 Gray's Inn Road, London

WC1 (the address of Gray's Inn Press, a prolific printer for the paperback companies), soon settled at Holbex House, 81 Lambs Conduit Street, London WC1 from where they began an extensive publishing schedule that was to see them become one of the most prolific publishers of the period, producing books at an average rate of seven books a month, with the majority of them published between 1950 and 1954.

The early books were 6d and 9d short novels, plus a few 24 and 32 page pulp size novelettes, most of these were written by the highly prolific Dennis Talbot Hughes, about whom very little is known. His output was tremendous, and seems to have been almost exclusively for the Curtis Warren/ Grant Hughes/ Hamilton & Co. group with the former being the publisher of the vast majority. Westerns poured from his typewriter, crime fiction, romances, and (when the call came) science fiction and jungle adventures. His style· was typical of the speed writers: short sentences and a profusion of "Then:" for quick switches in dialogue. Most surprisingly, although written at the rate of one a week, some of the later books which mixed science fiction (of the most basic type) and some rather imaginative fantasy were quite readable, and his Jungle Jim like stories of Rex Brandon under the name Marco Garron are also solid, fast-moving adventures.

Two other Curtis Warren authors were also highly capable of speed-writing: Frederick Foden was the author of many gangster novels under the names Brett Vane, Nick Baroni, Kirk David, and many others, whilst John Jennison started on the gangster novels, moved briefly to science fiction and later produced a high proportion of Curtis Warren's western line, all at the rate of one a week. Jennison and Hughes were Curtis' most pseudonymous writers, using 57 known pen-names between them for this one company alone!

Curtis Warren were interesting for another mushroom habit: in many cases the cover of the book was prepared by an artists agency, or by a freelance artist, with the name and title chosen by the publisher. The cover would then be sent to the author; sometimes an author was already half-way through the book, sometimes almost finished, and some marvellously contrived passages to explain the cover and title were often inserted. The names were rarely used by one author alone, and the process of choosing who would write as whom seems totally random, just so long as more than one author was used to prove that the name belonged to the publisher. Thus any one byline could conceal a number of different authors of varying quality, and very little continuity (or for that matter, reader loyalty) could build up around any one name, unlike (say) the gangster writers working for Scion who often had pen-names they used exclusively.

* * * * * *

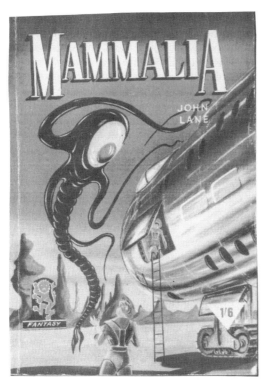

Curtis Warren Books may have given us some of the worst Science Fiction written, but they did use some of the weirdest cover art.

London was not the only home of the mushroom publishers, and the provinces had there fair share of small enterprises springing up. Probably the second busiest city was actually in Scotland: Glasgow had a flourishing publishing scene, with the with the likes of M.C. Publications Ltd producing the works of Rick Razio (whose work included the wonderfully titled *Blondie Beg Your Bullet* (c1950)) and D. L'Arnaud romances. The most prolific of these publishers were Muir-Watson Ltd. of 112 Bath Street, Glasgow C2., launched in 1948 with the publication of *My Confession* and *True Love* magazines. How these came to be is here explained by co-director, John Watson:

Published by
MUIR-WATSON LTD

> The growth of Muir-Watson took place before contraception was as sophisticated as it is today. In 1946 I emerged from the R.A.F. as a Flight Lieutenant with a D.F.C., some distinction as a pilot who knew how to bomb Germans, a wife and child and more or less bugger all else.
>
> As a lad I had started as a boy journalist on *The Glasgow Herald*, but they had forgotten career promises made during the War, so I decided to found a magazine which would capture the Renaissance-like feeling in the arts and politics which was prevalent in Scotland at the time. It was called *The Glasgow Review* and needless to say I had lost my shirt before I could say "cut"!
>
> One day a wholesaler in Glasgow pleaded with me as I delivered a new issue, 'Not that fucking thing again!' So I picked up something with exactly the same format and asked him if he would buy something similar if I produced it. It was *True Story*.
>
> The upshot was that I produced, double-quick, a thing called *True Love,* sold ten thousand copies and had my first profit. A guy in Manchester then brought a further eighty thousand copies and I was on my way. The trick being that I had an ex-service-men's paper-quota - which made me legit.
>
> The same people in Manchester, World Distributors, gave me an order for four hundred thousand westerns, and I was in the saddle. With that behind me I decided to be my own man ‑ there was John Muir (passive)...so I began producing romances, mysteries and westerns, until I met Mr. Turvey of Modern Fiction. He said I was wasting my time ‑ he being the publisher of Ben Sarto, very successful at the time...
>
> So I wrote *The Merry Virgin* by Nat Karta. Thorpe and Porter of Leicester approached me, and promptly agreed to buy fifty thousand Karta's a month. That was it. I then invented Hans Vogel and Hyman Zore which added another eighty thousand a month. I was in the money.

As Watson relates, Muir-Watson quickly established a western line which included many titles by John Russell Fearn as well as tales by W. Richard Hutton and Vic J. Hansen (whose name was misprinted as W.J. Hanson). The agreement with Sydney Pemberton of World Distributors for 400,000 westerns guaranteed a good profit, and further lines were quickly developed: Eileen Wilmot Graham wrote some romance titles as Eileen Wilmot, and Fearn turned in a detective tale, *Murder's A Must*.

Nat Karta, Hans Vogel and Hyman Zore were big-sellers, all three masquerading as real American authors. Short, gutteral names were an absolute necessity (according to the mushroom publishers) to fool the public into thinking these were the genuine American article, and to add credence to the claim that these were real authors, Watson ran a gag photo of himself on the inside covers of the books, and continued to write a number of titles himself.

One of the more prolific writers for Muir-Watson was Tyneside based Norman Lazenby, who had started writing at the age of 16 whilst apprenticed to a large electrical firm. He had sold his first stories in 1941 and followed them with a spate of novels to various publishers. In 1950 he produced his first tale for Muir-Watson, *Bad Woman* which appeared under the name Hans Vogel, and his comments about his work are a good guide to how novels were written in those days:

> Muir-Watson were always in a hurry and they supplied the titles and I wrote the stories at 4,000 words a day, each 4,000 a chapter which I sent off by mail that day. So they were actually printing the first chapters while I was writing the last few! I simply wrote the narrative as I went along, without plot outlines or notes.

> I note that I wrote *Shameless* and *Passion's Not For Noon* in nine days - two 45,000 word stories. So if they read lousy, you'll know why. I was taking a lesson from Fearn who told me in a letter one day that he was a seven day a week man and not a five day week guy as I had mentioned I was, and that he did 7,000 words a day. I figured if he could do that, so could I. On those two Muir-Watson books the wordage per day varied between 9,000 and 12,000 words, but, of course, when the two yarns were done I couldn't keep up working non-stop from eight in the morning to eight at night.

Although these were written at high speed, Lazenby feels that the Muir-Watson books were among his best at the time, and he received the unprecedented compliment of a raise in payment to a flat rate of £60 per novel where most publishers were paying him £1 per thousand words or less, or £15 less per 45,000 word novel.

World Distributors were just one of a group of companies based in Manchester run by the Pemberton family. The company had grown up around the beginning of the war, founded by one-time market-stall holder, Sydney Pemberton, who, like Gerald Swan in London, had discovered the selling power of magazines, comics and books imported from America. The publishing company established by the Pembertons, T.A. and E. Pemberton & Co. Ltd., was based at 11 Blossom Street, T.A. and E. Pemberton & Co. Ltd., although the company soon acquired further premises at 14 Lever Street. World Distributors Ltd., established in 1946, could be found at 22 Turner Street, all in Manchester. Fiction House Ltd., previously mentioned as the publishers of the Piccadilly Novels series, became an allied company directed by W.M. Stafford, and were giving three addresses in correspondence, their own in London, a Manchester office (the Lever Street address) and a third in Smith-Dorrien Road, Leicester, the address of printers Blackfriars Press. The Piccadilly Novels series had finally come to an end in 1950, but Fiction House quickly picked up the reins and began producing westerns at a terrific rate until the company finally folded in 1959.

Across: Fast moving spy thriller Fiction House's Piccadilly Novels line using typical artwork of the period to lure readers.

World Distributors were quite aptly named. Although most of their books were published in England, a number were published and printed in Canada by such firms as Export Publishing Enterprises Ltd. of Toronto who produced a novel by Canadian author and ex-boxer, Thomas P. Kelley - *I Found Cleopatra* - in 1946 for sole distribution by Pembertons of Manchester. Export, rumoured to have been set up by a British publisher attracted to Canada by the availability of paper, published under the Newstand Library imprint, producing racy-romances and crime novels until their Toronto-based warehouse burnt down in the Winter of 1950/51.

Bell Features and Publishing Co. Ltd., also of Toronto, produced a number of titles in their Bell Novels series for sole distribution by the Pembertons, whilst another Toronto firm, Pastime Publications Ltd., produced the first titles in the Action Novels series of westerns in 1947, the books distinguished by a red emblem on the cover. A number of other Action Novels were published by British publishers in the same period, namely Edward Foster of 362 Goswell Road, London, and Jonathan Press of Dawes Close, Worthing; the western novels published by Muir-Watson for Sydney Pemberton mentioned above were part of this series. Edward Foster and Jonathan Press also produced some titles under the Peveril Novels banner, reprinting old Piccadilly Novels.

Pembertons were also prolific publishers in their own right, and had produced romance novelettes as early as 1941. During the mid-forties they had published a number of full-length series', including crime novels as part of their Thrilling Novels series, which was later dominated by romances and became known as Thrilling Love Novels. A companion western series, Thriller Western, reprinted a number of British and American novels by the likes of Gladwell Richardson and Norman A. Fox.

As well as distributing the work of others, World Distributors became publishers themselves from 1949, one of their most popular authors being Dale Bogard, billed as the "Fastest Thriller Writer On Earth", whose tough gangster novels were strong sellers for the company. Author Douglas Enefer, attracted to the company because their rates were slightly higher and because they were based in his home town of Manchester, was one of the few writers to write in the American pulp style to graduate to the real thing, and his story "Homicide in Harlem" by Dale Bogard appeared in the American detective pulp, *Triple Detective*. World Distributors also attracted David Boyce who wrote a number of tales for them, including gangsters and romances, and other popular bylines included Larry O'Brien and Rod Callahan.

Another Manchester based firm was Cardal Publishing Co., who began publishing in the late 1940s under the direction of Archie Carmichael. Cardal were one of a number of firms hit by obscenity fines in the late 1940's which aggravated cash flow problems and soon put the company out of business.

In Bolton, author George H. Dawson set up Tempest Publications with Thomas H. Lane in 1949 and began to issue the novels of Nick Perrelli, the first of which, *Virgins Die Lonely* (1949), was written by Dawson himself. Dawson soon tired of the publishing business, and became a prolific writer for London based Archer Press under the name Michael Storme; he handed over the running of the business to Lane, leaving the Nick Perrelli byline to writer Thomas H. Martin whose work met with a great deal of success, and who recalled that:

> I wrote my first Perrelli in less than a week, incidentally, but I wouldn't have cared to write one every week! I had no contract with Tempest, but had straight dealing from the firm. At the time there was a lot of fuss about the violence and sex in the gangster novels (though they were tame compared to todays television plays) and after Dawson left I wrote Dope For Dolores for his partner Lane, a much less violent and sexy novel in accordance with Lane's new policy. Even when I was writing for Tempest I became so bored with the gangster stereotypes and American background that I introduced more complicated plots and more intelligent characters. While I was still writing for Tempest I also changed the background, as in *Terror In Tokyo* and *Gorbals Pick Up*. Before the latter could be published Tempest closed and handed over its unpublished MSS to Scion. But Scion's policy was for American backgrounds only, so the Gorbals novel (although Tempest had paid me for it) was never used. It was about a respectable Glasgow girl who, during a spell of amnesia, was picked up by the leader of a razor-gang. She soon replaced him as leader and proved capable of defeating rival gangs. At the end of the novel, a blow to the head obliterated her memory of her time as a gang leader and restored her memory of her former, normal life - to which she serenely returned and resumed her respectable routine. I preferred that novel to the American gangster novels of mine that *were* published.

A number of other provincial firms existed in the late forties, one founded by Rumanian-born civil servant Hyman Kanar in Llandudno in Wales to publish his own collections of short stories and novels, but in the main the publishing boom was centred on London where many more mushroom publishers were beginning to grow.

* * * * * * *

In 1947 Harry Whitby decided to go to Australia, and as backer of Pendulum Publications asked if his capital investment could be returned. In return he would sell Stephen Frances his share

Across: Many provincial towns had their own "mushroom" publishers. Besides George Dawson and his Tempest publications, Bolton, Lancashire also saw Dalrow publishing Phantom magazine (Illustrated by unknown artist RWS).

The town was also home to artist Denis McLoughlin, the major artist with TV Boardman. McLoughlin was also carrying out freelance work for local publishers, like Tempest and Jasmit.

of the firm. At the same time an outside offer was made to buy the company which was accepted and, with a small advance against full payment for shares, Frances became a man without a company. He would have been happy to admit that this was something of a blow ‑ he had never been in favour of authority *per se* and being his own boss was attractive, even if it involved being a "capitalist" employer of others. Unfortunately, all the plans he made were promptly ruined when Pendulum almost immediately went into liquidation and he was not paid the money he was owed. Frances now takes up the story:

> I had tasted economic freedom, enjoyed it and had no wish to return to working at the dictates of an employer. I'd rather work sixteen hours a day for myself than work a forty hour week for double the pay under a boss.
>
> I decided to gamble all to maintain my independence. I could have lived a year on my £250, but I put aside enough to live on for three months and regarded the balance as my capital. This capital I had to invest, and recoup the profit, within three months. The "profit" I made would have to be sufficient for me to live another three months while I repeated the operation.
>
> I couldn't afford to employ anybody but having had some business experience I didn't want to do so. I had enough know-how and energy to run a small publishing business single-handed.
>
> I hammered at my typewriter and wrote a Western almost non-stop in fifteen days. Meanwhile, I had an artist draw me a dust-jacket and a printer scraped up enough paper to print ten thousand paper-back books to sell for one shilling and sixpence.
>
> I visited Julius Reiter, Director of Kosmos International Distributors, and made him a proposition. "This is the dust-jacket drawing and this is the manuscript. I am willing to print and publish an edition of ten thousand and sell you the entire edition for fifty percent discount."
>
> A publisher normally allows a distributor forty percent discount. In turn, he gives the shopkeeper twenty five percent discount. If Julius bought from me at fifty percent this would mean almost double his usual gross profit. It was an attractive proposition and Julius' only risk was that he might not sell enough books to cover his costs, but in those days it wasn't very difficult to sell ten thousand western and Julius gave me a written order.

The western was entitled *Bushwhacked* and appeared under the name Tex Ryland (1948), published by Bernard Henry. Bernard Henry was another small publishing firm set up in 1948 by Bernard Henry Kornberg, who had worked at Pendulum. Kornberg also published a sports book, *Book of Boxing* by

Oswald Frederick (O.F. Snelling) as part of his short-lived venture. Snelling was himself a man with what he called "literary ambitions" and was co-director of Bertrand Snelling (Publications) Ltd. He recalls one of his books, *Battling Bruce* as "a hastily written biography of Bruce Woodcock, the then current phenomenon in British boxing, a subject which I knew considerably. It was written hastily in order to cash in before he got beaten, when nobody would want to read about him. We just about managed it. Our own publishing venture was doomed. For one thing, we were under capitalised, and for another we couldn't get the paper allocation needed to bring out a monthly magazine." Snelling wasn't the only one to discover that, and many of the one-man businesses which seemed to pop up overnight in the late forties fared as badly.

Julius Reiter, Frances' distributor, was born in Germany on June 28th 1907. As a lawyer he had defended communists early in the Hitler regime, and had soon been forced to escape, coming to England in 1933, where he made a living selling anti-Nazi literature and importing newspapers for displaced Germans which he distributed by pushbike. He launched his own publishing and distributing company, Kosmos International Agency, publishing newspapers, magazines, later expanding into westerns and detective thrillers. He gradually built up his business, only to be interrupted by the War. Arrested, he was taken to the Isle of White where he was stripped of all his possessions; he was subsequently sent to Canada, where he spent the rest of the War in a concentration camp.

Thanks to honest management of his business whilst he was incarcerated, Reiter picked up the threads after the War and launched Gaywood Distributors Ltd. in September 1947. Gaywood were one of the main distributors for paperbacks of the period and served a number of companies; Stephen Frances was just one customer amongst many, but was to become a vital part of the business with the arrival of Hank Janson in 1948.

Amongst the other companies distributed by Gaywood were those of Bernard Kaye. Kaye was a prolific publisher, starting in the late forties with the gangster novels of Ace Capelli and Johnny Grecco, and the racy romances of Andre Latour. Kaye ran his business from an office in Avenue Chambers, a large building on Southampton Row, London WC1. Other companies to be found at Avenue Chambers included Art Publicity and Kangaroo Books. Kangaroo had been publishing since 1942 and was mainly the vehicle for writer David Lynn who was by far the most prolific author for the company.

Gaywood were, of course, not the only distributors to handle paperbacks, which was a lucrative business by the late forties. Others included Thorpe and Porter of Leicester who were established in 1946, and Atlas Publishing and Distributing Co., Ltd. of Fleet Street, London who were particularly prolific in the production of British editions of American magazines, a lucrative line in the days of tight importation restrictions. Leonard Miller and Son, Ltd. of Hackney Road, London E2 are best remembered for their publication of British editions of American comicbooks and a steady line of British original comics, originating mostly from the Gower Street studio of Mick Anglo. Miller was also a large wholesaler for newspapers, books and magazines.

By 1949 the paperback industry was set for action: the publishers, printers and distribution lines had been set up, the most profitable lines were known, format and style had been established, and a host of authors (some known, others new to the writing game) were ready to turn out novel after novel to meet the demands of the public and the demands of their publishers. The mushroom publishers were in the driving seat, their business practises sometimes sounding like the concoctions of their authors, as Gordon Landsborough recalls:

Up to 1949, these publishers did not even employ sales representatives. Such were the shortages that they sold most of their product by telephone. It was astonishing to listen to them over the telephone. They would phone up a succession of wholesalers (many of them mushroom firms like themselves) and would quote the titles currently available. It was not a question of trying sales talk to get big orders either. The wholesaler would state his requirements and the publisher would tell him how many he could have, generally cutting the order because of restricted supplies. Astonishing publishing, but it only lasted about four years.

British publishing was poised on the brink of a phase that might, as Landsborough later said, be dismissed as a writer's fantasy. All that was needed was paper, and in March 1950 paper was deregulated.

3

THE NEW BRITISH PULPS

"To be truthful this little lot doesn't represent a very happy period of my life; chiefly, I think, because I was never as good a fictionist as Vic [Hanson] and the rest of them who made a success of moving into the clothbound field as commercial novelists. On the other hand, I managed to keep the wolf from the door with the aid of the old treadmill and for those days, when the war had hardly cooled and the Beatles hadn't arrived to bring in a new pop prosperity, perhaps it wasn't such a bad time after all. At least we had youth on our side then and if some of these titles make me cringe now, at least £1 a thou would buy more beer than it does nowadays."

David Boyce, private communication (1984)

When paper was deregulated, even the 'boom' of the late forties was nothing compared to what happened next. The paperback publishers which had grown up in the post-War years suddenly had the one commodity they needed; they went into overdrive.

In April 1950 John Spencer produced the first issue of *Futuristic Science Stories*, full of stories by Norman Lazenby, John F. Watt and Frederick Foden. Lazenby was the only one of the three to have appeared in any other science fiction magazine previously, and even he would be happy to admit these were not his best. The rate of pay was 10/- a thousand, and no author was going to craft his best work for such rates. Four magazines appeared in all, each as lamentable as the last. A few recognisable names contributed who were able to command slightly higher pay, amongst them Sydney Bounds who recalls:

At 15/- a thousand, I wrote the stuff directly onto the typewriter, and it went out with minimal revision. At this time I was not on the phone and Spencer's would send me a telegram; then I'd rush to the call box to phone them to learn their latest requirements. After a while I began to wonder why I was never invited to the editorial office. One evening, while travelling to visit friends in the area, I watched for No. 24 as the bus went along Shepherds Bush Road: and lo! It turned out to be a second-hand clothes shop.

As well as writing science fiction short stories, Bounds also wrote a number of gangster novels, his tales appearing under a number of house names invented by Spencers. The Earl Ellison byline, first used as a pen-name by Norman Firth, was taken over when Firth died and used as a house name. Amongst the authors who contributed were Lazenby and Lisle Willis, himself a contributor to the science fiction magazines. They were happy to use the same authors for westerns and foreign legion novels as well, and E.C. (Ted) Tubb (whose only experience was in SF) turned out novels in both *genres*. With the magazines established, Spencers also produced a number of SF novels, the first of which was written by Gerald Evans, who had failed to sell his latest novel to an American publisher. He decided to try Spencers:

> I needed quick money, and as Spencer had bought from me, I whisked it off to them at 10/- a thousand. (They should have been outlawed.) They cut 2,000 words out of the story by removing the centre pages and paid me £19 for it!

Even at 10/- a thousand Spencers still attracted authors, and were responsible for a great deal of *genre* fiction in the early 1950s, developing a team of authors who were able to turn to any field when necessary. W.H. Fear was one of their regular western and foreign legion writers, a capable second stringer, but the two authors most associated with Spencers were John Glasby and Lionel Fanthorpe. Both started in the science fiction magazines and expanded into novels, with Fanthorpe producing most of the science fiction and supernatural lines. Fanthorpe was still producing the two lines in the 1960s, often writing a novel over the weekend with the help of a tape recorder and five typists: as the tapes came off the recorder they were farmed out to the least busy typist who would type and return that section of the manuscript. By adding up the number of words in each section, Fanthorpe would know how much space remained for him to tie up all the loose ends in his book...it often came down to one last page and something of a cult following has since built up around Fanthorpe's contrived endings.

The scientifically trained Glasby, an expert in astronomy attracted to writing science fiction by the very direness of the mushroom product, turned to crime, romance and war, especially the latter field where he turned out over 100 novels, all at the same rate of 10/- a thousand. Spencers were notoriously tight: when Tony Glynn was asked to write a crime novel he was sent a copy of the first novel in the new series, written by Ted Tubb under the name Mike Lantry; once Glynn had studied the story, Spencers requested that he return the sample copy. Another incident recalled by Lionel Fanthorpe was a visit to the firm's offices: seeing issues of magazines which contained his stories he picked up one copy of each, and as he was leaving was charged the 1/6 cover price for them.

Below: Spencers' Story Magazines Futuristic & Worlds of Fantasy gradually transformed into the popular long running Badger SF & SN series.

Hamilton & Co., increased production accordingly under editor Gordon Landsborough. As seen earlier, Hamiltons were striving for a more diverse line in their fiction than most publishers, and Landsborough, horrified by the poor standard of the usual gangster novels, tried to avoid them as best as possible. He instigated a number of new lines, including a Crime Doesn't Pay series, and a Crime and Romance series, the latter featuring a female lead in Rusty Brown, the stories written by Cass Regan (Leslie Barnard). The new style Hamiltons line included such characters as con-man Gutsy Morgan, and The Rostron Outfit which had begun as a crime series and switched half way to a western series. The stories certainly lived up to the ever present claim on the covers which boldly stated "We Never Publish A Dull Story". Landsborough was not afraid of rejecting stories which didn't fit the bill, and one author received this reply to the idea of a projected series:

> Your Queen of Sheba fills me with misgivings. I hate these kingly atmospheres, partly because everyone goes around theeing and thouing each other in stilted language that makes for stilted reading. Also, writers seem incapable of giving us kings and queens with personality; they're always exactly alike. When I get a king who's trying like hell to win a football pool, and is scared stiff of his footman, and he's got hay-fever too, I might become pro-fiction-royalty

Amongst the most prolific companies were Curtis Warren who had the ubiquitous talents of John Jennison and Dennis Hughes on their books who, between the two of them, wrote almost half of Curtis' total output. Curtis had a regular output of gangster novels and westerns in 1950, with Jennison and Frederick Foden writing most of the former under house names like Brett Vane and Nick Baroni. In March 1951 they dropped all page counts, from 128 pages to 112 pages, but the contents were much the same. Curtis were one of the most regular producers of science fiction from 1950 on, with Hughes and David Griffiths producing the first titles. More notable authors to turn up in 1951 were John Brunner and Ted Tubb. The gangster novels were almost dropped in 1952 and Jennison turned back to westerns at the rate of one almost every week. The regular Curtis lines in 1952 were westerns (with Jennison writing 21 of them in 1952 alone) and science fantasy (Hughes wrote 15 of them that year).

Edwin Self, one time editor with Hamilton's, was co-director of Curtis Warren until 1950 when arguments over policy with Joseph Pacey caused him to leave. Self, at the age of fifty and with over twenty years experience in publishing, quickly contacted his regulars with the news that he was setting up his own company with immediate requirements for sex-gangsters, science fiction and westerns. He attracted a number of Curtis

Below: Curtis Books mixed bag of mainly SF and Western paperbacks were spiced up with Gangster as well as Jungle adventures.

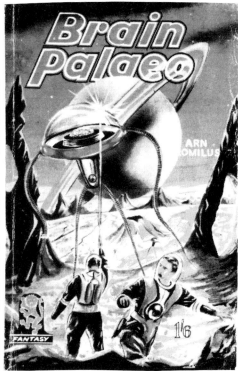

regulars, Jennison, Hughes and Albert Garrett amongst them. The gangster line was quickly established, and featured such names as Bart Banarto and Pete Costello. Self was operating out of 42 Gray's Inn Road, the address of printers Grays Inn Press, soon moving to 157 High Holborn, London WC1, where he styled himself as Publisher and Publishers' Agent, although how much agenting he did is unknown. Few authors bothered with agents in the early fifties, simply because there was a profusion of markets and the rewards were small enough without having to split them with others.

In the same way that the above companies formed something of a small group, sharing directors, editors and writers, a second group of publishers was formed around Gaywood Distributors.

Julius Reiter had founded the company in 1947 and over the years he had built up a solid distribution system, not limited to paperbacks alone. Gaywood Press was a major distributor of all types of books and magazines, and sold to a dozen major book chains such as W.H. Smith & Sons, Gordon & Gotch, Wyman's, and others. The paperbacks under his umbrella included a number of popular gangster authors, led by Hank Janson, and followed by Ace Capelli, Johnny Grecco and others. Gaywood acted as publishers themselves, securing Ralph L. Finn to write a couple of pot-boiler science fiction tales, and translating half a dozen of the popular Spanish 'Coyote' western series by Jose Mallorqui as well as the inevitable gangster line.

In early 1950, Reiter was approached by Reginald Carter, who represented the Racecourse Press. The R.P. Ltd., of 151-153 Curtain Road, London EC2 had been set up to print a newspaper for Polish refugees; unlike most presses, which were flatbed machines printing one sheet at a time, R.P. Ltd. had a rotary press. The rotary press, although it printed much faster, needed a much longer print run to make it profitable. With paper rationing coming to an end, Carter offered the presses for the printing of Hank Janson novels which, at the time, had a print run of 30,000 copies per title. With the new presses the print run went up to 35,000, and a number of titles were reprinted each month, lifting Janson to even greater heights and runaway sales.

Carter had his own plans to expand. In 1951 he bought up Poetry Editions (London) Ltd., a company founded in 1947 but which had subsequently gone bankrupt, and took over the publishing of Hank Janson under the New Fiction Press imprint. At around the same time, Julius Reiter also launched a new company, Paladin Press, to produce hardcover novels by genuine American writers.

Also in 1951, Ralph Stokes, an ex-editor and writer operating from 104 Southampton Row, London WC1 (Stephen Frances' old stockroom from the days of Pendulum Publications) took over from Bernard Kaye in the publication of Ace Capelli gangster novels, as well as launching other bylines such as Slim Brandon. The Hollyfield Printers Ltd. of Friern Barnet, London N11, responsible for the printing of many of the books published by Gaywood, Stephen Frances, Bernard Kaye and others distributed by Gaywood, also launched their own gangster series of novels in 1951 under the byline Clark Macey. Hollyfield was jointly taken over by Carter and Reiter in March 1952 and renamed the Arc Press. Carter installed a new rotary press and took over most of the printing of the Gaywood distributed companies from the summer of 1952.

Scion Ltd. were one of the companies to discover the lucrative gangster and western fields quickly, and amongst their first authors were R.C. Finney, Norman Firth and Stephen Frances, who was asked to repeat the success of the Janson novels; unable to add this new workload to his already busy schedule, Frances wrote only a couple, and rewrote novels submitted by others. These appeared under the name Duke Linton, one of the typically short, punchy house names invented by Scion for gangster novels. Amongst other authors were Bevis Winter, the ex-editor of *Stag* (one of the first magazines for men) and director of W.B. Ltd. (Stag Books) who wrote many tough gangster novels as Al Bocca and Sammy Coburn; Donald Cresswell began a successful run of novels under the name Ross Angel, and Vic. J. Hansen appeared under his own name as a popular western writer and under the name Brad Shannon, whom Steve Frances was to refer to as "the best of the bunch". Michael Barnes became a regular author for Scion under the names Ricky Drayton, Karl Medusa and others, writing whilst travelling throughout Europe. One prolific writer was Dail Ambler, a pretty, blonde ex-journalist who had spent some time in Hollywood and whose submission of a crime novel to Scion quickly led to an invitation to write a book every week. Her first tales appeared under the name Danny Spade - also the main character - in 1950, and she became a popular addition to the Scion gangster line. Scion made much of the fact that she was a she, offering a signed photo of her as a competition prize. There were only a few women writers writing for the new breed of paperback publishers although both Eileen Graham and Aida Reubens had successfully adapted to the call for crime novels.

This highly popular line-up of American gangster was backed up by the westerns of Hansen, Jim Bowie (Victor Norwood) and John Russell Fearn. In 1950 John Russell Fearn approached Scion with a science fiction novel, and was soon put under contract by Immanuel to supply two novels a month under the newly invented pen-name Vargo Statten who was quickly to become the leader in a science fiction boom, selling some five million copies of his books between 1950 and 1955.

The increase of production was fueled by the increasing availability of paper, but the novels could not be produced without authors who were willing to supply manuscripts.

Many of the mushroom publishers attracted journalists who had been drafted during the War and, on demobilisation, found their old newspapers had folded or were in a bad state of disarray. Authors found their old markets had collapsed or struggling to survive the severe paper shortage. Many publishers had more authors on their lists than they could comfortably cope with, and opportunities for freelance or new writers were virtually nil. The paperbacks were the only expanding market for fiction, and many new writers plunged onto the tread-mill with a vengeance. The publishers found it easy to fill their schedules.

As more companies entered the field, there seemed to be an endless supply of new writers, but with the use of house names it was impossible to make a name for ones-self. The busy freelancer may have been writing for as many as half-a-dozen different companies, and contracts tying an author to one company were very rare. If a publisher wanted to increase his output it was usually a matter of asking his regular authors to write faster, and few authors would turn down the opportunity of earning more money! The situation was perhaps best summed up by writer Raymond Buxton who also acted as an agent. In 1950 he wrote in reply to an enquiry: "I had such a tremendous response from ads. that it may take the source I was buying for a long time to get them *all* in print. I cannot however promise more than a pound a thousand at the moment, the market is terribly dull, as you perhaps know, and there are a crowd of hack writers 'muscling in' who take less."

The paperback market was seen by some authors as an easy, if gruelling, way to make money until the prospects for British publishers looked better. Others treated it as an education: although the paperbacks offered little in the way of editorial guidance they offered a constant market for the beginner in the same way that the American pulp magazines launched many excellent authors. Amongst the writers who felt that the paperback market held many similarities to the pulps was Norman Lazenby; at the time of writing his article on the subject of paperback publishers (reprinted below) Lazenby was 37 years of age and had been writing since the age of sixteen. He had sold his first story in 1941, a romance novel to Gerald Swan who published it as *You Can't Escape Love* (1942). Staying in reserved occupation during the War allowed Lazenby to develop himself as a writer, producing stories in any field from racy confessions to fairy tales for the very young. His article, published in *The Writer* in March 1951, gives a good contemporary view of the paperbacks from one of their most prolific writers:

THE NEW BRITISH PULPS

In this country today there are several publishing companies which have began operations since 1945. With the advent of paper "freedom" in March 1950, these publishers have become very active and they put out the equivalent of the American pulp magazine. But in Britain it is paperbacked books of crime, western and science-fantasy that are popular and not magazines of short stories.

Having sold about 170 stories, of which half are 20,000 to 65,000 word yarns, I can write authentically about this market. The usual fee is £1 a thousand words, although some receive more. I have received up to one-and-a-half guineas but not for the bulk of my output. Assuming £1 per thousand words as the minimum payment - and no writer should accept less - the fertile fictional mind can make this pay in full-time authorship, this means at least 3,000 words per day in order to earn a living wage, assuming that the slave toils for five days a week! My top output was once 12,000 words in one day. That same week I turned out 55,000 words of gangster fiction in five days. Actually over the eight days - Friday to Friday - I wrote exactly 80,000 words of this fiction and sold it all at £1 per thousand words.

Why did I do it? Well, I was working hard to gain time for a fortnight's holiday!

It may be argued that the novice writer cannot hope to compete with these methods. That may be true to a certain extent. But I believe most part-time writers can write about 2000 words in an evening, usually on cheap westerns or gangsters for this new pulp market. Anthony Trollope used to place a watch before him and write 250 words every fifteen minutes. Arnold Bennett worked to a schedule and was very upset when he failed ¯ as he did occasionally, as most writers will.

How is this done? This is how it is done. To write fiction quickly and without revision you must know instinctively the structural image of a story whether it be long or short. The writer must sense the proportions of conflict, characterisation, suspense and plot and weave them into one convincing whole. A convincing plot is one that is plausible whatever methods are used to make it so. Detail of setting and characterisation makes a story plausible. Naturalness is another ingredient which makes a yarn ring true.

One of the quickest ways to achieve production is to sit down with an opening idea, write it out competently and then try to build a story from this start. By the time you have finished the opening, new ideas to continue the narrative will be flashing into your mind. Most of these ideas would never occur to you if you had to detail a complete synopsis before starting. And the reason why ideas begin to stir is because you have begun to create a character or two and *they are suggesting the story*. This they would never do as cold embryos in a synopsis.

Some aspiring fictioneers wonder how they can possibly write a Western or a gangster story set in Los Angeles when they know nothing first hand of either. The answer is that one can learn all there is to know about any subject under the sun by reading extensively. If you would like to write a Western for £1 per thousand words, read nothing but Westerns for a month. Read some stories five times. Copy passages until the Western setting is absorbed. See Western films, and sit in the cinema until the film is screened twice. That way many points can be remembered. The same methods apply to crime or science-fiction.

Of course, it has taken me about twenty years to learn to write. This statement will either shock or amuse some people. But I began writing at sixteen years of age, and only now am I reaping any real benefits.

The new British pulp market is wide open. Only recently one company advertised for writers with offers of commissions representing *full-time employment.* Where was the announcement? In THE WRITER, brother and sister!

The market is mostly for male readership. The western is a sound proposition in lengths of either 40,000 words or 45,000. Gangster yarns on the lines of *No Orchids For Miss Blandish* are wanted in 45,000-word lengths. Science fiction, dealing with the futuristic world and life on other planets is needed in 40,000-word lengths. Honestly, the fictioneer who is prepared to work and who has shed his fond delusions of authoring best-sellers at the speed of one or two sentences a day, should reel like a drunkard passing a free-beer public-house!

In America the pulp magazines are rightly regarded as a stern training ground for new writers. Many writers who are now at the top in America started in the pulps and went on through the mill. In my opinion, it will happen here. The "names" of the future are not among those who, at the moment are "thinking" about work or looking for agents to peddle their one or two short-shorts. The "names" will arise from the pulp grindstone because of the rigorous training they are getting.

There are some who can leap to the top while others crawl - but not many. Brother, if you are good enough with the words you tap on to quarto paper, you can write your way round the world, put mink on your wife, live in Hollywood or the Sahara Desert, sail a yaught in the Caribbean, fly your own 'plane or drink until you wish you were back at the old office desk! But, to come back to Earth, why not try a year or two on the pulp mill?

Now, if you do me out of a job I only have myself to blame!

Lazenby followed his own advice successfully throughout the mushroom era, although much of his output was short stories for saucy magazines: "A story a day was my motto at the time!" he recalls. This worked well for him, and he sold about 280 to Paget Publications alone between 1949 and 1957, as well as many other stories to other publishers.

There were many particularly prolific writers in this period who were capable of writing a book a week, or at the outside one a fortnight. John Russell Fearn wrote 7,000 words a day, seven days a week, and Norman Firth was capable of writing 6,000 words at a sitting. Victor Norwood was invited to, and wrote, a book a week, and a study of the Curtis Warren publishing schedule reveals that Dennis Hughes and John Jennison were both writing a book a week for the same company, and there is no reason to believe they were the only writers capable of turning out the novels at similar rates.

There was one remarkable author whom I have not managed to trace who would no doubt have been able to tell some equally remarkable tales of his work for the mushroom publishers:

I met a publisher who kept a writer in a cellar.

It was a dark and chilly place, one of a warren of cellars along an echoing stone passage. The writer sat on a stiff kitchen chair at a small kitchen table, centred under a naked electric lamp suspended from the ceiling. A low-wattage lamp, I remember; the room never seemed more than half-lit. Against a wall was a hospital-type metal bed, and on it was a disorder of army blankets, brown and uninviting, and over-coats and clothes to keep out the night's seeping cold.

The writer was a thin and wasted creature, wan and blinking behind his glasses. I never knew his name. He sat at that table from morning to night, tapping timidly away at an old typewriter. I never saw him eat, though he must have. He was said to work all day and far into the night, and kept working weekends too.

He was supposed to write two books a week!

They were short books, of course, but...70,000 words a week, ten thousand words a day! I don't know how far he failed (if he did fail) in his target, but the task was beyond human endurance and this boy was in no fit condition even to attempt it.

The publisher, a man for whom I can say no good at all, paid him £7/10/- a week for his work. But first he deducted £2/10/- because the boy slept on the premises, and then was reluctant to part with what he owed to the unfortunate "staff" writer.

On first telling it sounds like one of those apocryphal stories that grows up around publishers and publishing, but further research revealed it to be true: the publisher was Scion Ltd., the author was real and the final evidence came from an editor who at one time shared offices at 37a Kensington High Street, and is now a respected newspaper editor and journalist, Peter Knight. It was he who provided a name, or at least a surname: Quinn. Or to quote Knight: "I remember Quinn (or "Quinny") working in the basement, and Maurice Read giving him ten bob at a time. It inevitably went on drink. He was the only author ever, I imagine, who was locked in until he had finished 10,000 words."

The story does not end there. Tales of people advised to use the cellars as bolt-holes if the police arrived and mysterious men in black overcoats are just some of the rumours, and the reputation that the cellars were haunted is another. A veil has been drawn discreetly over these tales by time, and the whole truth will never be know. Perhaps in some cases this is for the best. One editor recalls the tale of a writer arriving in his office with a manuscript: looking terribly thin and ill, the writer desperately wanted payment for it immediately because there was a long holiday weekend coming up and he desperately needed to buy food and medicine. Not having the authority to do this, the editor went to a higher office and got the reply "Tell him we are not made of money". The writer was later found dead from malnutrition.

All history provides anecdotes, not all as grim as the above, although some of the tales told during the research of this volume were particularly sorry: Ron Embleton, who later went on to become one of Britain's top comic strip artists, told the story of his first visit to a publisher at the age of 17; nervously clutching his folder he waited outside the editors office... "There was another character in the room - a writer, also waiting for an audience. When the secretary left her desk to announce me he got up and emptied the contents of the ashtray into his raincoat pocket. A moment of truth if there ever was one!"

Gordon Landsborough, following his departure from Hamiltons in 1951, acted as a trouble-shooter for a number of publishers, which brought him in touch with a side of publishing which "made Hamiltons, by comparison, look as sober and earnest as *The Times.*"

I won't dwell on some of the tales Landsborough recalls - the publisher chased around his office by an irate author wielding a fireman's axe, the publisher who welched on a printing deal which cost the printer £8,000, and instead close this chapter with the story of the publisher who used to burgle his own warehouse:

It was a rather tricky business, this. He used to leave a window unlatched, so that he could open it from outside. There was a bit of an area to cross, for the window was below ground level. With more ingenuity than most of his writers showed, the bent publisher would leave a decorator's plank leaning against the wall of this area. After dark, he would come along, reach down for the plank, prop it across the area, crawl across, open the window, go inside, parcel himself some books, which he sold to a pal around the corner.

One night he was crawling across the plank when a dispassionate voice invited him to answer the question, "And what d'you thing you're up to?" It was a cynical London bobby. Explaining things from the middle of a plank presents difficulties in the way of plausibility, and his statement that "this was his business and if he chose to enter via the window, then what of it?" only resulted in his being marched down the police station. His wife gave him hell when she got the story!

4

THE MUSHROOM JUNGLE

"Now for a header into the cesspool."

George Orwell, "Raffles and Miss Blandish" (1944)

To appreciate the paperback boom there is one source that can speak, literally, volumes: the books themselves. Although these mushroom publishers were generally small enterprises in the ten years following the War these 'minor' publishers published thousands of books, a vast store of information which reveals a great deal about every aspect of the publishing scene.

The books were all the same basic shape and size. The average was 112 or 128 pages in length, approximately 36,000 to 40,000 words in length, only half the length of what today would be considered a fairly short novel. Some later books were longer, 160 pages and 50,000 words in length, whilst many of the early books could run to 10,000 words and less - these 24 page pulp size 'novels' were often little more than long short stories. All the books were printed on whatever paper was available, often a mixture of different grades of paper, and made up in 32 page blocks, hence the steady jump in page counts: 64, 96, 112, 128, 160, or sixteen page half blocks. The blocks of the longer novels were held together by two wire staples stabbed through the side of the book, making it impossible to lay the books flat when opened. The laminated covers were full colour and action packed and more often than not featuring full-breasted, scantily-clad *femme fatales*. The shorter books could often be found at 9d or 1/-, but the magic price was 1/6, sometimes creeping up to 2/- for some of the more *risque* titles; in later years, as printing and other labour costs rose, 2/- was the average with some titles weighing in at a hefty 2/6.

The stories themselves were written to a formula. E.C. (Ted) Tubb, who wrote his first novels during this period, found this an education:

I had not written anything as long before and neither had I used the formula they wanted. This was to have twelve chapters, each of 3,000 words, each chapter, if possible, to end on a high-point. It was a mechanical style and led to stories which were more a series of episodes rather than a closely plotted story. But I enjoyed writing them and found the concentration on action easier to handle than the interplay of deep characterisation, a style both difficult to do within the confines of the length and unwanted by the publisher. They wanted big, fast, outright action, with heroes larger-than-life and villains who were just that. Fast moving adventure stories against colourful backgrounds - a formula which is still the best for easily assimilated entertainment.

The basic pulp format did not change from one publisher to the next. In fact most of the books were printed by the same firms and had covers by the same artists and were virtually interchangeable in all respects. *Genre* fiction was the call of the day, the blurbs and adverts on the front and back covers invariably served as a pointer as to what you could expect. No subtle sales features were required, no advance copies submitted for critical examination and no compelling quotes from reviews by top authors. The blurb was almost certainly written by the production manager/ editor - more often than not one of the directors filled this role. Gangster novels were advertised as "America's toughest writer gives the lowdown of Gangland!" or similar, whilst the more racy novels promised "the oldest

profession exposed" in their adverts. The occasional back cover biographies made equally extravagant claims about their authors, one example being Bart Banarto which reads in part;

> BART BANARTO grew up on the sidewalks of the East side of New York. He learned the facts of life in a hard and vicious school - and writes as he has lived - brutally, truthfully, and without fear of the public enemies whose evil lives he exposes.

Despite this claim, Banarto was a pseudonym invented by his publisher to hide the identity of a British writer living on the outskirts of Manchester.

Advertising played an interesting role in the paperbacks. Whereas advertising outside of ones own products is almost unknown in modern day novels, it was not impossible in the most popular magazines, the *Strand* for example, to have almost as many pages of advertisements as text, and that could be up to 100 pages. The novels were popular and reached a wide audience, and attracted advertisers seeking mass-saturation of their products, from cures for smoking and books on banishing "the torture of nerves" to constipation pills and gland regeneration. Amongst the more interesting advertisers was the Flexible Earth Co. who promised to make plants of all kinds grow much larger thanks to its carefully composted, completely organic "soil structure". With praise from many testimonials ("Lettuce seeds up in 7 DAYS!") one wonders if gardeners had room for growing bamboos, supplied by the British Bamboo Groves, Ltd. who operated from the same address in Lanivet, Bodmin, Cornwall.

The queen of all advertisers could be found just down the road in Lanivet, that lucky Cornish pisky, Joan the Wad, a charm which graced the inside covers of thousands of paperbacks from 1930 onwards and brought success and wealth to many lucky buyers, testified by many thousands of praise-filled letters. Along with her friends, Jack O'Lantern and (of course) Chad*, who peered over the wall delivering his message of "Wot No Luck!", Joan the Wad was a small but essential part of the paperbacks.

* Chad, a simple line drawing of a head with an elongated nose, dewy eyes and a single curl of hair, was the creation of George E. "Chat" Chatterton who, whilst based at RAF Cardington in Bedfordshire in 1938, used him on posters for dances and socials. "Later," he recalls, "I served at Farnborough and Little Rissington, and used him again there. By this time the fellers had picked it up, and he was appearing all over the place. It was the lads in uniform who made him, particularly the army boys. The first time I saw him abroad was on a wall in Tobruk. Those guys were short of just about everything you could think of." *George Chatterton, quoted from an article by John Hudson (Gloucestershire & Avon Life, October 1976).*

The Sophisticated novel with its "femme fatale" from publishers like Modern Fiction, Curtis Warren and Sporting World. Heade and Perl were amongst the best and most popular cover artists. Even Daniel Defoe's "Moll Flanders" gets the "oldest profession" treatment.

THE SOPHISTICATED NOVEL

The large majority of the original paperbacks fall into the two categories which were known as the "sophisticateds": gangster novels and the French-style novels of low-life. These two types were also the most popular and attracted the most attention, especially in the eyes of the Watch Committees who were set up around the country as watch-dogs over the purveyors of 'obscene' novels. The two can be considered together since the overall aim of the novels was to excite and even titillate, both relying on a sense of sensationalism to sell, although the contents were quite different.

The typical novel of low-life, often set in France, were written by typically continental writers: Henri Le Fontain, Paul LeStrange and Andre Latour, to give some examples - all hiding British writers who, in all probability, had never been to France in their lives; if they had it was probably only as part of the invading force on D-Day which hardly adds up to an extensive knowledge of a country and its mores. Still, the readers of these novels almost certainly had as little knowledge themselves.

Their covers showed alluring ladies dressed in the briefest wisps of lace, often preparing themselves in the boudoir, or "ladies of the night" plying their trade in the streets of Paris. This compares to the blowzy 'dames' who figured on the covers of the gangster novels whose well formed breasts were always prominently displayed. They fall into two categories: the confident moll who can give as good as she gets, the ghost of a smile playing on her lips and promise in her eyes, or the anguished beauty caught up in the ganglands, her clothes torn, her breasts heaving as she prepares to fight off her tormentor who (if visible) brandishes a gun or some other weapon.

The two *genres* may have been grouped together by the publishers, but the contents were two extremes of a similar path. The French-style novels have titles like *Streets of Shame, So Sad My Heart, Penalty of Love, or Love Denied*; the gangster novels would never mention "shame", "love", or "sadness", nor would love in the physical sense ever be denied in any of them, whether it had to be taken by force or otherwise. The gangster novels had short, terse titles which either implied violence *(Scar on a Corpse, Johnny Gets His)*, or sex and violence *(Angels Bruise Easy, The Corpse Wore Nylons)*.

The average French novel concerned a very basic story of love and romance which in itself would not have been out of place in one of the many romance libraries or women's magazines that were available at the time. The difference between the two markets was in the presentation of the novels and in some added pages of spiciness, although even the latter was cliche-ridden and relied on innuendo. To take an example of the typical French 'sophisticated', this blurb appears on the novel

Temptation by Andre Latour:

> [Temptation] is the story of every girl's romantic dream.
> The story of a young and beautiful girl's dream of love
> and romance in Paris. YOUR dream. It is the story of how
> this dream eventually came true, but the path of true love
> is fraught with dangers and temptations and only love that
> is strong enough and prepared to sacrifice enough can win
> through.
>
> Ellen and Nicky thought their love was strong enough but
> there were many pitfalls to be overcome before they
> eventually found happiness and romance.
>
> This tender and dramatic love story, of romance and
> thwarted passion, is beautifully and simply written against
> a background of Parisian Nights.

Despite the heavily laden romanticism, the book was eventually
taken to court, charged with being obscene and found guilty.
This was the first title by 'Latour' but was not to be his last,
nor the last to be destroyed by the courts as being obscene
literature, amongst them *Flames of Desire* and *Shameless*.
These were only a few of the titles that were prosecuted, but
only rarely did the books describe anything approaching graphic
sexual acts. A typical example comes from *Tragedies of
Montmatre* by Rene Laroche (1950):

> The hotel was a small and very discreet one in one of the
> streets that radiated from the Place Pigalle. He booked the
> room and, presently, she found herself being whisked up
> in the lift with him. They were shown into the room and
> the door was closed. They stood there for a little while,
> looking into each other's eyes.
>
> He took a step towards her. Her heart was beating
> frantically. Then she felt his arms about her and, with a
> little cry, she nestled up to him, her arms going round his
> neck and pulling down his face. His hands were trembling
> slightly as they caressed her. He was whispering to her,
> telling her how much he loved her - how much she meant
> to him.
>
> Then he swept her off her feet and she lay in his arms -
> thrilling with the joy of that moment.

But at this point the chapter ends, and the next begins: "Yvonne
left the hotel early in the morning, for she had much to do."
Sex is only intimated, never described, and although there were
usually at least two 'sex scenes' per book, invariably the story
dissolves into a series of dots, or cuts to a later time of day.
Later books did take the story a little further and one publisher
is known to have instructed his author to "increase the sex
angle" and use "a little more descriptive matter regarding sex."
In reply the author said that he was "adding three pages of

sophistication" to his novel, which earned the book a charge of obscenity, and its author a large fine.

The gangster novel on the other hand was concerned with sex in stronger terms, but emphasised the violent potential of the act. The gangster novels relied on violence in all forms, whippings, torture, punishing brutality; the descriptions were long and drawn-out, with close up detail on every blow:

McWilliams beamed at me: "Son, there's no fake about this. You're going to take the kind of beating you won't forget in a hurry. And afterwards I'll keep you here until you're ready to go back wherever you came from, and then you'll be on your way."

Again I said: "I don't get it." But I got it all right. I had been around long enough with the Gestapo boys during the war to know that when a prisoner is naked he is twice as scared as when he has his clothes on. It's one of those psychological tricks the Gestapo used to play in Columbia House and other of their twentieth-century torture rooms. And I also knew that McWilliams was being clever. If he killed me, there could always be an inquiry - sometime, somehow. If he beat me up and then had me nursed back to health, the mental scars of the beating would remain, even if the physical ones were healed. I'd be too scared to squeal on him.

Eddie appeared again. He carried a short length of rubber in his fist. I didn't like this. In fact, I was plain scared....

He nodded to Eddie. I braced myself. Eddie said: "We'll get along." The rubber hose swung viciously against my kidneys.

I writhed with the pain, and before I could utter a single word the rubber had whisked again, cutting across the small of my back and knocking the wind out of me. I know I screamed, and I heard McWilliams say: "Keep him quiet."

The tango-dancer stuffed a towel between my teeth. I bit on it to keep down the agony. Eddie was doing the job scientifically, not beating the upper half of my body at all, but working his way down from the small of my back, across my buttocks, along the backs of my thighs, down the calves of my legs. He did it without emotion, simply as a necessary job. He went down one side of me then the other.

After he had finished beating the hell out of my back, he switched to the front and punished me from my stomach to my knees. Behind the gag I was screaming hysterically, and the tears were running down my cheeks. The whole of the lower half of my body was a howling mass of pain. I would have done anything to have stopped that cold, scientific laying-on of the rubber truncheon, but all I could do was to bite the towel and take it.

(*She's Dynamite* by Jim Kellan, 1953)

Here, the writer has taken the action into the most minute of details, almost photographic, but the quality of the writing often dropped dramatically between the scenes of violence. The characters show little or no emotion except when inflicting or being made the victims of violence, nor is the writing emotive.

In his book, *The Uses of Literacy*, Richard Hoggart compared the writing between the French style of novels and the gangster novels appearing in the early fifties. In a section entitled "Sex-and-Violence Novels" he discusses, using invented examples, the style and general trends in the novels and details his final impression thus:

> The Laforgue writers really belong to the same world as the writers for the older women's magazines; or, like the authors of the 'spicy' weeklies, they are naughtily disobeying the edicts of the world just as the writer's in the women's magazines are obediently upholding them. But both recognise the edicts. The thrill, such as it is, comes from appearing to flout the edicts. Just as the women's magazine writers have simply to point to the stock moral situations by using the stock moral cliches, so the Laforgue writers have simply to point to the stock immoral situations by using the stock cliches of immorality. It is all no more than a mild excitement-of-situation derived from the relation of these situations to an agreed code. Therefore the writing can be, and almost always is, perfectly flat, a mere pressing-down of the known keys to produce the required moral/immoral play of relations.

> But the aim of the later writers is to make their readers feel the flesh and bone of violence. They cannot invoke the stock and formal thrills of anti-code behaviour, since there is no code: they must directly stir their readers' senses. They are, therefore, oddly enough and in a very limited way, much more in the situation of the truly creative writer towards his material than are writers of the Laforgue type, or the writers of love-stories in the women's magazines. The gangster writers have to ensure that the physical thrill is actually communicated.

> The writing at places such as this has often a kind of power; it strums on the nerves of the readers. But it is a narrow power; where it moves away from the situations which excite it falls into banality. One author has explained how much he enjoys 'living through' the fight and sex-encounters he writes about, in terms which suggest that the 'living through' is a very intimate matter.

The statement seems to throw light on the limited but undeniable power of novels such as these.

Despite the claim that the gangster novelists could not rely on "stock cliches" there were cliches that appeared time and time again. The violence itself was a cliche, in many cases the books being little more than a series of beatings, tortures, killings and brawls held together with the smallest amount of linking material. This is not to say that the majority of the books had no plot at all, simply that the plots varied little and were simply vehicles for introducing as many scenes of sadistic brutality as possible. Yet these scenes, as Hoggart records later in his essay, have the power to move closely along the nerve. "It moves then with a crude force as it creates the sadistic situation; the images cease to be cliches and catch the nerve-thrill. It turns directly on to its object and immerses itself in the details of pain."

The dreadful truth hit her like a blow. She was in a house of ill-fame and the man with her was obsessed with lust. She sprang at the door and hammered with her fists. Bonazi came up behind her and swung her round by the shoulders. His arms closed round her and his mouth clamped her lips in a frenzy of desire.

She struggled but he bent her backwards until her spine was on the point of cracking. All the time, the hot pressure of his lips increased - a mist formed before her eyes and she hung limply from his arms.

The pressure relaxed and he laid her on the bed. Through half-closed eyes, she watched him stand back and look at her. She gathered her strength and tensed her muscles. At all costs she must get out of the room and down the stairs. Surely there would be someone there who would help her?

He turned his head for a minute and she took a chance. Bonazi smiled cruelly as he watched the direction of her eyes in the mirror. He allowed her to grasp the handle of the door before he caught her.

"Sister," he said slowly. "You 'aint what I call restful. A guy don't wanna chase his skirt all over. Are you gonna play or 'aint you?"

"Let me alone," she panted. "I'll have you lynched for this. There must be some good guys in N' York..."

"Okay, sister, this is where you get yours," grated Bonazi. "You wanna learn the hard way, huh?"

He swung his hand and hit her across the mouth. The blow sent her reeling backwards but he reached out a hand and caught her. He held her poised in front of him and then spun her round with her arm twisted behind her. She bent under the pain and he took a brush from the dressing table and brought it down endways across her back in short, chopping blows. She shrieked under the stinging pain but she was helpless. A dozen times, he hit her, and then flung her face downwards on the bed. She lay sobbing like an animal in pain.

His grip tightened and again the awful pressure of his mouth descended on her. She struggled vainly. He edged her across the room. One of her arms came free and her hand brushed against the top of the dressing table. It came into contact with a glass powder bowl. She seized it and banged it hard. It broke and a sliver of glass cut her finger.

He turned his head to see what she was doing. A blind fury suddenly seized Karel. Raising the glass bowl, she rammed it into his face, screwing the jagged edges into his flesh.

He howled like a wounded wolf and staggered away from her, his hand clasped close to his face. Blood streamed through his fingers and puddled on the carpet.

"Take that, you lousy swine," shrieked Karel. "I wish I'd killed you, you beast. Now get out and I'll have the cops hunting you before morning. I hope they shoot you, you...you..."

She stopped suddenly as he took his hand away from his face. Almost, she was appalled at the sight of her own work.

The left side of his face was deeply scored. It looked as though he had been clawed by a tigress. Most horrible of all, his eye hung out on his cheek and the ball was split like a rotten orange. Bonazi would never see with that eye again.

(*Turn Off the Heat* by Nat Karta, 1949)

Apart from these brief moments of power the novels were padded with weak linking passages using a poor imitation of American speech, trying to imitate the way the tough gangster or American cop might have spoken. Thus there were long passages packed with weak dialogue which was supposed to convey an air of reality, but often sounded stilted and slowed the pace of the novel. The tone is always that of a low snarl, the characters rarely speaking to each other: they gritted, hissed and snapped at each other when they were not shrieking or crying; the guilty muttered and the dames whispered or growled huskily at the slightest sign of impending passion. There was an over-use of such phrases as "He said:" or "Then:" which allowed swift dialogue to take place when the pace of the novel was moving at breakneck speed:

Jek said: "We'll quit foolin'. Got the dough, sister? It'll be jes' too bad for you if you 'aint. Your old man 'aint gonna laugh when I spill that yarn to him about the way I caught ya with that beach guard."

Popsey said: "You won't hafta tell him. He knows."

"The hell she does," said Jek. "Who do ya thing you're kiddin'?"

(*Old New York* by Hyman Zore, 1951)

The volatile anger that steeps the novels carries itself over into the sex-act which rarely happens through love, as it may do in the French novels. The attraction is always physical and without morals, when it is not forced as in one passage quoted above. Even if the partners are consenting, the thrill is in the overwhelming animal passion:

> She pressed up to me, meeting me halfway. I tear the girdle of her robe away, see the whole of her lovely shape. She is a true blonde all right.
>
> Her lips grope for mine. I tell myself I wish I had found this dame a week ago. I could have enjoyed her every night more than those other dames.
>
> Her hands are all over me. I don't think nothing of it. I am thinking it's just that she can't get enough of me.
>
> She bites me on the lips in her passion. Hard. It hurts. I smash her in the face. She just laughs. She is like an animal. She clings to me tight, gripping me with her lovely hands.

(*Brooklyn Daughter* by Brett Vane, 1950)

In his classic essay, "Raffles and Miss Blandish" (1944), Orwell looks at the "new departure for English sensational fiction" typified by James Hadley Chase's 1939 novel, and insists that *No Orchids For Miss Blandish* glorified crime and made no distinctioon between right and wrong; a deeper reading of the novels published in the early years of the gangster boom proves that there was an undercurrent of morality despite the domination of violence. The hero, or narrator, may use identical methods to those used by his enemies and in parts he is often indistinguishable from them but he may show an occasional streak of sentimentality, and although the tone of the book is "kill or be killed" the moral at the end of the story is always that crime does not pay. The criminal is always killed violently, or on the verge of death on the "hot squat".

If a charge of immorality were to be brought against the books it should not be for the supposed lack of distinction between right and wrong, but against the void in which the heroes live. For the hero, the ending brings only emptiness as, time and time again, the novels instill the feeling that the only time the characters come alive is when inflicting pain or receiving pain. The overriding impression from reading these novels constantly is that the time spent between violence is meaningless: the characters come together, act out their parts until only one survives; there is no sense of gain or education from their actions, a reaction, perhaps, to the ceaseless violence many of the writers had encountered during the war.

This atmosphere pervades so many of the novels of this kind. The French style novels almost reach the same conclusion, but replaces true love as the stimulus as opposed to violence. The lives of the characters are shallow and empty without that one thing, whichever it may be.

Of course, there are exceptions to the above outlines, where a few authors tried to break away from the usual cliches, but these were few. Most illustrate one point clearly: when removed from the scenes of violence many authors flounder and became banal. Some of the better writers tried to inject a little humour into their novels, for example *I'll Take the Body* by Brad Rigan (1953) or the Kinsey Target novels written by F. Dubrez Fawcett - *Brooklyn Moll Shoots Bedmate* (by Griff, 1951), *Back Alley Blonde* (by Griff, 1951) and *Vice Squad* (by Hank Spencer, 1954) - and a number of private eyes who were in the wise-cracking, one-liner mould.

As with all writing, some were successful whilst others fell flat. The local of the stories rarely escaped Chicago or Brooklyn; some portrayed Soho *(Soho Spiv* by Ben Sarto (1948) and *Soho Girls* by N. Wesley Firth (1948) being two examples) and others were placed in South America *(Mexico Deadline* by Johnny Grecco (1950)) or *Tigress of Brazil* by Ben Sarto (1952)); Thomas Martin writing as Nick Perrelli took American gangsters to Japan in *Terror in Tokyo* (1950). Europe was the stage only for the French novels which, not surprisingly, rarely left Paris. If they did leave the shadow of the Eifel Tower it was as white slaves to the traffickers of human flesh. These combined the two styles of sophistication in their atmosphere of violence and descriptive torture, coupled with a dash of lust and animal passion. These were given more exotic settings and titles, *Cargo to Cairo* by Rene Laroche (1954) being set in Egypt, whilst *Auctioned* (1952), *Persian Pride* (1953) and *Desert Fury* (1953) by Hank Janson was a trilogy set in the Arab deserts. Author Stephen Frances was one of the few writers who tried to vary the locations of his books, taking Hank Janson on a trek across America in the first series of twelve novels before even he settled in Chicago for the majority of his books.

But for all the exceptions the general trends remain the same, with the violence and passion

Below: Moring edition of Hank Janson's desert escapade in "Desert Fury"

giving way to a final emptiness of meaning, and once the power of narrative had slipped into the background, the "punch-line" that crime does not pay would be lost to most readers; most of the critics of this type of fiction (mostly the police who were bringing prosecutions against the books in court cases throughout the country) saw only the sex-violence and none of the moral overtones which certainly existed, even if only to legitimize the sex and violence.

Across: Sophisticated images to make the heart pound. *Road to Hell* must show the skimpiest costume to defy gravity, whilst what more can be said about Perl's portrayal of *Blonde Rod*.

More conventional fare from Brown Watson's fledgling "Digit" imprint together with an example of the popular theme - innocent beauty meets cruel world.

THE MUSHROOM JUNGLE

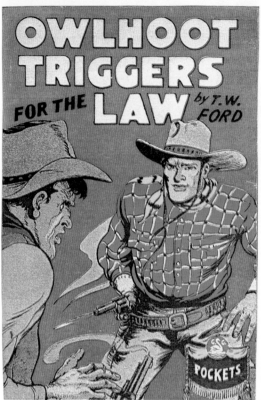

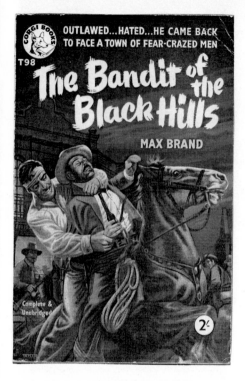

THE MUSHROOM JUNGLE

5

RIDERS OF THE RANGE

During the mushroom boom, the western ranked second only to the gangster novel in proliferaton. During the thirties and forties there was a marked increase in the number of western authors writing for the British market in competition to the many imported novels. One problem that faced early British western writers was that it was almost impossible for them to sell to the American magazines, as one author found: "they have an exclusive way of their own of doing them," he told a fellow scribe. Hardly surprising since the western was exclusively an American genre of writing, developing real-life heroes and anti-heroes in the same way that tales of our own folk-heroes Robin Hood and Dick Turpin had grown up.

Many of the dime novels chose Buffalo Bill Cody as their hero. Cody, still alive when most of the tales were written, was one whose adventures became more and more outrageously fictional as the years went on. This growth of legends around the legends has been a rich source of material for fiction writers over the years. The western in Britain was more on the lines of Hollywood, many of the heroes in the novels owing much to the exploits of Randolph Scott, James Stewart and later John Wayne. The John Ford movies *Fort Apache* (1948) and *Rio Grande* (1950) were influential at a time when cinema was highly popular in Britain, and the stars of film westerns were regular visitors to these shores: Roy Rogers, the singing cowboy, toured with his Rodeo, and Tom Arnold's Western Spectacle brought Tex Ritter (another singing cowboy!) to England's Harringay Arena. Cal McCord was made famous here as a rancher on the radio show "Riders of the Range", and William Boyd's "Hopalong Cassiday" (based on the novels of Clarence E. Mulford) was shown in the 1940s by B.B.C. Television - at the time the only TV channel available to the British public, independent television only arriving in Septem-

Across: Westerns proved popular with many of the "mushroom" publishers. Typical examples from Scion and Swan, with later developments from Hamiltons' improving *Panther* imprint and Transworlds sucessful *Corgi* line.

ber 1955.

The first original British western pulp had appeared in 1935, and pulp action was what the public got from the mushroom publishers. The cowboy was king, and the mushroom publishers had a market for fiction that was large and seemingly insatiable. The novels were a type dubbed "bang-bang" westerns, and it was considered to be the easiest of all the fields to write in; certainly this was the view taken by one publisher as recalled by Gordon Landsborough. When Landsborough joined Hamilton & Co. in 1949 as a production manager the wages were so meagre that he offered to write for the company. He had never written a full-length novel before, but he had a family to support and (having read some of Hamilton's previous efforts) felt that he was a match for most of their authors. The publisher, Harry Assael, had never seen a single example of Landsborough's writing: "However," Landsborough recalled, "I was assigned to write westerns. 'Anyone can write westerns' said the publisher, amiably."

As westerns were the 'easiest' type of fiction to write they were subsequently rewarded at a lower rate of pay to the sophisticated novels. At the time the average pay for the latter was between 15/- and £1 per thousand words, whereas the westerns in general brought in only 12/6 per thousand, and often less. One author received the princely sum of £10 for his full-length novel, and that was not an isolated case.

The emphasis of the novels was on action, and the westerns were perhaps the most stereotyped stories in the British pulp field. The hero was invariably tall, muscular and range-hardened; bronzed from his constant travelling and toughened by outdoor life, the heroes were usually drifters (at least when the stories opened), noted for their swiftness with a gun whenever they were required to draw their many-notched Colts, although they were equally at home using a rifle or Bowie knife. Similar to the gangster novels heroes who lived by the code of violence, the western hero only lived because of his ability to out-draw his enemies - his was the law of the gun as much as his counterparts in the gangster novels. The covers of the paperbacks invariably showed the hero with his gun blazing, more often than not with a gun blazing in each hand, although historically few real-life heroes of the west ever used two guns (if they did it was usually as a back-up, as guns frequently jammed).

The stories were a series of shoot-outs, conforming to certain rules whereby the hero was never allowed to draw first, nor allowed to deliberately shoot anyone in the back, and certainly never allowed to shoot any innocent bystanders. The villains of the stories had no such qualms, and were capable of any dirty deed; sometimes they were cowardly, power-crazed gamblers who surrounded themselves with hired guns, or tough rogues with their posse of bandits. The story would follow the characters through shootings, hold-ups and stampedes until the hero could face the villain at the bloody climax.

The heroines fell into three broad (sic) types: the ladies who had travelled from the city and looked upon the cowhands as little more than animals; the bar girls and saloon dancers who laughed and jested with the customers, plying them for drinks and money; and the tom-boy ranch girls who could match any man and give as good as they got. Whoever they were, the end of the novel would find them in a clinch with the hero and the thought of wedding bells ringing in their ears.

The stories were written in a stilted language in which all cowboys supposedly spoke. Whilst the gangster novels relied on the occasional Americanism and terse, corner-of-the-mouth speech, the cowboys would drawl, as in this example:

> "It's a nice layout," Rip told him. "How come yore dad tuh settle this side uh the Rio Grande anyways?"
>
> "Got hisself in wi' some Mex big shot," Walcott explained. "Done him a favour one time, an' by way uh reward the greaser deeded paw the spread. Usta be a fancy Mex outfit. How yuh happen tuh know my sister?"
>
> Rip told him, and the giant chuckled. "Allus figured she'd grow up tuh be a honey," he said. "Our maw was the purtiest woman I ever seen. I'll git hell offen Pam. She never did hold wi' me slopin' fer timber country."
>
> "Reckon she'll shore be surprised to see yuh," said Rip. "Yuh bin in town long? Reason I asks is I was wonderin' iffen yuh'd seen a hunch uh jaspers I'm lookin' fer."
>
> Walcott regarded him shrewdly in the moonlight glow. "Yuh got the look of a badge toter tuh me," he said. "Ranger mebbe. Are yuh trailin' fer the Law?"
>
> "Hell no! I ain't no lawdog," protested Rip. "Nope! This is a kinda pussenal mater between me an' a buzzard named Dobe Shang. Yuh heard uh him?"

(*Buffaloed* by Jim Bowie, 1951)

It may seem surprising that, for the huge amount of westerns that appeared in the mushroom era, only a few of them dealt in any way with the American Indian. Very few stories introduced any native Americans as characters apart from the occasional rogue Apache; to read these westerns without the benefit of any knowledge, the reader could easily be forgiven for thinking that prior to the arrival of Columbus, North America was the sole property of the buffaloes and a few shady Mexicans. The stories did not offer much in the way of historical background except for references to well known historical characters such as Bill Cody and Jesse James. Unlike the gangster stories, there was little that raised the average story towards any great standard,

Below: Note the "self pirateing" of cover art by the unknown artist in the Badger and Brown Watson books. Both were printed by the Dragon Press. A coincidence?

The days of *Indian Fury* in the old South-west are brought to life in this fast-paced novel...

APACHE TRAIL

A.A.GLYNN

WHEN THE TOM-TOMS BEAT, DEATH IS ON THE

CHIEF UNGOW

WRITTEN BY AN INDIAN WARRIOR ....
Complete and Unabridged

RIDERS OF THE RANGE   89

nor were there any moments of intensity that could lift a story and thrill the reader directly.

There were a few well written tales which relied solely on the writer's power of narrative to bring the story to life, but too many of them were so stereotypical that the field was over-whelmed by sheer lack of new ideas. Things were so bad that one author was able to plagiarise his own novels for plots and characters and sell virtually the same tale twice to the same publisher, as well as novels to other publishers which were slightly re-written versions of earlier tales. Hamilton & Co., mentioned above, surprisingly had an excellent line of 'oaters' in the early 1950's, attracting the work of Richard Conroy, Gordon Landsborough (who turned out to be a pretty good writer), Jack Trevor Story and the prolific American writer Lauren Bosworth Paine who had started writing for the pulp's in the mid-forties, and who turned to novels ten years later, selling his first to Hamilton's Panther line in 1955. For two years novels poured across the Atlantic, mostly under his own name and the pen-name Mark Carrell. Since then, Paine has established himself in the record books as the most prolific novelist in the world, having written some 900 westerns, crime thrillers and romances at the rate of over 25 books a year.

The best western line did not belong to the mushroom publishers but to Transworld Publishers, a division of the American publisher Bantam Books Inc. set up at the instigation of Ian Ballantine. The Corgi Books imprint began in 1951 and who could number the first British edition of Jack Schaefer's perenial classic, *Shane* amongst their first releases. The earliest selections were made from the parent company, and followed the Bantam numbering, although with the appointment of Michael Legat in 1952, Corgi began purchasing the rights to books previously available in the UK in hardcover and were independently numbered from early 1953, developing a highly collectable line.

Unfortunately for every good writer there were twenty bad ones, and flagging sales in the over-burdened market - even Corgi were financially unstable until the early 1960s - caused the publishers to look at other fields and, whilst the western held its own in terms of prolificy, a number of other *genres* were explored.

Whilst the novels in the gangster and western fields were often cliched and poorly written they were, in the main, following a style that had been formulated for them, and these traditional elements were not only acceptable but were expected by the readers. The violence of the gangster novels and the gun-toting, range-hardened cowboys of the westerns were simply following pre-set standards, perhaps taking them a step further than before in some cases. Both fields were to survive the mushroom days with no real loss of face, with westerns losing ground naturally as their time passed.

Below: Popular western fiction from Scion & Gannet and the later Corgi & Sombrero (Muller)

MUSHROOM MEN FROM MARS

Science fiction, however, was one field that suffered greatly in the hands of the mushroom companies since it had never been firmly established in Britain. There were few magazines which dealt with this form of literature, and no large pool of well-established writers to call on when the opportunity arose for science fiction to take its place in the mushroom jungle. There were exceptions but these proved rather than disproved that rule: quality science fiction had appeared in Britain for many years, with H.G. Wells seen as the father of British SF; the thirties and forties had such classics as *Brave New World* by Aldous Huxley (1932) and *1984* by George Orwell (1949), but these were by mainstream authors whose imaginative writings were more easily classified as science fiction than anything else; they were using the field as a way of making social commentary. Olaf Stapledon made a great impact with his novels *Last and First Men* (1930) and *Star Maker* (1937), two philosophical blockbusters written on a grand scale.

The American's again led the field when the first specialised SF magazine, *Amazing Stories*, appeared in 1926, and many pulp titles were imported into Britain throughout the 1930s. A small but vocal hard-core market was built up, and a number of British authors were producing comparable material for the American magazines (notably John Beynon Harris, later better known as John Wyndham), but there was no home-produced adult magazine in Britain until 1937 when *Tales of Wonder* appeared, and even this was soon put to the wall by the War. Science fiction did, however, have a place in many general magazines, and was a firm favourite in the boys' papers, prompting the release of *Scoops* in 1934; aimed initially at a young audience the editor soon found he had many adult readers to whom he also tried to cater. Unfortunately the magazine never quite catered for either, and folded after 20 weeks.

The nearest to a regular British science fiction publisher during the war was Utopian Publications, directed by Benson Herbert (himself a writer of SF) and Walter Gillings, an important figure in the history of British SF magazines, but even this company produced only around a dozen booklets, almost solely reprint material, between 1944 and 1946, and the majority of the output was 'art' folios and racy magazines.

In 1946, Pendulum Publications launched a series of booklets as part of their Pendulum 'Popular' series, and a chance meeting between the editor of the line, Frank Arnold, and Edward (Ted) Carnell led to the launch of the classic British SF magazine *New Worlds*, with Carnell as editor. The company folded after only three issues appeared, and three other magazines launched in the heady days of post-War Britain folded as quickly - *Fantasy, Futuristic Stories* and *Strange Adventures*, the latter two the sole work of Norman Firth who had no background in science fiction at all, but would happily turn his hand to anything for £1 a thousand. In 1948 there were no British magazines at all and the hoped-for advance of quality sf was back to square one. It was taken over by the mushroom publishers who found they had an almost monopoly in the field where the only quality opposition was a fan-backed relaunch of *New Worlds* - which went on to become the back-bone of British science fiction.

Stephen Frances, ex-director of Pendulum Publications, launched S.D. Frances (Publishers) Ltd. to publish Hank Janson but had the foresight to know that science fiction was a field that could be exploited at a time when the markets were overloaded with both gangsters and westerns. To this end he invented the byline Astron Del Martia and published *The Trembling World* (1949), written by John Russell Fearn. The title went virtually unnoticed, and Frances concentrated on the more lucrative Hank Janson novels.

The mushroom SF boom exploded in the Spring of 1950 when the end of paper rationing for periodicals prompted the arrival of the first mushroom magazines and of Vargo Statten. The two could not have been more different.

The magazines were published by John Spencer & Co. and are generally held to be the worst SF magazines ever to appear, yet 50 issues crept out, spread over four different titles, selling an average 8,000 copies apiece. The Vargo Statten novels, on the other hand, were a tremendous success: written by John Russell Fearn, who was a noted SF writer for the American magazines (and the first British author to ever make a living solely from science fiction writing), there were eventually 52 Statten books selling an advertised five million copies and a magazine bearing the name was launched in 1954. The initial success of the Statten novels quickly led to other publishers requesting books from their regular authors, most of whom had no idea what was required of this new literature. What resulted was a mixture of gangster violence and cowboy stories set in space. What was sometimes called "the literature of the imagination" was soon reeling under the weight of endless alien invasions, whether from Mars, Venus or further afield. Few polished SF writers wrote for the mushroom publishers, although a few placed stories (usually under pseudonyms) that had failed to sell to the higher-quality markets: "If I couldn't sell a story anywhere else then at least Spencer paid for the cost of the overhead in producing the story," Lan Wright, a regular contributor to *New Worlds*, wryly recalls. Even these 'failures' were far better than the average attempt that appeared.

The science content in the science fiction was virtually non-existent; many scientific terms were misused and time and time again, planets became stars, galaxies became universes, etc, etc. The erratic use of astronomical terminology was so bad that any author trying to sell to a better market found their efforts quickly rejected. Once the mushroom boom was over, many authors never appeared in the field again.

Accuracy was not a feature in many stories. Apart from errors in terminology there were countless others. Spacemen put the last rivet in their cigar-shaped rockets just before blasting-off into space, and there is one story which I can happily recommend as the worst single piece of fiction ever published. The offender is *Pirates of Cerebus* by Bengo Mistral (1953), where the atmosphere actually fills the gaps between the planets, the solar system is divided by a barrier of "atomic molecules" which burns up meteors, and characters have a habit of shouting such meaningful phrases as "Speed up the breakaway radio active sun heading towards Saturn" before going off to lunch and a spot of skiing. The hero, Casper Carylon races to save the heroine, Regina Zelda from Magoth the Wizard (a real wizard!) and his walking trees in a spaceship that travels five times the speed of sound; the story has dragons, storms in space that can toss spaceships around and the spaceships themselves are powered by a whirling propeller which (of course) only works once the pilot has inserted the ignition key!

The two most prolific authors of science fiction for the mushroom publishers were John Russell Fearn and Dennis Talbot Hughes, and they show the marked difference between the practised sf author and one new to the field.

Fearn was born in Manchester in 1908, his family later moving to Blackpool where he had a number of jobs. The two great loves of his life were films and imaginative fiction; he had discovered the American pulps in 1931 and quickly sold a novel to *Amazing*, followed by many to the leading magazine of the day, *Astounding*. He had been writing SF for almost twenty years when he started appearing as Vargo Statten and his other novels for the mushroom publishers, which appeared under numerous other guises such as Volsted Gridban, Lawrence F. Rose, Conrad G. Holt, etc., showed him to be a capable writer: his background knowledge of SF was firmly based in scientific theory of the time and whilst his books were limited to the standard format of the mushroom books, his stories were filled with action and imaginative elements which raised them far above the average SF tale.

Hughes, on the other hand, had no background in science fiction, and made glaring errors which spoiled even his very poor stories; when he wrote fantasy, as he did in the later years of the mushroom boom, he showed an ability to write imaginatively and the books are far more readable, but any straying into pure science fiction brought them crashing down to his previous low-level of craftsmanship.

SF was one of the few fields to attract regular magazines: with the exception of confessions and adult titles, the mushroom publishers seemed to steer clear of magazines except for one-offs. The only regular magazine publisher was Gerald Swan, whose own attempt at a science fiction title, *Space Fact and Fiction*, was of laughable quality. As mentioned above, Vargo Statten had his own magazine, the *Vargo Statten Science Fiction Magazine* (which later became the *British Space Fiction Magazine)*, but it failed to attract top names thanks to the original editor's insistance that the authors should simplify stories for an unsophisticated audience. The best of the crop was Hamilton & Co.'s **Authentic Science Fiction**, the early issues of which featured full-length novels, later introducing filler short-stories and articles. The early tales were a mixed bag, but things improved under the editorship of H.J. (Bert) Campbell who had a solid scientific background in research chemistry, and *Authentic* attracted some excellent fiction. The best novel line was also from Hamiltons, with tales by H. Ken Bulmer, Bryan Berry, Campbell, E.C. Tubb (who later became editor of *Authentic*) and Jonathan Burke.

Romance of the women's papers type was a regular market throughout for most of the mushroom publishers, but it never achieved the popularity (or the sales figures) of other types of novel, almost certainly because it was a field in which the mushroom publishers could not dominate. There were many romance libraries produced by quality publishers, such as C. Arthur Pearson's *Silver Star Library* and *Lucky Star Library*, Amalgamated's *Oracle* and *Miracle,* and Thomson's *Red Letter*. Women's magazines were a regular source of romantic fiction, hardback publishers catered admirably for the library markets, and when the mushroom publishers put out a title it had comparatively lower sales; with paper so precious, they stuck to the bigger selling gangster and western market.

A plethora of SF burst
onto the scene. some
almost one shots.
Regal producing just
two Fowler Wright titles

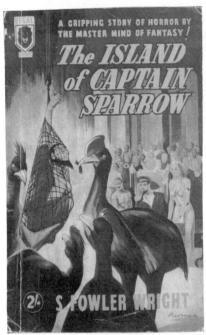

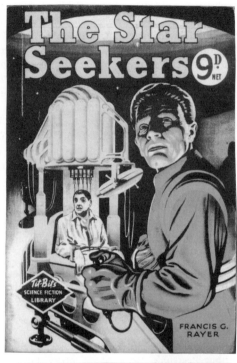

One of the few regular romance publishers was Pembertons of Manchester. They published a regular series of 48 page romance novelettes between 1948 and 1950, *Pemberton's Romantic Novels*, as well as longer novels in their Thrilling Love series. Other novelette series' included Popular Fiction's *Women's Popular Novels* of anonymous 24 page tales, later superseded by the longer *Real Life Series,* and the *Paul Dupont Romance* series from Martin & Reid.

The romance novel lacked the edge that made the French style novels so popular. They were far more moral tales, but a number of spiced-up confessions appeared, implying a more personal and intimate story. These were essentially the French-romances with a hint of immorality in the title, and the master of these was Paul Renin. As mentioned in an earlier chapter, Renin was the pen-name of Richard Goyne and the novels had been appearing since the 1920s.

Renin produced nothing direct, although one critic has suggested that this is even nastier since it is both sentimentally coy and furtively suggestive. A typical scenario for such a story could start with a run-away girl arriving in London with only the sad memory of her broken home; she meets a man with whom she finds forgetfulness, if not love, but who either later rejects her, or (far worse) stays with her and makes her life hell. In either case, our heroine finds she has married the wrong man, but manages to find another whom she can love and respect. The books were moral throughout: there was always an air of uncertainty in anything suggestive which the gangster novel lacked, a knowledge that the heroine would regret what she was doing, which she invariably did. As with the 'sophisticated' novels discussed earlier, there was no descriptive matter concerning sex and always those ever present dots to spur the imagination on:

> Presently, with only the dull glow from the gas fire, they danced to the haunting music from another land. It was all wonderful, just as sweet as their madness—but time and circumstance had ceased to be. They had stepped out of hard and bitter reality into a fairyland of their own making.

> What could the codes of reason matter, with this madness flowing through them and binding them together like a new consciousness?

> Locked in each other's arms they danced, now barely moving across the room, just holding each other. Dreaming...

> The music stopped, and with it came the chiming of a single note from a distant church clock. Jimmy whispered her name, and then her arms stole up and about his neck once more. In the darkness they found each other's lips.

Only their low breathing disturbed the silence...and then the closing of a door...

(*Carnival Kisses* by Paul Renin, 1953)

Gerald Swan was one of the few publishers to issue regular romance magazines, *Affinity* and *Romances* being two which achieved creditable runs. The main thrust of the romance magazines market, however, was in confessions, with numerous publishers disguising some very average "girl meets boy, girl loses boy, girl gets boy back" romantic tales behind titles such as *Intimate Confessions, Intimate Love Stories, My Story Confession Book, Personal Confessions, Revealing Confessions,* etc. etc. The only difference between the romance and the confession was generally that the boy turned out to be a murderer...

The racy, adult magazines had titles like *Peppy Stories, Snappy Stories, Spicy Stories, Reno Revels,* and could be summed up as "girl in silk stockings meets boy, girl in silk stockings loses boy". The snap of a taut suspender belt was the closest to sex the stories dealt with, although they were often decorated with line-drawings of nudes and (in some cases) the offer of art-folios and photographs.

The proliferation of gangster and western novels on the stands by the early 1950's led to flagging sales for the mushroom publishers, and with the deregulation of paper (and always with an eye for profit) some of the more adventurous publishers began to experiment in other fields. Those that stuck to the overburdened lines were soon forced to experiment, but invariably the experimentation came too late, and any sudden switch usually heralded the end for the company.

One company which had gone to some lengths to provide a wide variety of stories was Hamilton & Co., and a sheet of editorial notes which was sent out during the early 1950s shows some of the variety they demanded from their authors:

These notes are intended to stimulate ideas. We hope that in the back of your mind you have ideas for stories and series of stories, and we want to encourage you to come forward with the ideas.

Remember that our market is not so sophisticated at the moment. We want rattling good yarns with strong plots, stimulating characterisation, suspense, mystery, drama, but above all, humour. Humour especially of dialogue.

We are out to lift our stories above the common run. We

don't want stuff written with an adolescent ring. Best way is to avoid writing about immature personalities. We want adult reading, because our market is the adult reader. It is easier for most writers to give this adultness by employing American characters, though we do not want exaggerated American styles. Intelligent, educated Americans have a racy talk, not much different to our own. We must have this raciness.

BACKGROUND: At this moment we have a series of French Foreign Legion stories building up, a pseudo-Tarzan series, boxing stories, some Alaskan (Jack London) type. And a few other stories which are labelled Secret for a few more weeks. In addition we are bringing out stories with themes not as usual in the current paper-jacketed field...a negro seaman on the run in Benghazi, hunted by American seamen because he hit out at a nigger-hating first mate. He is hunted through the Arab quarter, on to Italian settlements...out into the desert. He kills an English soldier accidentally...gets a jeep and a tommy gun, tries to battle his way out. Dies in the desert in the end through lack of petrol. Twist: it was a negro who killed him - sold him water in petrol cans...

Another: four American war criminals traced on a plane flight to Australia. Learn this accidentally in mid-air. Force plane down on a deserted island used as emergency landing strip in Jap war. Criminals - fat business men, not conventional gunmen types - intend to burn plane out with passengers, escape themselves with new identities. Crew and passengers escape, are hunted over South Seas island by men who must kill them if they are to save their own lives. They hide up - have a battle with thirst and hunger. Then find island is a graveyard for American war equipment (a quite usual thing), derelict planes, guns, trucks, ammunition - but no small arms. Petrol too. It becomes a race against time. Their radio op starts to build a transmitter from scrap. Will take him a few days. Criminals are closing in. They start to use a tank which the flight engineer puts into action. They don't know how to use it, how to fire the gun, but they have a good try. Keep off the criminals...and then Japs come from a neighbouring island. They want to wipe them all out, because they think they might be taken for trial as war criminals. That's a ripe situation.

What ideas have you in this line - apart from series? Our writers must surely have ideas, rich, colourful ideas. They should let us know them. We are in experimental mood.

The stories themselves must have this note of adventure, but mustn't be boys' paperish. But the personalities must be built up so that they are recognisable human beings.

OTHER GENRE FICTION

We don't want stock characters. And physical characterisations aren't a patch on mental indiosycrasy for establishing personality. It's the mind of man - and woman - that's important.

We don't want conventional heroes, too upright to tell a lie; villains who sneer and snarl and have dago names; and heroines who toss their heads proudly or cast their eyes modestly on the ground...

We don't want conventional types - the Indian who is stolid, says nothing more adventurous than "Ugh" and rolls his eyes with superstition after dark. As a difference, one writer is building up an Indian who reads back numbers of the Saturday Evening Post. He likes the ads. He's bothered at all times about what he wants for his hut. Goes for a TV for a while, then switched favour to a washing machine, finally plumps for a refrigerator. He hasn't a bean and he lives in the Arctic Circle. That's a bit more unusual and interesting that the usual character we get. And we want writers to work up new characters. It's easier to write about characters with personality than it is to use synthetic creatures.

We don't want stories pitched on a Chekov note. Grey, dreary hopeless lives aren't for us. Write about up and coming people; people who get somewhere and do something. Don't write about frustrated people, because we only share their ulcers.

One of the developments mentioned above was in the foreign legion field. This new field was first tried by John Robb (Norman Robson) in 1951 who recalled in an article written a few years later for *The Writer:*

From the days of P.C. Wren up to a few years ago, this field was scarcely touched. I laid the foundation for the current boom with two novels entitled *March of the Legion* and *Broken Ramparts*. That was four years ago. They were an experiment. Both my publishers and myself kept our fingers crossed. The sales, without being high, were encouraging. Very soon other authors were following.

The foreign legion story quickly established itself in the paperback canon, and was another field in which the mushroom publishers dominated. Some were highly inventive tales, notably those by Robb himself, and his novel *Punitive Action* (1954) was filmed in 1955 by United Artists as *Desert Sands*. Another excellent tale was *Zone Zero* (1954) in which a small band of legionnaires are trapped in a remote Legion post in the Algerian desert, only thirty miles away from where a hydrogen bomb is due to be exploded. This topicality set Robb above most of the legion writers that were to follow. Hamiltons, sensing a good line building up, had regular legion novels by Alex Stamper (James McCormick) and Bruno Schwartz (George Mann), again of good quality, but there was a rush of titles whose plot invariably consisted of lonely Legion outposts surrounded by the angry local Arab population. An offshoot of the legion novel was a short series of Bengal Lancer novels published by John Spencer, but the idea only lasted for four titles.

Historical novels seemed very unpopular with the publishers, although in the last days of the mushroom boom a handful did appear: Curtis Warren published four novels by Cecil Alexander set in 18th Century Europe, whilst Hamiltons (again as part of their experimentation in other fields) had produced a number of pirate novels by Shaun O'Hara and Konrad Murray set in the West Indies and South Africa. Gannet Press tried to produce a new series of Dick Turpin highwayman novels by Arnold Ryden (John Russell Fearn), but only two appeared, amongst the last titles to appear from that publisher. Fearn had earlier been invited to submit a horror novel to Scion, but the finished novel never saw print at the time, and Scion instead retained Fearn's services as their leading science fiction writer, and as a writer of Tarzan-esque adventures.

The jungle adventure, a *genre* made popular by Edgar Rice Burroughs, whose *Tarzan of the Apes* first appeared in 1912, was an early experiment for the mushroom publishers, a slew of titles appearing around 1950 and 1951. In 1943, ex-provincial journalist Mark Goulden had taken over the firm of W.H. Allen, and in the late 1940s reprinted many of the Tarzan stories under the Pinnacle Books imprint, prompting Curtis Warren to release *The Missing Safari* by Marco Garron (1950) featuring 'Azan the Apeman'. Azan, an ex-R.A.F. pilot who lost his memory after crashing in the jungle, was a little too close to Tarzan, and after only six books was threatened with copyright infringement by Burroughs' executors, E.R.B. Inc. The publishers recalled many of the books and destroyed them, but rather than lose a line that appeared to be growing in popularity, continued the Garron byline and featured Rex Brandon in a series of jungle adventures written by Dennis Hughes. There wasn't a hint of the apeman about these, but more than one nod to the adventures of Alex Raymond's famous jungle explorer, Jungle Jim.

The Gold of Akada and *Anjani the Mighty* (by Earl Titan, both 1951) introduced a new Tarzan-esque character: Anjani was one of twin babies born on an expedition. The two babies are spared when the expedition is wiped out by a hostile Monango Warriors, and are bought up by different tribes. The two novels centre around jewels and lost cities, an evil queen, a beautiful widow, and the struggles of the two brother, one pure, the other evil. Highly entertaining though they are, the author, John

The Jungle novel spin-off from *Tarzan* led to an exciting genre. The Scion novels shown are illustrated by Turner at his best. Curtis Warren's *Azan* proved a bit too close to the original.

Russell Fearn's Vargo Statten science fiction novels were selling far better, and the series was halted. Publishers Scion Ltd., however, detailed another writer to launch a new series, and Victor Norwood produced the Jacare series, a dumb strong-man in a South American setting. Norwood recalled the series with some affection, and commented:

> I credit the Jacare character to a lively imagination enriched by extensive prospecting expeditions I made to Guyana and Brazil, etc. The character of Jacare was a 'natural', and making him dumb spared me a lot of verbal agitation, I mean, what COULD a hulking wild-man of his type say? He existed on action, not words, and his affliction added the authenticity lacking in most jungle adventure stories.

The other jungle adventures were a mixed bunch, ranging in quality from *Zamba of the Jungle* by John Raymond, which was badly written but accidentally amusing, to the two 'Shuna' novels by John King (Ernest McKeag) which are a mixture of Conan Doyle's *Lost World, Boy's Own Paper* and pure space opera, behind highly attractive Heade covers.

A few of the novels fall into the detective rather than gangster field, but these were rare and few fall into the 'Whodunit' mould. Some English detective series' appeared such as Mary Archer's Denis Chad (a British P.I.) and R.C. Finney's Inspector Bourne; John Russell Fearn reintroduced his scientific detective, Dr. Carruthers, who had proven popular in a series of hardcover novels published by Stanley Paul. Two paperbacks, one each under the names Hugo Blayn and Nat Karta chronicled his further adventures. Another Fearn invented scientific detective was Adam Quirke who appeared in two novels under the name Volsted Gridban.

A derivative of the gangster novel was the boxing novel, a highly popular sport at the time (even moreso than today), and mixed violence in and outside the ring. These were essentially gangster novels with a little sport thrown in as the mobsters battled for the fortunes of their "boy". Sporting novels outside this limited plot rarely appeared, although an interesting example of this was *The Black Wraith* by Raymond Buxton and Ben Bennison which concerned dog-track racing. A few horse racing novels from the 1920s were reprinted, but in the main the mushroom publishers stuck to the tried and tested ground.

THE ANGUISHED ANGELS

The covers of the mushroom paperbacks have become a source of great collecting interest and it is often the case that the novel itself is of secondary importance to collectors.

The most collected of the post-war paperback artists is Heade whose beautifully rendered dames graced the books of many companies, particularly those of the Locker group and the Hank Janson novels. Heade, born Reginald Cyril Webb in 1901, had exhibited at the Royal Academy in the 1930s, and turned to dust-jacket illustration during the War, via the prestigious London art agent, W. Partridge. In the late 1940's he changed agents, linking up with Maurice Hall Agency of Hammersmith, run by Charles Montague Hall and his wife, through whom Heade began producing covers for the Paul Renin romance stories. Heade's strength was in the boudoir, with a succession of leggy lovelies draped in enticing lingerie facing some menace, often a gun coming from off-frame, or the reflection of an intruder in the vanity mirror. These were typical of the paintings that covered the gangster and racy-romance novels, the scantily-clad beauty under threat.

Few other artists gained the respect or reputation achieved by Heade during the paperback boom; some have achieved more success in retrospect, their work only now attracting the attention of collectors as individuals. The "good-girl" art has always given the gangster novels in particular a wider appeal than they would otherwise have had, although the silk-stocking art of artists like H.W. Perl and Len Potts always looked static in comparison to Heade's. Perl had been a prolific cover artist in the 1930s for numerous publishers, and was probably the most prolific cover artist for paperback novels during the late forties, a position challenged in the fifties by Leonard Gard and John Pollack.

The two most prolific western artists were Jas. E. McConnell and Nat Long. McConnell, born in 1902 and working for many years in advertising, was one of the most sought after artists for covers, by both mushroom publishers (particularly the Fiction House Smashing Western series, which he almost single-handedly illustrated) and quality publishers like Amalgamated Press. Over the years his artwork appeared on the covers of many leading publishers, Pan, Digit and Corgi amongst them, making him one of the most collectable of cover artists nowadays.

Denis McLoughlin provided a number of early covers to the mushroom publishers, such as Pembertons and Kangaroo, but his fame was made with T.V. Boardman, for whom he provided dust-jackets and paperback covers for twenty years, even designing their famous bloodhound logo.

David Wright, whose leggy pin-ups had been a wartime attraction in the *Sketch* magazine, produced covers for the American Hurst group after the war, as well as advertising posters and pin-ups for *Men Only*. His attractive artwork graced a few of the mushroom paperbacks published by Harborogh Publications in the early fifties, before he found wider recognition amongst the general public as the artist of the superb *Daily Express* strip, "Carol Day". Another artist who was to gain a huge following in later life was James Holdaway who worked, briefly, as a staff artist for Scion, having a small studio set up in the infamous cellars - his artwork on "Modesty Blaise" for the *Evening Standard* began in 1963 and continued until his death in 1971.

Other artists found more fortune in comic strips before turning to covers: Ron Embleton had his first strips published by Scion at the age of 17 before producing a small, but none the less remarkable, number of covers for John Spencer and World Distributors. He later work took in everything from the juvenile educational weekly *Look and Learn* to the satirical "Oh! Wicked Wanda" in *Playboy*.

Another Scion artist was Ron Turner, born in 1922, and working after the war on the staff of Odhams Press. He began to freelance in 1948, producing strips for Scion comics at the rate of £1 a page, script and art, and soon branched out: his most notable covers were for the Vargo Statten science fiction novels, Turner showing the influences of Chesley Bonestall and Alex Raymond in accurate space-scapes, often using a symbolic motif to summerise some of the plot points of the book. Turner was the leading science fiction artist of the paperbacks, leading to an offer by Pearsons to produce *The Tit Bits Science Fiction Comics* for which he scripted and drew a series of excellent adventures.

The only contender for Turner's crown was the action-packed sf art of Norman Light, whose work, although never attaining the technical excellence of Turner's, had a vibrant, colourful excitement, making him a popular choice with John Spencer for their sf magazines.

Scion favoured the work of Philip Mendoza on their gangster covers, often signed as 'Ferrari' or 'Gomez'; Mendoza had been an illustrator for newspapers and a cover artist for Pendulum in the late 1940s, and the connection with Steve Frances led him to design the Hank Janson silhouette.

Curtis Warren, on the other hand, relied on H.W. Perl for a stream of silk-stocking and cami-knicker gangsters moll artwork (his best during the early 1950s), whilst Ray Theobald provided some lifeless spaceships for their science fiction line.

Hamiltons used the prolific talents of John Pollack for most of their non-sf titles, and introduced Josh Kirby on the covers of *Authentic Science Fiction*, now heavily associated with the best-selling novels of Terry Pratchett and other humorous fantasy titles.

Payment for covers varied: Hamiltons, for instance, paid 12 guineas and that included all the lettering, later rising to 15 guineas without lettering. During the 1960s, when the fully painted cover had its heyday on paperbacks, the payment went up, varying from publisher to publisher, but rarely above £45 - the Pan line paid up to £60, but cheap second-rights covers from Europe could be bought for £25 - and some as low as £7. Some publishers paid as little as £10 for their original covers. The illustrated cover began to fade in the late 1960s as more photographic covers began to appear, eventually superseding the work of Mortelmans, Peff, Boldero, Osborn, McConnell, Mortimer, Blandford, and many others who had provided the stunning painted book cover art for Pan, Panther, Digit, Four Square, Ace and many other paperback firms.

6

"ONE AND SIXPENNY DREADFULS"

"In my youth books were written called 'Penny Dreadfuls' and 'Blood and Thunders'. This is a rather apt description of these books, which can be called 'the one and sixpenny dreadfuls'."

Mr. C.H. Gage (Maidstone Quarter Sessions, 28 July 1954)

Whilst the books themselves have become forgotten and any upset they caused in the literary history of British publishing pushed into the background, the mushroom publishers left behind a legacy which could be called their contribution to British Literature. Their contribution was unintentional, perhaps, but it had such a staggering impact on the laws of obscenity that it deserves a study at some length.

As previously described, the vast majority of the books relied on exciting the reader for sales. In an earlier chapter we studied the general form and tone of the gangster novels, and the overwhelming conclusion must be that they portrayed violence in the most microscopic detail, the writers wording their descriptions, frame by frame, with almost photographic accuracy. This gives the reader an extremely intimate relationship with the characters and the contention that the novels move "closely along the nerve...turns directly on its object and immerses itself in the detail of pain" (Richard Hoggart) is one that needs expanding upon.

These novels were intended to stimulate, to carry the reader along on a wave of excitement. Much of the stimulation came from violence, and more often than not from violence against women; at least one editor, Gordon Landsborough, found he could not stomach the unfettered violence, later saying:

In almost all of these stories, the girl was a nymphomaniac

who could be most brutally ill-used. Imagination on the part of the authors often extended to violence during the sex act, or the sex act related to violence and under sordid conditions. Ripping a nympho's stomach at the climax of the sex act appeared in more than one story I read; beating her almost unconscious and yet she still crawled for sex participation was another theme. I felt such stories, while unpleasant, might have no influence upon balanced readers, but with scores of these stories going out yearly, it seemed to me to amount to a wave of propaganda which could have some effect. I cannot see how it helps humanity if the female half is constantly portrayed as worthless and deserving of brutality.

That the publishers and editors wanted sex in some way included is beyond doubt, although perhaps the above comments emphasise sex as being the predominant obsession of these books. Not true. The publishers were (at least at first) very mindful of sex in their books, and blue-pencilled vigorously any offending material that could have taken them to court. But violence...that was encouraged. Norman Lazenby received this letter from Edwin Self in 1950 which sums up the situation as concisely as one could want:

> I read *Bad Woman* and thought it quite good. Perhaps there was a little too much emphasis on the sex-angle...Generally with this type of book there has to be a sex-emphasis and I usually find it works out better if the central character of the book is a gangster-type with plenty of brutal beatings-up, etc., and, of course, the sex-angle is brought in by his affairs with female characters who have rather minor roles.

It was violence that was the stimulation, not sex (although sex was the focus for the covers). But many minds find it impossible to separate the two, and whilst sex was often intimated it was never described. The books could not be described as pornography; according to the definition given by Norman St. John Stevas in his book *Obscenity and the Law*, a pornographic book is one "deliberately designed to stimulate sex feelings and to act as an aphrodisiac. An obscene book has no such immediate and dominant purpose, although incidentally this may be its effect."

The definition of obscenity has been the cause of arguments for countless years. A dictionary definition usually gives a list of synonyms such as impure, indecent, or lewd, which are alternatives but hardly a definition for such a subjective term. But when the word is used in relation to obscene books there is a rigid definition which has not changed in the eyes of the Law for many years. The first Obscene Publications Act was passed in Parliament in 1857, and the law was not updated to take into account more modern taste and morals until 1959, over 100 years later. What was known as "the test for obscenity" was formulated in 1868 and it was under this definition that many cases were brought against the paperback publishers and their books; over eighty years of change, in education, in art and in public taste were bypassed in laws defined by and administered by "grey ones, left over from the last century, the century of mealy-mouthed liars, the century of purity and the dirty little secret" (D.H. Lawrence, "Pornography and Obscenity").

* * * * * * *

It is not my intention to detail here the full history of books the law has deemed to be obscene, but it is important to put the history into perspective before the events of the 1950s can be understood.

Whilst 'obscene' literature has been with us as long as we have been writing, the subject matter that is considered 'obscene' has changed with the ages. From the days of the middle-ages many books were banned, mostly on the grounds that they were heretical, speaking out against injustices within the church. Over the years the focus changed as the church, especially after the days of the Inquisition, gradually gave way to more local systems of government. The focus became the banning of political tracts which attacked the government and royalty and was essentially an extension of the laws of libel. The first real case that links libel with other forms of 'obscenity' that were attacked in the 1950s date back to 1708 in which year a publisher was taken to court for the publication of *The Fifteen Plagues of Maidenhood*. During the case it was noted by Mr. Justice Powell that "It is stuff not fit to be mentioned publicly. If there is no remedy in Spiritual court, it does not follow there must be a remedy here. There is no law to punish it: I wish there were: but we cannot make law. It indeed tends to the corruption of good manners, but that is not sufficient for us to punish."

Here we find that obscene literature is outside the scope of the law. Unless it contained some other form of libel, the law could not act against it. The first book to be prosecuted as an obscene libel was in the case of Edward Curll who had published *Venus In the Cloister, or the Nun in Her Smock* (1724). The case against Curll was that, although there was no physical breach of peace, the book tended to corrupt the morals of the King's subjects, and was therefore "against the peace of the King". Although there was a great deal of indecision as to the validity of the argument it was eventually upheld and for the first time "obscene libel" became a misdemeanour. This small change in law occurred in 1727 and was the lynch-pin of the charges brought against the paperback 225 years later, all charged with being obscene libels.

The Victorian age has long been held as a time where sex was a taboo subject and this attitude is reflected in a great deal of Victorian literature. Of course, with such strict morality in force on the surface there was a great undercurrent of pornographic literature; a great deal of it was kept in check by the many vice societies which existed, particularly the Society For the Suppression of Vice which was founded in 1802. The trade in explicit pornography was so great that an Act of Parliament was passed in 1857 to try and stop the trade for good. Lord Campbell's Act gave magistrates the power to order the destruction of books and prints if, in their opinion, their publication would amount to a "misdemeanour proper to be prosecuted as such." To enforce this Act, magistrates were empowered to grant warrants to the police so that they could search suspected premises.

Once this first Obscene Publications Act had been passed it finally put the law into words, but it wasn't until 1868 that the real test for obscenity was laid down in judicial law. The case involved was that of Henry Scott, a metal broker from Wolverhampton and zealous Protestant, who had sold many copies of a pamphlet entitled *The Confessional Unmasked*. In 1867 Scott's stock was seized under Lord Campbell's Act and the justices ordered that they should be destroyed. Scott appealed, and the Recorder, Benjamin Hicklin, found in his favour on the grounds that although the pamphlet was obscene and its indiscriminate sale was calculated to influence good morals, Scott's motives in circulating it was an innocent one of promoting the Protestant Electoral Union (the publishers of the pamphlet). As the pamphlet was an attack on Roman Catholics, they, not surprisingly, appealed to the Queen's Bench and it was here that Lord Chief Justice Cockburn gave his definition of obscenity which was quickly picked up and recorded in a number of text-books. Although not law, the words were to be repeated at almost every obscenity trial since:

The test for obscenity is this, whether the tendency of the matter charged as obscene is to deprave and corrupt those whose minds are open to such immoral influences and into whose hands a publication of this sort may fall.

It was under this test that the gangster books of the 1950s were prosecuted. Over the years there had been many celebrated cases against books now considered classics of literature and which were even at the time discussed widely in literary circles. These are not the subject here but it is interesting to note that the focal point of moral outrage in the thirties and forties was more often against sex manuals than particular works of fiction. There was a puritanical drive against them which seemed designed to keep the open discussion of sexual matters by the working classes firmly in the offices of doctors and the church confessional.

During the war there had been something of a clean up

campaign, possibly related to the draft of American soldiers to these shores (even the man on the street believed that the Americans were "overpaid, oversexed, and over here"), although nudity seemed acceptable, most memorably the *Daily Mirror's* Jane, who bared all in 1943, much to the delight of the American magazine *Round-Up*, who noted that the British 36th Division immediately gained six miles. The earliest known cases of gangster books being prosecuted occurred in May 1942 at the Central Criminal Court when Jarrold Publishers (London) Ltd. along with author Rene Raymond for publishing *Miss Callaghan Comes to Grief* by James Hadley Chase. The book was found obscene with the publishers fined £100 plus fifty guineas costs, and Raymond fined £100.

In the wake of that trial, publishers Wells Gardner, Darton and Co. withdrew a plea of "not guilty" and pleaded "guilty" to publishing two obscene books entitled *Road Floozie* and *Lady Don't Turn Over*, written by Harold Kelly under the pen-name Darcy Glinto. Both publishers and author were fined £50 on each charge, with 50 guineas costs against the publisher.

Below: They may have "flouted" moral standards but the gangster novels proved so popular that they even crossed over to their US locations with American editions.

UK Milestone & US Leisure Library.

The first cases against the mushroom publishers occurred in Glasgow in 1949, followed by many many others. The vast majority of the cases were destruction orders issued against booksellers. If a complaint was made to the police that a shop was selling obscene material a magistrate had the power to send the police to the shop where they would pick up anything that looked remotely questionable. A great many complaints were lodged against nudist magazines such as *Sun Bathing News* and *Health and Efficiency*, and when these were picked up so were many other publications. The gangster and romance novels with their attractive 'dames' and threatened women were a prime target. At no point were these books or magazines tested for obscenity - these cases did not go to court and therefore no judicial rulings were made as to their nature, obscene or not obscene. The magistrates would simply issue a destruction order which was then served on the bookseller. If the bookowner did not appeal against the order the books were destroyed, and if the bookseller did appeal, the onus would then be on him to prove that the books and magazines were not obscene. To fight the destruction order would mean a long and costly court case to obtain a judicial ruling, and few booksellers bothered; the loss of a few pounds worth of magazines compared favourably to fighting a court case which, considering the puritanical sweep that was overtaking the country, he would probably lose.

A typical case is that of shop owner Bernard Shrensky whose shop in Bethnal Green was raided by police. Four items were seized: two issues of the magazine *Razzle*, and the novels *Trading In Bodies* by 'Griff' and *Flame of Desire* by Andre Latour. When the case came before the magistrate in July 1954 it was quickly dealt with: the clerk of the court asked Shrensky if there was any reason why the books should not be destroyed to which Shrensky replied, "No, Sir." Harold Sturge, the magistrate then asked, "There is nothing you want to add?" Shrensky replied, "No. Nothing at all." Mr Sturge then said: "Very well. There will be an order for their destruction." End of case.

An increasing number of prosecutions were being brought against the publishers themselves amongst them Raymond and Lilian Locker who were warned about publishing obscene books when one of their Paul Renin novels featured a whipping scene. Both Bernard Kaye and Gaywood Distributors were fined £50 each plus costs at Blackburn Magistrates Court in August 1951 for publishing and distributing *Temptation* by Andre Latour. By then the publishers had already been calling for a committee of censors similar to those who governed the issuing of certificates for films. B.Z. Immanuel, the director of Scion Ltd., summed up the situation by saying "We have always insisted that authors should cut out suggestive sex. And we always make sure in all our novels to point out that crime doesn't pay. On our children's comics for instance we run such slogans as 'You Can't Beat the Law'. But there is still no ruling or guide whatsoever to publishers on gangster novels. I certainly don't want to publish anything that would corrupt the morals of certain sections of the public, and I think it is time a national advisory body was formed." *(Sunday Pictorial, April 24th 1951)*

Despite Immanuel's claims and wishes, Scion were fined for publishing an obscene book and were almost forced into liquidation in the summer of 1952.

Amongst the publishers who approached Scotland Yard for advice was Julius Reiter of Gaywood Press, but the answer was always the same to such questions: "The police don't know what is obscene until it has been published, taken to court, and found to be obscene!" Scotland Yard did keep a list of books that were subject to destruction orders, but refused to release the information.

Obscene publications was the main topic of conversation at the International Criminal Police Commission in Oslo in September 1953, the conference concluding that obscene literature was an important contributory cause in the rise of sexual offences since the war. It was suggested that the Commissions members should take the strongest action against the trade.

But in Britain, a great deal of action was already being taken.

The appointment of Sir David Maxwell-Fyfe as Home Secretary in 1951 led to a three-pronged attack on vice which included the witch-hunting of homosexuals, the harrying of prostitutes and a crusade against pornography. The latter culminated in 1953 when 197 prosecutions were made against obscene literature. Some newspapers took up a stand against Maxwell-Fyfe, particularly *The Recorder* in which editor Edward Martell attacked his campaign against obscenity, saying "a book that may have been selling regularly for 20 or 30 years without a word of objection from anybody may suddenly be seized and condemned." Maxwell-Fyfe was supported in his action by then Director of Public Prosecutions, Sir Theobald Mathew.

The biggest obscenity case of all was that of Hank Janson. Widely reported in the press, the case led to a flood of prosecutions against reputable publishers, and eventually to a change in the obscenity laws. Janson was probably the biggest selling author of the paperback boom, and the two trials that were brought against him will be studied in the next chapter.

But, first, let us see how the various companies were faring under the twin attack of overproduction and prosecution...

* * * * * * *

B.Z. Immanuel, director of Scion Ltd, found himself the head of a very successful company, with an excellent line-up of writers capable of spinning a good yarn at high speed. In 1951 the directoral line-up was augmented by A. Lou Benjamin, brother of Esther Immanuel, and on the editorial side both Peter Dewhurst and Julian Franklyn joined. Franklyn was a respected writer on language and heraldry, and 'ghosted' a number of books for Scion in a way which was probably not unique. Victor Norwood, himself a prolific writer for Scion, recalled: "He used to write the MSS then put it into the Scion input stream, and subsequently 'accept' it for publication, using some established writers name, and picking up the payment—then averaging £30 a book, no royalties. Just one of the crafty dodges going on in those days." Franklyn was also well known for his blasphemous outbursts against his employers, claiming that he had been tricked into joining the firm.

Scion was only one of a number of companies running from the offices and cellars of 37a Kensington High Street. One company was Chariot Books, who may seem odd bedfellows for Scion, publishing, as they did, top-quality novels by recognisable literary figures, amongst them Nicholas Monsarrat, H. Rider Haggard and E.M. Delafield. The books were printed in France (where Scion also printed a number of their comics, in particular their Americanised comics which had alternate pages printed in colour), as printing costs were lower. The selection committee for the series was Louis Golding, R.T. Minney and Nancy Spain, who held many raucous meetings at the home of the former in Hamilton Terrace trying to decide which books should appear. With all the activity at 37a Kensington High Street, most of the book business was handled by Lou Benjamin from Scion's distribution warehouse at 6 Avonmore Road, London W14. As well as having a solid line-up of gangster novels of their own, Scion also bought up a number of other lines.

Muir-Watson had been successfully publishing gangster novels since 1949 from their base in Glasgow, with distribution from Thorpe and Porter of Leicester. John Watson, however, was unsatisfied about his life as a director of a publishing firm:

> Churning out that kind of crap was not really my idea of a life fulfilled, apart from which there was some faint writing on the wall. The background to all this was a constant struggle with banks and printers. I chucked it. But I had learned a lot. I had learned how to control a narrative, and long before my time a lot of good writers had learned their trade at the rubbish end of the market.

Watson sold all the rights and unused manuscripts of Muir-Watson to Scion in 1952. With that came the rights to use the highly popular bylines Nat Karta, Hans Vogel and Hyman Zore. At the same time Thomas H. Lane sold all the rights to Nick Perrelli, a pen-name inven. ' by Lane's co-director at Tempest Publishing, George Dawson. Dawson had set up the firm in the late forties, but had left the running of the company to Lane, returning to writing under his popular Michael Storme pen-name. Perrelli had been handed over to Thomas Martin, who continued to write novels under the byline after the Scion take-over, recalling:

Dawson had written the first book under the pseudonym (*Virgins Die Lonely*) and I had written the second and subsequent Nick Perrelli books. When the pseudonym had become established and Tempest closed down, he turned up at Scion, where I was continuing the Perrelli series, to claim the pseudonym as he was legally entitled to do. He was willing to share it, but that didn't appeal to me, so when Milestone was launched I soon launched my own pseudonym, Max Risco, which soon overtook Perrelli in sales. Dawson sold the Perrelli pseudonym to Milestone, and then I believe it was used for the work of several authors.

The apparent success of Scion Ltd. was soon shattered by a financial blow that almost put the company under. In the summer of 1952 Scion were fined for obscenity and immediately suspended business.

The first to be affected by the fine were the authors who were owed money, some as much as £300. The directorate split into three factions.

Milestone publications was set up by a number of Scion authors and editors, amongst them Peter Dewhurst who became one of the company directors. The company was set up with little backing but was able to start publishing immediately thanks to an agreement with a paper supplier who offered them credit. Amongst the early group of authors to write for the company were Victor Norwood, Gray Usher, Donald Cresswell and Jack Trevor Story, all of whom had strong connections with Scion. Ted Tubb and John Russell Fearn were both invited to write for the company and turned in novels. Tubb recalls that the Milestone set-up was slightly more in the authors favour:

I was asked to write for the new company and this time was paid by the thousand words instead of a flat rate, and, more important, received a contract for each book. The terms were not much better than before, but the contract did include certain 'escape clauses' and was an improvement over the old system.

The 'contract' meant that Tubb, who had previously been working for a flat rate £42 per novel was able to get £45 for a novel of similar length, a small but vital increase. But more importantly, the contract now only took first British rights rather than all rights and authors were able to negotiate foreign sales. Some took up the challenge and hired agents: Richard Steel was the leading agent at the time for sales abroad, and translations of many of the novels appeared in countries ranging from Italy to Norway. Some companies had already been selling the novels abroad and in one case were paid ten times as much money for re-selling the novel than they had paid for it! This was the case of Bryan Berry who had sold a novel to Hamiltons for around £35. The story was then resold to the American pulp, *Two Complete Science Adventure Books*, and a complaint from Berry resulted only in an invitation from Hamiltons to write more novels under the same conditions. A letter to the American publishers, however, led to Berry selling his first work to America, and three stories appeared under his own name in one issue of the companion magazine *Planet Stories* (January 1953). The subject of contracts led one writer to comment "my contracts with Scion and Milestone meant something only as long as the directors wished them to mean anything." Norman Lazenby was offered a similar contract by Scion with the muttered warning from editor Julian Franklyn that the contract wasn't worth the paper it was printed on.

The slightly higher rates offered by Milestone attracted some of the top names of the time, and amongst them was Frank Dubrez Fawcett, who revived his female protagonist Miss Gaby Otis for a new series of Ben Sarto novels. The popular Danny Spade (as written by Dail Ambler) appeared in many new adventures, and science fiction writer Vargo Statten (John Russell Fearn) was all set to appear alongside Volsted Gridban (Ted Tubb) when suddenly Scion Ltd. re-emerged.

Lou Benjamin re-launched the company from their 6 Avonmore Road address and at once tried to attract his authors back to the fold. A better deal was offered to compete with Milestone, for instance John Russell Fearn who had only fulfilled three years of his exclusive five year contract was offered the chance to sell elsewhere. Fearn had an excellent market in Canada, the newspaper supplement to the Toronto *Star Weekly,* where he had been writing a highly popular science fiction series featuring the Golden Amazon since the mid-1940s; for these Fearn was receiving the top-rate, and was appearing alongside the likes of Erle Stanley Gardner.

Fearn's renewed contract meant that a number of stories he had agreed to write during the hiatus were withdrawn from the other publishers, although some books already written would appear during 1953. One tale, sold to Milestone and for which a cover had already been prepared, was withdrawn, and this left Milestone with a cover, a title, and no novel. Ted Tubb was requested to concoct a tale and the book appeared, although it had nothing to do with the cover which illustrated key elements of the Fearn story. Scion Ltd. also put a halt on the use of some pen-names which were owned by them, including Nat Karta and Volsted Gridban.

For most Scion authors this meant they now had two markets for their work, both of which were paying slightly better rates than before. Once the dust settled the new arrangements seemed attractive and authors continued to write for both companies.

1952 was a turning point for many companies, not least for those associated with Hank Janson. In March 1952 Reginald Carter and Julius Reiter took over the Hollyfield Printers in Friern Barnet and installed a new rotary press. In August the newly named Arc Press took over the printing of Hank Janson, running an edition of 100,000, by far the highest print run achieved by any of the gangster writers at this time. To make full use of the presses, Carter also launched a new company, Comyns (Publishers) Ltd., taking over another defunct company. From August 1952 Comyns began a regular schedule, attracting work from a number of Scion authors who were at the time uncertain of the companies future. Dail Ambler supplied a Danny Spade novel before linking up with the newly launched Milestone, and both Victor Norwood and Vic Hanson produced gangster novels, the latter launching the Red Benson series under the name Max Clinten, taking over the name from Stephen Frances.

Bernard Kaye, operating from his offices in Avenue Chambers on Southampton Row launched Kaye Publications with brother Alfred Kaye. The new imprint had grown out of the Bernard Kaye Agency and continued a number of old lines, including the french-romances of Andre Latour, the gangster writer Johnny Grecco, and new 'french' style writer Josh Wingrave.

Gaywood themselves launched a new byline, Dirk Foster as well as continuing their exclusive distribution of a number of lines, chief amongst them the Janson novels.

Amongst some of the other companies there was a period of steady output. Modern Fiction, for instance, were putting out an average two titles a month, mostly under the Griff and Ben Sarto bylines, many of those written by Frank Dubrez Fawcett; Modern Fiction were to increase their output in 1953 to first three and then four titles a month, introducing or reintroducing a number of new bylines including Spike Gordon and Hank Spencer.

Curtis Warren were as prolific as ever, and in March 1952 had changed the format of their books to give them an extra boost on the newsstands, increasing the page count at the same time to 128 pages, up from 112. They all but dropped their gangster line and introduced a number of new house names to disguise the authors of their western and science fiction novels, written mostly by John Jennison and Dennis Hughes respectively. In late 1952 Curtis began to issue each book in a simultaneous hardback under their Lion Library imprint, a library edition of maybe 6,000 copies priced at 5/-. These library editions were identical to the paperbacks but printed on slightly thicker paper and each book was issued with a dustjacket.

Hamilton & Co. instigated a new line in 1952 that was to long

A Panther Book

outlast the company. Panther Books was an imprint used on a number of titles which showed little difference to the usual Hamiltons output, but quickly developed into a solid numbered series. The average page count increased to 128 pages, and later to 144 in early 1953, at which point Hamiltons began to issue their books in a simultaneous hardcover edition with a panther symbol stamped in gold on the cloth cover. As with the Curtis Warren titles each book was issued in a dustjacket.

By this point, Hamiltons editor Gordon Landsborough had left the firm, handing over to two editors. Landsborough had instigated a science fiction magazine/book series in 1951 under the banner of *Authentic Science Fiction*, which he edited under the pen-name L.G. Holmes, and this had become a great success in the days of overproduction and consequent falling sales. *Authentic* was soon selling some 20,000 copies where gangster novels were selling 17,000 and westerns as low as 13,000. The days of instant sales of 40,000 were long gone except in the cases of the most popular gangster writers.

When Landsborough left he handed *Authentic* over to H.J. (Bert) Campbell, a prolific writer of science fiction for the series who had a solid scientific background and had acted as scientific advisor of the series for some time before assuming full control. The other books were put under other editors: the

first was Derrick Rowles who had worked for Hamiltons under Landsborough between 1950 and 1952 before moving briefly to Scion Ltd. as Art Director. It was Rowles who suggested the use of a logo for the new line of books, and was instructed by the publisher to think of one. He thought of Panther, and had to phone the zoo to find out what they looked like, but that small suggestion was to pay off in later years when Panther Books could be counted amongst the top five paperback publishers in the country. The other notable early editor at Panther was W. Howard (Bill) Baker, an ex-journalist who was to bring many new and excellent writers to the line, later to leave when Panther all but axed their original novels line; he joined Amalgamated Press where he began a long association with Sexton Blake, as editor and prolific writer for the *Sexton Blake Library*.

Sinful Sisters

ROLAND VANE THIS CHALLENGING & REVEALING NOVEL WILL HOLD THE READER SPELLBOUND UNTIL THE VERY LAST WORD

DECEPTION

Timothy Trenton

Blonde on the Spot

8,000,000 SALE
12TH REPRINT

HANK JANSON

2/-

BEST *of* TOUGH GANGSTER STORY AUTHORS

VICE RACKETS *of* SOHO

This story exposes the White Slave Rackets which flourish unchecked in Londons Square Mile of Vice

ROLAND VANE

THE MUSHROOM JUNGLE

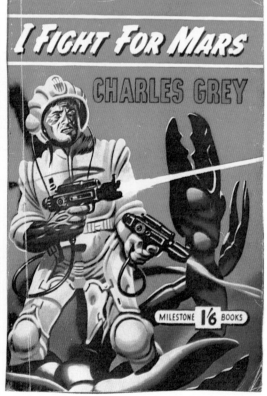

THE MUSHROOM JUNGLE

The three companies run by Raymond and Lilian Locker had built up a solid financial backbone on the strength of the Paul Renin reprints. The R & L Locker imprint was phased out in 1951 with preference going to Archer Press and Harborough Publications. Archer had developed a strong line-up of gangster writers as early as 1949, most of which were later taken over by the Harborough imprint. Most were the work of two authors: George H. Dawson, the ex-director of Tempest Publishing, wrote an excellent series of novels under the byline Michael Storme, many featuring Nick Cranley, and William Newton, writing as Spike Morelli and Gene Ross, produced some equally popular stories featuring regular characters. Archer was used mostly thereon as the publisher of Paul Renin and the french-flavoured novels of Roland Vane, the pseudonym of the groups third prolific author, Ernest McKeag.

Archer and Harborough found a very useful additional source of income from selling the books abroad, and many of the novels were issued in America by Kaywin Publishers (actually British printings with an overprinted American price) and Leisure Library, many using the attractive Reginald Heade covers. Kaywin, of Cleveland, Ohio, produced sixteen novels under their own Archer Books imprint, almost identical in every respect to their British counterparts, whilst Leisure Library of New York would eventually publish 24 titles. A number of mushroom companies were selling novels abroad, and in one case a publisher knew nothing about his novels being resold, but soon closed the pipeline when he discovered it! American companies such as Universal, Lion and the Canadian publishers Harlequin all featured gangster novels from Hamilton & Co. and World Distributors, and a great many titles found their way to America as exports.

THE
ARCHER PRESS LTD.

The various movements of publishers in 1952 were reflected in a massive increase in production in 1953. Curtis Warren and Hamiltons were each publishing in both paperback and hardback, Curtis reintroducing their prolific gangster byline Brett Vane amongst many other new names, and Hamiltons introducing Russ Ames, Scott Jefferson, and revitalised their own gangster line with tales by Bart Carson, Joe P. Heggy and Jeff Bogar. Modern Fiction increased their output of Ben Sarto, Griff and a number of french romances; the newly formed Milestone produced a regular schedule of gangsters and westerns, whilst Scion relaunched a number of bylines as well as many tales under those acquired from Muir-Watson, Nat Karta, Hans Vogel and Hyman Zore. Kaye Publications kept up a regular schedule of french romance and gangster titles, whilst other publishers such as Edwin Self were publishing along much the same lines, with authors such as Lisle Willis providing many french romances under the names Marc Lavelle and Jean-Paul Valois, as well as publishing the gangster novels of Bart Banarto and Paul Costello amongst others. Brown

Watson and John Spencer were also equally prolific, although the latter favoured science fiction to the french romances as their second line.

1953 also saw the formation of a number of other companies. Since the split-up of Scion Ltd. B.Z. Immanuel had retained the offices at 37a Kensington High Street and by May 1953 he was publishing again under the imprint of Ken Publishing Co., allied to another company called O.K. Fiction. In June the first books published by Gannet Press Ltd. appeared, with gangster novels by Jim Kellan and Jack Diamond, plus science fiction by Bengo Mistral and Vektis Brack, two of the more ridiculous names that were put on science fiction. Gannet, even as early as June 1953, were attempting to diversify their product, a state of affairs that was reflected by all publishers as the gangster and western markets became overburdened. Their schedule was set to include "Gangster, Science Fiction, Westerns, Romance, Foreign Legion, Highwaymen, Spy, Detective" according to their order sheets, although it was only in 1954 that they showed any great move away from the regular output in the first three categories.

Also in 1953, Ralph Stokes, who had been the regular publisher of Ace Capelli for two years changed the name of his company to R.S. Gray Ltd, reflecting the involvement of the Gray's Inn Press, also of 42 Gray's Inn Road, London WC1. The two directors were Ralph Stokes and Leonard Slater, who continued to publish Ace Capelli and attempted to launch a new line of Slim Brandon novels, although only one appeared.

* * * * * * *

1953 was a year of overproduction. The paperback market was swamped with books by the mushroom publishers and other firms increasing their output now that paper rationing was a thing of the past. The last restrictions were lifted in June.

TRANSWORLD PUBLISHERS
LONDON

As well as the prolific output of companies such as Penguin, Pan and Collins in the general fiction market, there were also the numerous crime novels published by T.V. Boardman, Cherry Tree Books and the Collins White Circle series. During the early 1950s Hodder and Stoughton, famous for their Yellow Jacket novels, relaunched their paperback line, as did Cassell who launched a new Pocket Novels series in 1950. Pocket Books (G.B.) also began publishing in 1950, whilst 1951 saw the arrival of Corgi Books. 1952 saw the arrival of Cooper Book Company, who as Cooperbooks published gangster and western novels in typographic covers before going on to the usual pictorial covers; another new company was Stanley Baker, who soon established two series, Futuristic Science Thriller and The Thriller Library, both rather short lived.

That same year saw W.H. Allen take over the Pinnacle Books line from Mark Goulden Ltd., who had previously concentrated on Edgar Rice Burroughs titles. Goulden had bought W.H. Allen in 1943 when the company was all but extinct. Goulden revitalised the company, selling it to Doubleday of Garden City, New York, around 1951. The new Pinnacle imprint covered a much wider range, including true crime as well as a wide range of fiction.*

1953 saw even more paperbacks fighting for space on the stands. In January Gold Medal Books were launched in Britain by Frederick Muller, and the following month saw the arrival of the Arrow Books imprint from Hutchinson. Fontana Books, an imprint of Collins, first appeared in October. Paperbacks were a volatile market, and more than one company found that by the end of 1953 they were struggling, with falling sales.

It was the beginning of the end for the 'big' little companies, and the final blow to many of them was the increasing number of companies being taken to court over gangster obscenity. Events came to a head when the Hank Janson novel *Killer* was named in a murder trial, the book having been found in the possession of the murderer and the method of murder (the victim was clubbed to death with a chair leg wrapped in a cloth) being similar to one in the book. It was inevitable that Janson would be taken to court. Julius Reiter and Reginald Carter were questioned and asked to make statements about the publishing of Janson in August, and in November were charged under the obscene libel laws. The subsequent court case would rock the publishing world.

*Goulden, still in charge, bought the company back seven years later and retained it until 1970 when it was sold to the American Walter Reade Organisation; almost immediately it was re-sold to the British theatrical group Howard & Wyndham. Throughout all these changes, Mark Goulden remained in editorial control, and would do until his retirement at the age of 80, in 1976 (he died in May 1980).

7

"THE BEST OF TOUGH GANGSTER WRITERS"

"Never liked the everyday kind of person

The uninteresting or ordinary folk,

I always wanted action and that's the great attraction,

Of this guy who looks on danger as a joke.

Walking around with nowhere to go,

Only myself to amuse,

I feel so tired and a new kinda low,

I've got the Hank Janson Blues."

The Hank Janson Blues by Peter Cornish & George Korel,

as sung by Anne Shelton (1953)

The world of publishing has its heroes and its heroines, it's best-sellers and those whose work is immensely popular for a while and then sells steadily from the back-catalogue, leaping ahead again if a new *magnum opus* arrives or a forward-looking studio picks up the option to film. The ebb and flow of publishing can bring names to the surface whilst allowing others to drift into obscurity as tastes change or as styles and subjects become dated. In the mushroom boom, the hero was Hank Janson.

Stephen Frances' name will forever be linked with that of Janson; when he died of emphysema in 1989 at his home in Spain few people knew about it, apart from a few close friends. His name had not appeared on a book for over ten years, and during the last years of his life it was his wife, Theresa, who supported the family. Yet during the 35 years between 1946 and

1971 his novels sold over 20 million copies, were reprinted in America and throughout Europe in translation, and his Spanish Civil War saga, *La Guerra*, written over two years in the mid-1960's, was praised by one reviewer as the best historical novel since *Gone With the Wind*. *La Guerra* garnered comparison's from other reviewers with *For Whom the Bell Tolls* and *Dr Zhivago* for its epic treatment and compelling power, yet it's publication in America (in one 629 page hardcover) went almost un-noticed: the day of publication co-incided with that of *Inside the Third Reich* by Albert Speer, and it was the latter that received most of the attention of the national press's critics to the exclusion of all else. In England it was split into four volumes and invisibly entered the market as a series of paperback originals.

Frances was never a 'great' author, and never thought of himself as anything more than an average wordsmith, later recalling his surprise at the publication of his first article by saying, "what was surprising was that I could write anything an editor considered worthy of publication. I'm a terrible scholar. I hated school so much I made great efforts to avoid being taught anything. Engish grammar was a mystery I had no wish to unravel." Instead of learning, parrot-fashion, the rules and regulations of verb, noun and predicate, he made up for it by reading voraciously: "My mother worked until late at night and when a child I had to spend long and lonely hours in a gaslit room with only books for company. I pored over those books, gradually extracting meaning from them, and eventually books became as important to me as food and drink. I didn't merely read books, I soaked them up. And I suppose that without knowing it I absorbed the principals of grammar. I know, or 'feel' when a sentence is right. Or wrong. So my writing is more or less grammatically acceptable, but I tend to be impatient with spelling, negligent of spelling and more than ignorant of grammar. When I split an infinitive I don't know I'm doing it and don't care anyway. I don't think it matters two hoots to a reader who is eager to get on with his reading." The truth of this statement was proven by the followers of his Hank Janson novels, which were selling at the rate of around 100,000 copies a month.

Stephen Daniel Frances was born in Lambeth, South London, in 1917. His father, also called Stephen, was a shop assistant who had married May Isabel Abbott in 1916, but was soon to be conscripted into the army. On the day his son reached one year of age he was killed whilst serving in France, and Frances was raised by his mother on the pittance of an army pension. "My earliest memories are of depressing sights," he later wrote. "We lived on the top floor of a tenement house. Wooden stairs with a rickety bannister led up to our 'landing' and gas cooker. One door opened on to our bedroom and the other to the kitchen. This had a shallow scrub-sink and a water tap. We had gas for lighting and a coal fire for heating. The toilet was an outhouse down three flights of stairs and into the back yard. It also catered for the other twenty or so occupants of the dwelling. Everybody in my world was wretchedly poor. Whenever my mother was hard-up she hid with me in the basement coal-cellar until the rent collector went away. As I grew older unemployment increased and living conditions became worse. Bread and jam was the staff of life, eaten in large quantities to keep bellies filled. A little girl who was ill became the talk of the street because the doctor had ordered she should be fed chicken. Chicken was then a luxury and the family had to pawn to buy it. Everybody speculated upon how chicken tasted."

The family was dominated by Frances' grandmother, known as the Old Girl, an alcoholic nymphomaniac whom he recalled with mixed emotions. "I never once saw my Grandma sober; neither did I ever see her completely drunk. She lived at a staggery, boozy level that she maintained with a steady intake of whisky." She lived with two of her sons in a two-roomed tenement flat, Podge (because he was slender) and Charlie (known as Long'air because he was prematurely bald - he later died of appendicitis and was given a pauper's burial. The Old Girl was so drunk she fell into the grave). With his mother at work, the burden of looking after the child fell to Podge who tried to make a little money selling anything from hot-water bottles to children's toys around pubs, or to the Old Girl, who spent most of her time returning Podge's meagre earnings to the pubs' landlords.

His formal education at elementary school ended at fourteen when he took up the position of office boy to a Trade paper in Fleet Street and followed it with various other short-lived jobs; at fourteen he also joined the Labour Party League of Youth and at sixteen was an undercover member of the Communist Party. "However," he recalled, "the Communist Party soon became disenchanted with me. At the time the Party were organising meetings throughout Britain to raise money to aid the Spanish Republicans fighting Franco. At the same time the Spanish Republicans were shipping barge-loads of Spain's gold reserves to Russia. When I began to enquire why with so much available wealth the Spanish Republicans needed the Communist Party to take up collections, I was denounced as a Trotskyist and ejected from the Party."

It was whilst working as a shipping clerk with an import and export firm that Frances' first article appeared, a double page spread in the *Daily Worker* under the bold headline "THE VICTIMISATION OF SHIPPING CLERKS". He continued to submit articles to various papers, but the urge to write stories was always present. "My early ventures in writing were stimulated by my resentment of the poverty in which I and so many others lived. I wrote articles which were political arguements. Then I discovered that I also liked to write fiction. In my spare moment, in the office, on the tram going to work, or even waiting for the bus, I scribbled ideas, or character sketches on the backs of envelopes or scraps of paper. At the back of my mind hovered the dream that one day I might be paid for what I wrote and be able to earn a living at writing."

Frances was a conscientious objector during the war, and launched a magazine in December 1939 entitled *Free Expression* from his home, at the time a converted single-decker bus on a plot of land by the Thames at Shepperton. It was here that he met Harry Whitby, a doctor who also had a private source of income and a scientific fascination for gambling. In 1945 the two met again, and it was at Whitby's suggestion that they went into business, going halves in the venture with Whitby supplying the finance and Frances doing the work. "I had walked out of my job and was facing a bleak and moneyless future," he recalled. "I didn't hesitate. I jumped off the treadmill!" At Harry's suggestion he went into publishing. "By the following day I'd already begun founding Pendulum Publications Ltd."

Pendulum offered as diverse a range of titles as could be found during the days of the war. Amongst the titles was his own first novel, *One Man in his Time* (1946), featuring a Frances-figure growing up between the wars in poverty, an outspoken young man who cannot find work in London, a travellor, an opportunist and an idealist. The book was told in first-person narrative by an un-named protagonist, part fiction and partly based on some of Frances' own experiences; one reviewer speculated what it would be like when the author attempted a novel rather than an autobiography!

Pendulum, like so many other publishing companies of the time, struggled to keep afloat during the winter of 1946/47. The weather was savagely cold; Frances found himself working in the dark during power-cuts, the distribution network was fouled-up by snowbound roads, and at the same time Harry Whitby decided to go to Australia and wanted to sell his co-director the other half of the business. Before reaching a decision, the two received an offer for Pendulum, which they accepted. Whitby was paid back his investment and emigrated, and the two received a small advance for their shares and promissory notes for the balance.

The new owners of Pendulum almost immediately went into liquidation, and the debts never honoured. Frances, now without a company and only £250 to show for it, decided to gamble all on a new company. Whereas Pendulum had become a respectably large concern with secretaries and employees, the newly founded S.D. Frances (Publisher) Ltd. was a one-man affair: Frances turned his typewriter to a western novel, written in fifteen days, and carefully planned a 10,000 copy print run.

Unable to handle the distribution alone, Frances made a proposition to Julius Reiter, who had recently set up Gaywood Distributors for the handling of books that were not covered by his already-established Kosmos International Distributors. Frances offered him a 50% discount if he would take the whole edition. It was an attractive offer, and Reiter accepted.

> "I had shaved down my profit to give Julius such a large discount," Frances later said, "but I was running no risk and my basic capital was secure. In addition I would earn an author's fee as well as my slim publisher's profit; I didn't have to employ salesmen, nor packers and a small desk in my Shaftsbury Avenue flat served as my office. Overheads were at a minimum. My only problem was getting the books delivered to Julius within three months. If power-cuts and printing failures dragged out delivery to six months my gamble would fail."

In between phone-calls to spur on the printers, and having no money to produce a second title, Frances thought up another money-making scheme: manuscript-vetting. He advertised, offering to assist would-be writers to get into print. "To those hopefuls who applied for details I sent a four-page leaflet I'd written, offering to read, correct and give marketing advice about a manuscript for a fee appropriate to its length. I pictured myself profitably time-filling while waiting for the printer to deliver the book to Julius. But only four hopefuls applied. I sent them leaflets and one was sent back within days. It was a beauty. The man who returned it was probably a University professor. In bold, very red ink he'd corrected all my grammatical and spelling mistakes, modified my faulty punctuation and under-scored clumsy sentences. I hung my head in shame."

The economics of the business were simple: the total cost of producing the book was about £290. Selling 10,000 copies would bring in £750, less 50% to the distributor. The profit was £85, which allowed an average weekly wage of £7 (about average for the time). But only if the books appeared at regular three-monthly intervals. Luckily the first book was delivered on time, and Frances returned to Reiter with a second western and an offer to repeat the deal. But this time the reception was lukewarm. So Frances offered him a gangster novel.

* * * * * * *

Hank Janson had first appeared in the days of Pendulum Publications. A printer had phoned up with the news that he had enough paper for a 25,000 print run on a 24 page book. This was manna to any publisher, but the manuscript had to be in on Monday. It was Friday. "I rang around," Frances recalled. "No writer I contacted had any manuscript available of the length required. A distributor telephoned. He wanted another two thousand copies of a glossy Film Star book. 'We can't deliver until the end of next week,' I told him. Then to console him I mentioned I'd soon have a twenty-four pager to offer him. 'What category,' he asked. 'I don't know yet. I'm selecting a manuscript.' 'Avoid romance,' he warned. 'Too much on the market. Crime, westerns or gangster are preferable.'"

Still unable to find a suitable manuscript, he turned to a friend, Muriel. "I asked her if she was willing to work over the weekend. She was. 'It's going to be hard work,' I warned. 'I'll dictate and you'll type.' We worked all Saturday and until after midnight on Sunday. But by then we had the exact number of typed pages the printer needed. I was hoarse from walking up and down while dictating and Muriel's shoulders ached from hunching over the typewriter."

The book was delivered, appearing under the title *When Dames Get Tough*, the author given as Hank Janson, quickly followed by *Scarred Faces*, a sixty-four pager containing two short novels ("Scarred Faces" and "Kitty Takes the Rap"). The three stories were relatively well written, with each story continuing from where the last left off. However, it was not until the next series of books was launched that Janson became the bestseller of his time.

With the lukewarm reception of the second western novel (which later sold to Scion Ltd.) Frances quickly turned back to the gangster novel, and over the next few weeks wrote *This Woman Is Death*. Whilst waiting for the printers he wrote another, *Lady Mind That Corpse*, and even as the first title was being delivered was already into a third. He delivered the second novel to Reiter and offered him *Gun Moll For Hire*, and was given the news that sales were good. Reiter wanted fifteen thousand of the third book, and another five thousand each of the first two. However good this news was, it was tempered by the knowledge that he only had the finance to print 10,000. Reiter immediately offered to finance the additional printing, and a bond of friendship was formed between the two. "I couldn't believe it," Steve later said. "In almost all my dealings in business everybody was obsessed with getting their hands on money and then never letting go of it. I never forgot this, and later on, when powerful book distributors made extremely tempting offers I never for a moment considered taking the distribution of Hank Janson away from him." The fourth novel, *No Regrets For Clara*, had a first printing of 20,000.

Janson was another reflection of a fictionalised Steve Frances. The stories were violent, fast-paced and written in a style that was easily read. Janson was a traveller who roamed America finding women and adventure in equal quantities. The fictional America he travelled was a stark contrast to an England still in the grip of rationing (in a later interview Frances said, "I got all my background material by seeing as many Hollywood gangster

Across: *No Regrets For Clara*. Frances' fourth Hank Janson novel. Sales must have been boosted by Reginald Heade's superb "menaced dame" cover art.

and crime movies as I could, by reading up John Gunther's *Inside America* and various travel guides"). Frances himself tried to think himself into Janson's shoes: "I aimed at making Hank Janson seem a real living person. I invented a biography for him which was widely accepted as true. So many readers believed Hank Janson was flesh and blood that Hank Janson fan clubs were formed around Britain that appealed for Hank to pay them a visit. When writing, I completely identified myself with Hank Janson. If a girl slapped his face my cheek stung. If he smelled rotting fish I felt nauseated and if he exhausted himself I had to gulp whiskey to revive myself. Because I could identify myself so thoroughly with Hank Janson, my readers were probably also helped to identify with the book's hero, which is what many readers like to do."

The books were becoming a runaway success, the print run soon up to 30,000, and Reiter was asking for a more regular supply. "I am a very slow and very bad typist," Frances admitted. "But I was being urged to provide more Hank Janson books, more quickly." The answer was a second-hand dictaphone which recorded on a wax cylinder. "When I completed a stack of cylinders I carried them around the corner to a typing agency. I developed my own writing method. I dictate the book hot and fast. I put in everything that bubbles into my mind. Often the sentences don't make sense but the words conjure up an emotion. I can dictate so very much more quickly than I can type that I can quickly record a first 'rough' novel. Then, when

I get back the mass of typed material from the typist I cut drastically, edit ruthlessly, change, adapt, correct and edit until I feel I can send the ammended copy for its final typing."

The dictaphone solved the problem of delivering manuscripts, but there was still the problem of erratic printing. This was solved by the arrival of Reginald Carter, a representative of The Racecourse Press, a printing firm on the lookout for new business. The rotary press at Racecourse was able to print at high speed, but required a larger edition to make it profitable, and the presses ran best printing five titles at the same time. The next book was launched with 35,000 and a new batch of reprints made up the first print order. Julius Reiter wanted a new title every six or eight weeks. "I kept my dictaphone going day and night. While my corrected copy of one book was being typed for the printer, I was already well into the next book, the early chapters of which were already typed and being passed back to me for editing. Incredibly, juggling with reprints we did achieve the target of printing five titles simultaneously. I felt more like a factory than an author."

In 1948 Frances had taken a holiday in Spain, and spent many weeks in the village of Rosas. A second visit convinced him that he wanted to escape from the hectic treadmill of British publishing, and he bought himself a flat in a new block that was under development. A new style of battery-powered dictaphone meant that he could continue work without worrying about the fluctuations and vaguries of the Spanish power supply, and the move was all set. He spent some weeks in Spain once the flat was completed, organising his new home. "Fitting out the flat and buying all the odds and ends to make it habitable would be a long and tedious task. I was urgently needed in London so my Spanish friends offered to undertake the chore for me. When I set off for London I took with me the completed dictation of another Hank Janson book. When driving up from the coast I passed through the Elephant & Castle crossroads and while halted at the traffic light saw a news placard outside a newsagents shop that read: "Read Hank Janson. South London's Best Selling Author." This was the first time it occured to me that Hank Janson might become an established best-seller."

Daniel Farson was, at the time, the presenter of a half-hour television show entitled *Success Story*, one of which featured Hank Janson. "Many readers believed that Hank Janson was flesh and blood," Frances recalled, "and I saw no reason to dispell this illusion. But because I don't much resemble Hank Janson I insisted on being interviewed wearing a mask. We chose a stripclub as a setting with girls stripping in the background while I sat at the bar, chatting with Daniel Farson and wearing a Fedora and two overcoats that gave my shoulders an impressive burliness. Carter was in his element as a company director. He was as competent as a movie-star as he strolled around a large warehouse with Farson, nattily dressed and indicating the mountains of Hank Janson books, parcelled and ready to ship out, and reciting the sales totals of each title."

Hank Janson had risen to the leagues of the multi-million sellers when the climate in British publishing was showing a downswing. Paper rationing was deregulated in 1951 and more and more books jostled in the bookstands. Publishers were collapsing regularly as competition became more fierce, yet Janson's sales were increasing. The success story of Hank Janson was summed up when Frances said, "Writing is hard work and very demanding, but I enjoy it. And those who are lucky and can enjoy their work are lucky indeed. I was content to work hard and have the advantages of a simple, natural life, far away from the hustle, bustle and greyness of city life." It was as perfect an existance for him as he had ever hoped for. "I had no dreams of attaining wealth and fame." To which statement he added the fateful words, "Which was just as well!"

* * * * * * *

"Hank Janson, born in England during the First World War. Janson stowed away on a fishing trawler at the age of nineteen and started a series of adventures that took him pearl fishing in the Pacific, whaling in the arctic for two years, and through most of the States of America. He obtained American nationality and worked in New York as a truck driver, news reporter and assistant to a Private Detective Agency. During the Second World War he served in Burma, returning in 1948 to England for the first time since he had left in his teens. By 1950, as he began to reach the peak of his popularity, he was living in Surrey with his wife and children, spending his time gardening and writing about his personal experiences in a fictional form."

So ran the 'official' biography which appeared in a number of his books in the early 1950s. Of course, in reality, Janson and author Frances shared only one similarity, that of being born during the First World War. But many readers believed that Janson was a real person, and his adventures to be the "genuine article".

Hank Janson avoided a number of the problems faced by his rivals; with Frances in both the writing and publishing seat, a certain standard *had* to be maintained or he would have been cutting his own throat. Frances was certainly a capable writer, a fact testified by his popularity and longevity. As early as 1949 he was invited to write for various other publishers, so as well as his commitment to Janson he was also producing books for Bernard Kaye Agency under the names Ace Capelli, Johnny Grecco and Steve Markham. He also sold his second western to Scion Ltd under the name Tex Ryland, and was invited to write gangster stories under the name Duke Linton. For his own company he also wrote a novel as Link Shelton and one as Max Clinten, and launched Astron Del Martia as a science fiction byline with a novel by John Russell Fearn.

Despite this increase in output, Janson still reigned above all the other gangster bylines. One of the reasons for his popularity was probably that Frances was able to build from book to book, the stories being serial rather than episodic, and the character of Hank Janson was drawn in fully as the stories progressed; too often the gangster novels featured paper private-eyes and cardboard dames to fill the gaps between sadistic torture scenes and brutality. Janson, although capable of violence, did at least show himself to be capable of other emotions; cynical about his dealings with others, and often taking the law into his own hands, Janson had an instinctive sense of right and wrong throughout his adventures, a sympathy for the underdog which mirrored Frances' own; he was capable of feeling jealousy (as in *This Dame Dies Soon*), or deep love (as in *The Filly Wore A Rod*). The first series of books took Janson across America, and although each title was self-contained, there was a continuity to the stories, for instance, *Lillies For My Lovely* saw Janson in Des Moines trying to solve the mystery of a girl's sudden death. The girl, Sally, he discovers is still alive, and at the end of the book they leave Des Moines together, a thread picked up at the start of *Blonde on the Spot* which sees the pair driving into Oklahoma and more adventures. After the first series of twelve books, the second series saw Janson as a newspaper reporter on the *Chicago Chronicle*, a position he was to hold for nearly twenty years. The serial nature of the Janson novels allowed other characters to reappear, amongst them the Chief, Janson's long-suffering boss on the *Chronicle*, Detective Inspector Sharp, who tries every trick in the book to pin something on Janson (another of the cops is coincidentally called Blunt), or Sheila Lang, the fiery-tempered writer of the Woman's Page of the *Chronicle* with whom Janson has a love-hate relationship; all were given enough space to develop as characters rather than incidental trimmings.

The success of Janson was immediate: within two years the books were announcing that a million copies had been sold, an average sale of over 60,000 per book, far above average for that type of novel. The novels began to sell in even greater quantities throughout 1951, with the arrival of the third series. This new series included a number of stories which did not feature Janson as the lead character as well as stories of Janson the newspaper reporter, who continued to appear in most of the books. The first title in this series was *Baby, Don't Dare Squeal* and was the first to be issued by Frances from offices at 104 Southampton Row (actually a stockroom he had inherited from his Pendulum days), and the cover (by Heade) appeared to have had the price of 1/6 overprinted by a new price of 2/-. This overprinting of price continued for the next three books, *Death Wore a Petticoat, Hotsy, You'll Be Chilled*, and *It's Always Eve Who Weeps*. The next title, *Frails Can Be So Tough*, saw an even more startling change - rather than the usual Heade dame, the cover showed a silhouette of Hank Janson, the title and the price of 2/- only. This move was made after the increasing number of prosecutions being made against newsagents and publishers; if the police received a complaint about risque magazines or books on display at newsagents they would usually pick up anything which looked similar. Rather than waste valuable board, and cover the cost of preparing a new cover, it was easier and cheaper to overprint the silhouette. This continued for another two novels, *Milady Took the Rap* and *Women Hate Till Death*. Another change had taken place, Frances was no longer the publisher, this honour now going to New Fiction Press of 104 Southampton Row. This was an imprint of Editions Poetry (London) Ltd., a bankrupt publishing house which had been purchased by Reginald Carter for the sole purpose of publishing Hank Janson; Frances and Carter had a very close publishing relationship, Carter taking on all of the responsibilities for publishing and printing, allowing Frances more time to concentrate on writing.

An interesting experiment which should be mentioned here had appeared soon after the launch of the third series: a Hank Janson magazine entitled *Underworld*. Steve Frances later commented:

> The idea of *Underworld* was that bearing the HJ upon it *[Janson being the editor - SH]* would make it sell like HJ novels. We would have a mag at just the expense of an occasional HJ story. But the public didn't fall for it and although it sold 30,000 it was silly to do it if an HJ novel sold 100,000.

Originally intended as a quarterly, Frances only edited two issues. The stories in the first issue were all pseudonymous, with Ace Capelli, Max Clinten, and Dave Steel all being associated with Frances, a Hank Janson novelette (by Frances), and a story by Brad Shannon. Shannon was the pen-name of Victor Joseph Hanson, admired by Frances ("the best of the bunch") but by a quirk of fate, although Hanson did contribute a story, the Shannon byline appeared here on someone else's story by mistake. Hanson (proving the incestuous nature of the fifties paperback publishers) had taken over the writing of novels under the bylines Duke Linton and Max Clinten, both of which had been launched with stories by Frances. The second issue of *Underworld* contained a reprinted story by Damon Runyon, whom Frances ranked in his top three favourite authors, the others being O.Henry and Jack London. Although noted for his humorous stories, Runyon filled them with the underworld characters of Broadway and the many other cities he had visited as a reporter. Runyon would appear to have had a greater influence on Hank Janson than Chandler's Philip Marlowe, although Janson also reflected Marlowe's unswerving loyalty to a cause; as the series progressed the character of Janson seems to have evolved so that it rested comfortably between the two.

The second issue of *Underworld* also contained a Hank Janson novelette, but the magazine folded. Frances continued to write the novels, but in 1952 he sold all rights to the name to Reginald Carter for the sum of £4,000, bluntly admitting many years later:

I made a mistake. When Carter made this proposition I was solely in control of a very simple, but lucrative business. I was a one-man band. I wrote a book, paid a printer to deliver completed books to a distributor and received a cheque. Everything worked as smoothly as silk...With a sellout of an edition of 100,000 of each new title, and continual reprintings of previous titles, Hank Janson was a success story. My accountant told me that my little one-man business, operating from my small desk in Shaftsbury Avenue, showed a much higher profit than some of his other clients who employed two or three hundred workmen.

On paper I was financially well-off. But not in fact. I'd been pulling myself up by my own bootstraps. From the beginning all the money I'd earned I'd ploughed back into the business to pay for ever bigger editions of subsequent books. However, there was some spare cash I could shake free from the business that enabled me to live a little more extravagantly than previously. Now I could take a couple of girl-friends to dinner, pay by cheque, return to my flat by taxi, and provide for my guests from a well-stocked drink cabinet.

I trusted Carter implicitly. He rented a house in Sussex where he lived, and where there would always be accomodation for me if I gave up my Shaftsbury Avenue flat to become resident in Spain. With guidance from an accountant, Carter formed a new limited company.

I sold all my interests in my Hank Janson business for four thousand pounds. I suppose that I passed over to him about thirty thousand pounds-worth of books and debts, which made the sale nonsensical. Except that Carter and I had a gentleman's agreement. Hank Janson was the basic source of all the profit and as the author it was commonsense that I should be relieved of all responsibilities so that I could concentrate on writing.

New Fiction Press were incorporated as a company in November 1952 and continued to publish the third series, but during this period there were more developments with the covers of the next two Janson books. Both *Broads Don't Scare Easy* and *Skirts Bring Me Sorrow* were issued with partially silvered covers. The same silhouette was used, but part of the original Heade illustration could still be seen - the silvering only covered the dame on the artwork. The next title saw a return to the normal Heade cover, but even that title, *Sadie Don't Cry Now* later appeared with a different Heade cover with the 1/6 price tag overprinted with 2/-. Both *The Filly Wore A Rod* and *Slay-Ride For Cutie* had attractive Heade covers painted for them, but were only published in silhouette covers. The next title, *Kill Her If You Can* brought the third series to a close after a somewhat confusing period.

The fourth series of Janson novels started with *Murder* in 1952. The stories were appearing at regular six-weekly intervals with a print run now at 100,000 copies per title. With earlier titles being constantly reprinted, the sales figures of Janson were phenomenal: by mid-1953 over eight million copies had been sold in five years.

Carter's business was by now on a massive scale, his companies including Comyns (Publishers) Ltd., New Fiction Press, and the printers Arc Press. In all he employed over 100 people. Arc Press was jointly owned by Julius Reiter, who was also director of Gaywood Press, the distributors who also published books themselves, and of Paladin Press which was launched in 1951. Gaywood were not only paperback distributors - they also distributed children's books, newspapers such as the *Daily Mirror*, and magazines such as *Illustrated*.

Soon after taking over the rights to the name, Carter instituted a new series under the Janson byline, the 'Hank Janson Special', and used Janson on a number of American reprints by Gil Brewer and Edward Ronns (Edward S. Aarons) which were given the 'Hank Janson Seal' ("Hank Janson says 'read this book'"). The Special was a novel written by Janson which featured a completely different background to the usual stories. Although some of the main series titles had not featured Janson as the lead character, eg *Broads Don't Scare Easy*, *Death Wore A Petticoat*, etc., they were crime novels; the first Special was *Auctioned* which was set in the deserts of Persia and dealt with slave-trading. It was the first of a trilogy completed by *Persian Pride* and *Desert Fury*. The fourth Special was a science fiction novel, *The Unseen Assassin*, whilst the fifth reprinted Frances' first novel, *One Man In His Time*.

By the end of the fourth series Janson was under serious threat from the Director of Public Prosecutions. During 1953 both Carter and Reiter were visited by Scotland Yard, Reiter preparing a statement on August 11 1953 and Carter on August 28th. On October 19 both made further statements, answering specific questions concerned with the printing, publishing and distributing of three Hank Janson titles, *Amok*, *Vengeance* and *Killer*.

These titles all appeared as part of the fourth series after the name had been sold to Carter. During the period in question Carter put New Fiction Press on hold and issued a number of Janson novels under the imprint Top Fiction Press, from his offices at 139 Borough High Street, London SE1. The fifth series which took Janson on an assignment to Europe, had just been launched with *Silken Menace*, but only two appeared, the last being *Nyloned Avenger* in the Autumn of 1953. Four further titles were advertised and covers had been prepared for advertisements, namely *Woman Trap*, *Perfumed Nemesis*, *Blonde Dupe* and *Dainty Dynamite*, but these did not appear: on November 23 1953 Carter and Reiter were charged at Guildhall Justice Room with publishing obscene libels in the form of seven Hank Janson novels with their case to be heard at the Old Bailey.

Across: Hank Janson continued to be popular well into the '60s. After the New Fiction/Gaywood era, Moring and then Roberts & Vintner published in the UK. The character also crossed the Atlantic to be published in the USA by Gold Star.

Below.: Restrained and pensive
Heade beauty stands accused
of.......

8

THE TRIALS OF HANK JANSON

It is said you are here as members of the public to decide this case. That is true enough. But you are also here as part of the administration of the justice. To administer what? Surely the law, not some fabrication of unknown writers and publishers. Who are they to impose upon us their notions.

Gerald Dodson, summing up Regina v Reiter, 1954

The case against the publishers of Hank Janson opened on Thursday, January 14 1954, the charges being against Carter, Reiter, Arc Press, New Fiction Press, and Gaywood Press. These five defendants were charged that between March 31 1952 and October 1 1953 they uttered and published seven obscene libels in the form of seven novels: *Accused, Auctioned, Persian Pride, Pursuit, Amok, Killer* and *Vengeance*. In court, counsel stated that the books were on sale throughout the country at 2 shillings a copy. Five of the books dealt with murder, robbery and every other kind of crime. The other two had a background of slavery in some desert with nomads and Arabs being enslaved by the local Caliph. The main theme running through all the books was sex. The second theme was cruelty with descriptions of the hero being tortured and young girls being tied up. In the submission of the prosecution the only effect of these books would be to corrupt and deprave.

As well as giving the Jury the Hicklin test for obscenity, the prosecutor raised two further points of law: that the intention of the defendants to corrupt and deprave was not important (the authority being given as the 1923 case *Rex v. Montalk*), and that if part of the book was obscene, then the whole book was obscene (the authority being the 1952 case *Paget v. Watson Publications)*.

The prosecutor read brief extracts from the books and gave a synopsis of the rest of the book. At the end of the first day the Jury were allowed to retire between 2.12 pm and 4.00pm to read the books. The Recorder, Gerald Dodson, asked what the position was and the Foreman of the Jury replied that the Jury had read as much as they needed to fairly assess the contents. When it was suggested that the Jury might need a little more time to examine and read the books, Dodson replied, "No. They have said they have read enough and that they have been able to go through them. Why that statement should not be accepted I do not know. For my part, I accept it. I have glanced through these books myself and I was quite able to form an opinion, with no difficulty at all." This opinion was countered on the second day of the proceedings by defence counsel Gerald Howard, Q.C., acting on behalf of Carter, Arc Press and New Fiction Press, who maintained that the charges were being brought against the books as a whole, and the Jury should read the whole book; thus the Jury retired a second time between 10.48 am and 12.45 pm, at which point Dodson adjourned the case.

During the case it was pointed out that it took one member of the defending counsel an hour and a half to read each novel, whilst the Jury considered that three and three-quarter hours was sufficient to read all seven. Dodson's opinion seems to have been made up the first day, as shown by such statements as, "But there may be something in the Jury reading these books, although I am loath to inflict the task upon them. It seems a ghastly way of spending their time."

The case for the defence opened on Monday January 18 after the formal matters of proving that Carter and Reiter were the publishers of the books. The case was opened by Gerald Howard who introduced a number of books and film stills which in his opinion were indicative of the day's standards. The books were taken from Public libraries and had not previously been taken to court in London and charged with obscenity, the films being on general release. Howard also pointed out in his opening speech that it was the obscenity of the book that was being dealt with, what was actually written down, and not anything that the reader might infer from certain passages. It is important here to realise that these books were devoid of any precise sexual details. Stephen Frances said of his early Janson books: "My stuff was done on innuendo. One minute a man and woman were sitting side by side. You'd read a whole page, and get the impression of physical contact, but you couldn't pin it down." It was also interesting to note that Hank Janson himself had something to say on the matter: in the novel *Torment For Trixie* Janson attends a Church Literary Group meeting where a novel, *The Inconstant Lover* is under discussion; the lady chairman having read extracts denounces the book as a disgrace, at which point Janson interrupts:

> "Folks. There's nothing wrong with that book. The story doesn't say anything happened to the dame."

> The Chairman said quickly. "They spent the night together in that shack. Surely that's inference enough."

> I repeated slowly. "There's nothing wrong with that book. The only thing wrong is the way you folks look at it. You've got a suburban attitude. You see rottenness where no rottenness exists. This book isn't obscene. It's like life; maybe a little extra flavouring. The only vice and obscenity in this book is what your own minds read into it."

(*Torment For Trixie* by Hank Janson, 1950)

Of the seven books involved in the trial, *Accused* seems to have caused the most controversy and is the obvious choice for a closer study.

The following is the description of the book by Mr. Griffith-Jones:

> JONES: To take *Accused* as an example. That book is the story of a young man who starts off driving a car out on a drunken and rather lecherous evening with some other young men and women. On their way back he runs over somebody in the road... indeed, two young girls, if I remember rightly, going at tremendous speed in the car; they carry on and do not stop; blood, and so on, is found over the bonnet. Then he is on the run and jumps on to a lorry, and goes out into some deserted area of the country... this takes place in America... he is dropped off the lorry, he walks a long way and finishes up in a little cafe kept by a man called Freidman; he is down and out and has no food, so Freidman offers him lodgings and food if he will work for him, Freidman offers him lodgings and food if he will work for him, Freidman, in the cafe, and there he settles down to work. The story then revolves around what happens in the cafe. Freidman is a sadist; he has married a woman, a young girl, who is to all intents and purposes his slave, who he treats with the utmost brutality. He then treats this young boy with equal brutality and really enslaves him. One has descriptions night by night, as the boy sleeps on the floor outside the bedroom door, of Freidman torturing, in effect, his wife, and one hears her groans of agony coming through the door. Eventually this young man and the wife become attracted to one another; they have sexual intercourse with one another, and they are discovered in the act... I think upon the second or third occasion of doing it... on the

kitchen floor while Freidman is away; Freidman comes back and they are discovered in the act. There is a scene and Freidman says he will punish them; he puts his naked wife over his knee and with a knife is going, apparently, to slit her private parts and threatens to castrate the young man as soon as he is finished. The young man eventually can stand it no longer... the wonder is that he has stood it as long as that, you may think... so he siezed a flat-iron, knocks the villain on the head and kills him, puts him down the well, and then the boy and girl run off. They of course have sexual intercourse at every possible opportunity until the boy discovers that the woman is older than he thought and becomes less attracted by her; there is a beastly description of a woman's festering foot; eventually she takes an overdose of morphia and died, the boy goes off and is finally picked up by the police and then beaten-up, and one has a description of the sadistic and ghastly beating-up of the boy imprisoned by the police.

That is the general outline of the book. Now would you look perhaps as an example at page 58. We are in the cafe and the villain Freidman has gone down to the town to pay his money into the bank; then you see about a third of the way down the page:

"I followed him out on to the veranda, watched him come down the steps, cross over to his lorry and climb up into the driving seat. There was maybe an hour to go before closing time. But I turned back into the dining room, closed the door, locked it and switched on the 'Closed' sign.

She was waiting for me, her eyes anxious and apprehensive as I closed the door behind me. It was as though she didn't know whether to run to me, or away from me.

I knew we were crazy. but I also knew nothing was going to stop it happening. It was inevitable, something that had to happen, like a car going down hill with no brakes and no means of stopping until it hit bottom."

It appears in a moment, of course, what is inevitable; but if you have read all the book up to now it is perfectly clear that the only thing that is inevitable is the sexual intercourse that is about to take place:

"I walked over to the kitchen door, closed it deliberately, bolted it firm. There were shabby, sun-dried and sun-bleached curtains that I drew, covering the glass portion of the door.

When I turned around she was staring at me with a kinda wild, desperate look in her eyes. 'You can't,' she panted. 'You mustn't. There's folk coming in all the time.'

I crossed to the only window the kitchen possessed, jerked the curtain across, leaving us in a kinda half-light.

She shrank away from me, pushed herself back against the table."

And then he goes over and stands by her...

"'We can't stop this thing,' I said hoarsly. 'It's no good trying to fight against it.'

'No,' she panted. 'You mustn't. There was a thoroughly scared note in her voice.

It was like it was before, the palms of her hands against my chest but without the strength to push me away. And with the door closed and the sun beating down on the iron roof that kitchen was boiling us in our own perspiration."

And so on...

"'You mustn't,' she whispered. 'It's crazy. Anybody can come in.'

My shirt was wet, sticking to me like I had been rain drenched. I could feel beads of sweat forming..."

And so on...

"I could feel her skin through her dress, hot and slippery, soft and desirable, the quickening of her breathing increasing the fierce urgency inside me. I did what I'd done before, ran my fingers along her spine, grasped her hair, pulled her lips to mine.

This time she resisted, not too strongly but enough. 'Don't be crazy,' she breathed. 'Anyone can come in.'

'I've locked the dining room,' I whispered. 'Closed down for the night.'

I felt the tenseness inside her, the rigidity of shock and fear. 'You can't,' she whispered. 'You can't do that and...'

I pressed her head towards mine, cut off her words with my mouth. Her rigidity lasted for maybe a couple of seconds and then she was responding with a savage urgency that was almost frightening, grasping me fiercely, greedily. Her hands were as slippery as mine and the very fury of her passion was frightening in its intensity, sweeping me along with it.

It was like we were fighting each other. She writhing and biting; me clutching her tightly, our hands seeking and finding each other almost brutally. She panted frantically 'No. You mustn't!' But she wouldn't let me go and the rim of the table was at the back of her thighs, bracing her, giving her resistance.

There had never been anything like it for me before. I

knew that there was no stopping now, that this just had to be.

She panted again: 'No. You mustn't.' Yet her fingers were in my hair, pulling me towards her, her hands caressing my sweat-soaked shoulders and her lips searching greedily for mine.

Her dress tore. She panted 'No!' Then a few seconds later, 'No. It's crazy.'

I didn't say anything. I wasn't even thinking. Everything was a hot whirl of emotion, a perspiring whirlpool that grasped me in a delirious embrace, sucking me ever and ever down and down, my senses swimming with ecstasy as I plunged ever more deeply towards the tranquility and peace I would find when the urgent, heady whirling ceased."

There are plenty of other passages in that book and when you read them you may well think I have selected one that is by no means the worst. I spare you in open Court the description I had intended to read of the finding of the two on the kitchen floor by Freidman and the appalling scene as she lay across his knee, undressed, with a knife raised in his hands.

What you have just read is the prosecutor's interpretation of the passage. Read it again. Henry Farran, the narrator is kissing a girl in a torn dress, rather than the "inevitable sexual intercourse" seen by Griffith-Jones. Steve Frances later wrote: "All author's words trigger off images in readers minds. The reader usually adds something of his own invention to the author's words. If an author writes "cold, clear water glistening in the sun", one reader might think of a fountain, another of a goldfish pond, and a third reader of an Arctic seascape. The word 'woman' conjures u[p visual images in most men's minds, but they are sure to be very different images. An author can write: 'He and she clung to each other' and in the mind of a reader these words may seem to describe the act of sexual intercourse, although there has not been any such description."

The story of *Accused* is a drastically simplified, Frances-esque interpretation of James M. Cain's *The Postman Always Rings Twice*, first published in America and Britain in 1934. Cain's version has Frank Chambers, a drifter, who comes to work at a rural diner, falling in love with the beautiful, young Cora, - they murder her middle-aged Greek husband, Nick Papadakis, face the courts but escape punishment; she eventually dies in a motor accident and Chambers is wrongly executed for her murder; Cain essentially reworked the plot in his 1954 novel *Galatea* which has paroled convict Duke Webster working for Holly Valenty and her husband in a roadhouse: the two fall for each other, Val Valenty falls to his death, which the two are

Across: James M Cain's novels reached the wider public via publishers like Ace Books, the successors of "mushroom" publishers Harborough.

accused of, eventually being found not guilty in court. It wasn't the first time Cain had reworked the plot - the famous *Double Indemnity* (1943, filmed 1944) was another of his husband-murdered-by-wife-and-lover stories.

In *Accused* Frances brought together all the themes he had used with underdog Hank Janson, the brutality of police, the casual and uncompromising sadism of certain individuals, the trapped victim whose nightmare escalates beyond all endurance; Harry Farran is certainly a victim: far from opening with his involvement in a drunken, lecherous evening out it begins with a sadistic beating given to the captured Farran by the police. The story of Alfred Freidman's death is told in flashbacks, the hit-and-run incident remaining untold until half way through the book when we learn that Farran himself was neither drunk nor badly behaved, and the accident was caused by another member of the party who splashes alcohol into Farran's eyes whilst he is driving, was bullied into driving on only after agonising over what to do and was later blamed for the whole accident by his friends.

Griffith-Jones' "descriptions night after night...of Freidman torturing, in effect, his wife, and one hears her groans of agony" is a little more florid than the book, which talks of "little moans, punctuated with sharp gasps of pain" - but no groans of agony night after night.

Farran and Freidman's wife are attracted to each other, "they have sexual intercourse with one another, and they are discovered in the act," according to the prosecutor. That passage in the book reads: "The kitchen was the only place. But this time it was different, without timidity and without restraint. And when it was over it was a gentle parting, reluctant yet peaceful and satisfying." A whole page of dialogue later, Freidman arrives home early and catches them, hardly "in the act".

The passage relating to Freidman's threats with a knife as seen by the prosecution are even more imaginative: at no point is there any threat of castration and if Friedman intends to slit his wife's genitalia it is, again, open to interpretation: "Then he raised the knife, held her in such a way that both she and I understood in the same dreadful moment the horrible, unbelievable intention in his mind." The girl is sprawled face up across his knees: Freidman might just as easily be thinking of cutting her throat, her breasts - if he is thinking of cutting anything at all!

Following Freidman's death "they of course have sexual intercourse at every opportunity"...or, if you bother to read the book, once more.

The Jury had not read the books at this point, and were only allowed three and three quarter hours to read all seven books. Had any of them read the books from cover to cover they would have discovered other errors: a little girl raped for the sixth time in *Amok* was a twenty year old, perhaps raped in the back of a car, perhaps raped again later, only intimated at by the sounds overheard by the narrator, another for instance where Griffith-Jones makes a scene more devastatingly brutal in the eyes of the Jury, this time by adding four rapes for his "little girl".

Would *Accused* stand up to reading today? The sex is only intimated at, the novel short by today's standards, the dialogue terse and a little corny in places. The story has been written by others, and written better, but for all its faults it still makes exciting reading. Frances' power was in the sweltering heat and turmoil of human emotion. He occasionally batters his readers with strong, emotionally charged scenes, using repetition to hammer a point home which jars uncomfortably against dialogue elsewhere pared down to the bone. *Accused* is certainly not obscene - nor was it at the time, I believe. Its subject matter of lust and murder may not be to everyone's taste, but no-one could deny its dramatic verve and raw power.

In retrospect, *Accused* has lost its ability to shock because it has been exceeded by films and novels time and time again. Even a 15 rated film contains far harsher language and graphic scenes, as do modern newspapers, whilst the Jilly Cooper school of novels have made soft-core pornography, if not respectable, at least acceptable. Standards change; it is difficult to believe that anyone would deny it.

The evidence of standards was not one that Dodson wanted to consider; his own views were made quite clear on the matter, to the point where it appeared he was making his own personal stand, lawful or not:

DODSON: I do not think that standard has anything to do with it. Sooner or later I shall be bound to tell the Jury so, and Mr. Howard and Mr. Humphreys can hear what I'm saying. I do not think it has anything to do with it at all. The standard of morals may fluctuate from time - it is a pity that it does - but the law is the same and it is not much good talking about the case of Higgins, or whatever it was...

HOWARD: Hicklin, my lord.

DODSON: Hicklin - as having been adopted in 1932 and being nineteen years old; it is still law today. It has really nothing to do with standard but I cannot prevent the defence referring to these matters. I do not think it is relevant. Not a bit.

Yet the standard of books available and read by the public in 1954 was the main point of the defence. The majority of the third day and part of the fourth day was taken up with reading extracts from many different books, all as readily available as Hank Janson. Different aspects of sexual and brutal nature were selected from a list of 50 different novels; their reading was not made without interruption from Dodson who at one point said, "Well, Mr. Humphreys, how many more books have you got to inflict upon the Jury?"

Christmas Humphreys, Q.C., appearing for Reiter and Gaywood Press, closed the case with his speech, and Dodson began his Summing Up. That the Summing Up was open to question was not even denied at a later Court of Appeal hearing where it was said, "it would have been better if he had used some other expressions than he did use." Dodson repeatedly insisted that to look at the standards of today's [1954] books was wrong:

I suggest to you that it would be most dangerous to do anything of the kind. No doubt you are quite aware that you are being asked to slide, to let yourselves slide into the degeneracy of modern times as depicted in these books which have been produced on behalf of the defence. Somebody has been industrious enough to produce and select these books. If they serve any purpose at all, they may indicate to you the sort of abyss into which you are asked to assist by whitewashing these books with which you are concerned and so contributing to the general slide downwards of this type of modern literature to which your attention has been called. I suggest to you it would be a most dangerous standard to adopt; and, indeed, it is not the law, and it is not open to authors, whether in Spain, and publishers to alter the law by writing books of this kind which you have seen this morning.

Fortunately the law is prescribed for us by better authorities than people who can write descriptions which you have seen. I refrain as far as possible from using language other than that which is strictly judicial, but it is a little difficult. But that is what you are being invited to do, to really disregard the law as it exists today and to substitute another law made for us by these writers and the men who make money publishing this degrading type of literature. One may thank God that it is only a small part of literature of today, but, as we have heard, of course commands enormous sales. It appeals to the lower instincts and the passions of men, and these men have been making money out of it.

Fashions may alter. Of course they do. The bathing dresses of our grandmother's days are very different from the bathing costumes of today. Reference has been made to what is called the bikini bathing costume, which is apparently adopted all over the world. It is different to what it used to be, but unless it is calculated to deprave and corrupt, then there is nothing obscene about it, and nothing perhaps could be suggested as indecent, but we are not concerned with any other word than that which is here in these charges, namely "obscene".

An obscenity is something which tends to deprave and corrupt. It is said here by Mr Humphreys this morning that there is no evidence that anybody has been harmed by these books. That is not necessary. The wording of the definition is something which tends to do it, not neccessarily does it at all.

As I have said, standards of morality in particular may change. Alas, they do, very often for the worse, but the law does not; it stands fast. It is a bulwark against the incoming flood of immoral writings, if these books produced today are an indication of that flood tide, and no doubt they are. It might well be a privalege of a Jury to stand fast against it.

Dodson's Summing Up continued in the same vein until finally he began to cut away at the defence again with: "you have listened to ingenious arguments, so ingenious that at times you must have felt as though the old world, the old standards of morals that you have known, was gradually slipping away from you and leaving you and your children a miserable inheritance." At this point Christmas Humphreys stood up, threw his papers down in disgust, and left the court.

As his speech closed, Dodson, it could be said, spiked the Jury one last time:

> The whole of the argument seems to me not to be based upon the law as it is but upon a rule which is invented for the benefit of these men, upon the unauthorised alteration of the law. What you have got to see is whether fairly and squarely, remembering what you have read so carefully and diligently and at length in these seven books, this is a matter which tends to deprave and corrupt the minds of persons who are open to evil influences such as I have indicated all men are.

How many more instructions did Dodson feel the Jury needed? Modern standards were no defence, the fact that there was no proof that the books corrupted or depraved was no defence, only a tendency which all men were open to. "Perhaps you would now consider your verdict...but do not burden yourselves by taking a lot of literature with you to your room; it is all in your minds and you have seen quite enough."

The Jury retired, at 11.41am, returning at 2.30pm. When asked if a verdict had been reached it was found that the Jury could agree on only one count.

> DODSON: Is there any chance of agreeing about something?

> FOREMAN OF THE JURY: It seems highly improbable at the moment.

> DODSON: All right, Mr. Foreman. Of course you realise it is very desirable if you can agree one way or the other, because it involves everybody a great deal of labour and expense because it has all got to be tried again, except this one count; somebody has got to go through it all again. I do not know if it would help you at all, because I do not know how you are divided, but these words have received the approval of the Court of Criminal Appeal and they might help you if I repeat them to you:

> 'It makes for great public inconvenience and expense if juries cannot agree owing to the unwillingness of one of their number to listen to the arguments of the rest', which is another way of saying that juries come to an agreement by pooling their ideas, putting their heads together in the process of give and take, mental give and take. I do not know whether that in any way assists you, Mr. Foreman, or not. Would you like another five minutes or so to consider what I have said?

With pressure such as this upon them it is little wonder that twenty minutes later the Jury had reached a final verdict, finding all five defendants Guilty on all seven counts.

Before the final sentence, there was one further piece of evidence given. Dodson was given, for the first time, an indication of how much profit was made by the various companies: "the defendants have told me their net salaries were about £2,000 a year," said the witness. Dodson would seem to have thought that this was simply the profit made from Janson, stating in his sentence: "I am told that in six weeks there is a fresh edition made of 100,000 copies. It runs into a very large figure, and if only half the 2s is profit - or whatever it may be - it runs to many thousands of pounds, and it is a monstrous thing that anybody should be allowed to make money in that way." When sentence was finally passed each company was fined the sum of £2,000, a year's salary for each man, and almost certain to put the company's out of business.

Evidence was also given on the previous convictions, one each for Gaywood and New Fiction Press (as an imprint for Editions Poetry, already mentioned earlier). Dodson also asked how many destruction orders had been issued in respect of Hank Janson, the answer being 1,400 in respect of 52 books since 1950, an enormous and misleading figure since none of the books had been individually tried or defended. The individual destruction orders, including the number of orders which had been made in London, against the seven trial books were equally astonishing: *Accused* - 24 (2 in London), *Amok* - 8 (1), *Persian Pride* - 12 (4), *Vengeance* - 16 (2), *Auctioned* - 20 (3), *Killer* - 15 (1), and *Pursuit* - 17 (3) all in 1953 bar one against *Auctioned* in July 1952. Earlier evidence had been given about the sales figures of some of the books: *Accused* - 97,000, *Amok* - 78,000, *Persian Pride* - 140,000, *Vengeance* - 90,000, *Killer* - 98,250; the other two were given no figure, but were estimated between 90,000 and 100,000.

Despite mitigation from both Howard and Humphreys, Dodson said when sentencing:

> Giving this case anxious attention I have come to the conclusion that it cannot be met by mere repayments. Money fines are nothing to people who make money upon this scale, and it is high time publishers realised their responsibilities, as no doubt most of them do. In these cases we are told you were in doubt, and notwithstanding the doubt as to the obscenity of these books you went ahead with it. One can only hope that this trial will mean a step in the other direction, towards the realm of pure and exhilarating literature, and not this kind of debasing stuff which sooner or later will drag the whole reading public down into a veritable lagoon of depravity.

> Under these circumstances, the sentence of the Court upon each of you is one of six months imprisonment, and a fine of £2,000 on each of these companies.

* * * * * * *

Like many people, the Jury may have thought that Carter and Reiter would automatically take the case to the Court of Criminal Appeal and that the case would be reheard. Not so: an Appeal cannot be brought on the premise that the conclusion of the Jury was wrong. It can only be brought on a point of law, or mis-direction.

The case of Carter and Reiter was heard at the Court of Criminal Appeal on Monday March 15 1954 where it appeared before the Lord Chief Justice of England Lord Goddard, and Mr. Justice Slade and Mr. Justice Gerrard. The Appeal was brought on six counts, all concerned with the contention that Judge Dodson mis-directed the Jury as to what was allowed as evidence, that his own views were put so strongly, that it appeared he was almost ordering the Jury to find the books guilty; other points included that he did not direct the Jury sufficiently to judge each book separately, nor did he differentiate between the seven books accused and the many books the defence produced when he discussed the "incoming flood of gross immoral writing".

The Appeal judges were not without their own views as to the nature of the books; early in the Appeal Lord Goddard, having had the "misfortune" to have read the books, said "I cannot see that any Jury could not have come to the same conclusion other than that they were grossly and bestially obscene, " and later that "they are filthy, and if they fall into the hands of young adolescents, I do not wonder that there is juvenile crime today."

The attempt of the defence to introduce books books into court to show standards was argued against at appeal:

JUSTICE GERRARD: I do not understand the word 'Standards' of today in relation to this particular case. It seems to me that it is saying the biggest collection of dirty books you can get together the better view the Jury has of the standards of today. I do not understand that.

MR. HUMPHREYS: What I mean is this: my friend has referred to one book, *The Well of Loneliness* and I can think of another, *Ulysses,* which were banned and years later are openly allowed to be on sale, reprinted again and again and can be bought in London. Therefore, books held to be obscene at English law are now openly on sale. Therefore, today the standard or the test or level of what is indecent or obscene in English law is changing all the time.

LORD CHIEF JUSTICE: I very much doubt that. If a thing is filthy today I do not see why it should not be filthy in five years' time or, if it was filthy five years ago, why it should not be so today.

The latter statement ignores the facts given only seconds earlier!

During the Summing Up of the Appeal, Lord Goddard said:

> This Appeal is brought entirely on the Summing-Up of the learned Recorder. Let me say at once that the learned Recorder's Summing-Up was perhaps to a certain extent rather more rhetorical than one could have wished, but he evidently felt strongly, and it is very difficult for a Judge to control his feelings when he is dealing with the stuff such as there is in this case. I do not wonder that the learned Recorder spoke strongly...

The Appeal was therefore dismissed, as was the Appeal to reduce the sentences, Gerrard saying, "It is high time that the publication of this stuff was stopped and stopped in such a way as would indicate that other persons offending in like manner should know the view of the Court. We cannot say that the sentence passed by the learned Recorder in any way erred in principal and therefore the appeals against sentence are also dismissed."

* * * * * * *

In December 1954 Stephen Frances returned to England, later saying "A summons had been issued for me at the same time as Carter's and Reiter's, but could not be served because I was in Spain. When I learned about it I wrote to my solicitor that I would come back to stand trial with them, but that was not possible: Carter and Reiter had already appeared at the Guildhall and a trial fixed for them at the Old Bailey. My soliciter arranged that I should await the outcome of the trial. If it was favourable, the summons would be dropped. If unfavourable, I would return to the United Kingdom to stand trial.

"However, immediately after the trial, possibly at the instigation of the Recorder, a warrant was issued for my arrest. This was contrary to the agreement made with my soliciter. I considered that this released me from my undertaking to return at once to London, and instead to do so only at my own convenience."

On December 22 he appeared at Guildhall where Mr.E.G. MacDermott for the prosecution said that the case against Frances was that he was the author of the seven 'obscene' Hank Janson novels. Frances was committed for trial at the Old Bailey.

The case opened on February 1 1955, having been delayed from the original date of January 4, with Frances pleading Not Guilty to the charges. The Jury were then asked to read all seven of the obscene books and two further Janson novels which Frances admitted to writing, namely *The Jane With the Green Eyes* and *Milady Took the Rap*. Each day the Jury had to remain in their room between 10.30am and 4.30pm, apart from a break for lunch; the original idea was that the Jury would be able to take copies of the books home to read, but there were not enough copies of the books to go around. The case for the prosecution was that the Jury would be able to compare the style and phrasing in each of the books and be able to determine that they were all by the same author.

In a statement made on February 10 Frances said that he had not written the books and had not written any of them since he had moved to Spain; the seven books were the work of his successor. When the trial resumed the next day the Counsel for the prosecution, Mr. Griffith-Jones, announced that two receipts had been discovered during an examination of the accounts of New Fiction Press. One of them was for £20, and written on the back was the word *Accused;* the second was for £125 for various manuscripts, including *Persian Pride*, *Amok, Pursuit,* and *Desert Fury* (the latter being the third in the trilogy started by *Accused* and *Persian Pride*). These receipts were made out to a man called Pardoe and, said the prosecution, it appeared that the publishers were paying him for the stories. As the receipts had been in the hands of the liquidators of New Fiction Press, they could not have been in the hands of the defendants.

With this sudden turn of events the Judge directed the Jury to find Frances Not Guilty on the four counts concerning the books mentioned on the receipts, and suggested that they take the same course with the other three. Without retiring the Jury acquitted Frances of the whole indictment and he was discharged.

* * * * * * *

The question now must be, who was Pardoe, and what was his relationship to the Janson saga? The answer, is not as simple as the question. Very little is known about Geoffrey Pardoe: his first book, *The Baby Famine*, appeared in 1945 and concerned the social reasons for the fall in the birth-rate in Britain. The book did not sell particularly well, although it attracted some notoriety by being condemned in the press. Only two further books appeared under Pardoe's name, *This Is A Mystery* and *Traffic In Souls*, both of them non-fiction. The former was issued in a limited edition of 2,000, numbered and signed by the author, by Stephen Frances in 1948. Selling at 12/6 it was still being advertised some years later, and other cloth-bound books published by Frances were still available long after he had moved to Spain. It is quite probable that these publications were part of the reason why Frances was always in financial trouble despite the success of Janson. Pardoe, according to Frances, "was a speed-writer, churning out gangster novels at a great rate." Pardoe's connections with Gaywood have been established to a degree: he certainly wrote at least one of the novels published under the Dirk Foster byline, and it seems probable that he was one of the writers who took over the writing of books under the names Ace Capelli, Johnny Grecco, and Steve Markham, all associated with Gaywood distributed companies. It is believed that Pardoe died soon afterwards: he had lived for some years with a bad leg and walked with a pronounced limp. His doctors told him that if the leg was not amputated he would eventually die. Pardoe reputedly flatly refused the operation and died soon after.

From his books we learn that he was born in the late 1890s, the eldest of four children bought up in the Stoke-on-Trent area where his father was a headmaster at an elementary school. He spent ten years at school and at Birmingham University. He first came to London in 1912 and lived there during the Great War, later living and working in Hastings, Sussex, where he had three daughters (although there was no mention of a wife, and Frances did not recall one). He moved back to London, living in Kennington, and had a fourth daughter around the beginning of the war. One of Pardoe's publishers said that much of what he claimed should be taken with a pinch of salt.

His precise relationship to Janson requires some speculation; certainly £20 payment for a novel was far lower than most authors were paid. Could Pardoe have been paid for supplying ideas? Certainly Frances re-wrote novels supplied by others: when asked about some of his pen-names he later said, "I wrote some Duke Lintons - my pen-name - and something, I believe, under David Steel. Some of the others under these pen-names were written by a friend and I slashed and edited them."

Frances made a number of cryptic remarks in correspondence in later years about the books in question: he would say that his claim that he did not write the books was made because it was the "pure" truth. The "pure" truth of course is that he did not write them, rather dictated them using the battery-powered portable dictaphone he had taken to Spain which was his normal method of working, sending the small record away to have his words typed up into a manuscript, and then editing the manuscript for final publication. Could "speed-writer" Pardoe have been the typist? It seems likely.

Whatever the truth, the resulting stories were certainly the work of Frances, as any of his readers could testify, and a Jury would almost certainly have discovered that. The trick, as Frances saw it, was to have the Jury read the books as a whole and question the original obscenity ruling. As it was, the opportunity never arose. The re-trial was a failure in his eyes, and until the end of his life Frances remained bitter about the events which had branded his work filthy and obscene. In private correspondence Frances made plain his outrage:

> [The reason] why Carter and Reiter were made (not found) guilty...was the importance of HJ to business. The police

were accustomed to picking up a few books from a newsagents. When they set off to raid HJ they probably had no conception of what was involved. At the warehouse address they had to get vans to take away thousand's of HJs. At that time the monthly print run was 150,000 of a title. All titles were in stock, being reprinted as soon as they weresold out, 160,000 were being despatched. At the printers was 150,000 that had just been printed and most of the sheets for yet another 150,000 of the most recent title.

All these books were seized. It needs very little imagination to realise the tremendous damage done to the company raided in this way, had all its stock removed and dare not continue publishing and printing until the case had been heard because anything new that was published was liable to seizure.

If the prosecution failed, and immense claims were made for compensation, whose heads would roll?

As the "mushroom" publishers collapsed, they left behind a tortuous trail for future researchers. Who was Drax Ampax or Jeff Bogar?

The Whispering Gorilla in the World Fantasy Classics Collection from World Distributors is amongst the rarest of titles today. Until recently only a couple of surviving copies were known.

The book is actually a reprint of an earlier novel, even the original US author was unaware of its existence.

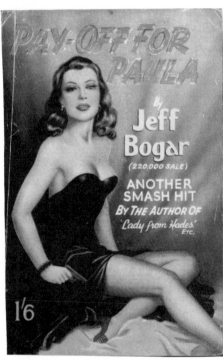

The whole of the dark continent is terrorised by a gigantic gorilla, a gorilla who is not a gorilla, but a man.

9

AFTER THE STORM

"I knew them all, a weird bunch I do assure you, ferret-eyed and dead keen to make a fast "buck" without the slightest scruple."

Victor Norwood, private communication (1983)

The notoriety of 'banned books' and their consequent public demand was clearly shown by booksellers during the Janson trial in 1954, one bookseller saying "Since the books were first brought to the public attention there has been a rush to buy them. I sold all I had in an hour." Little evidence as to who actually paid their two shillings for copies of the books could be brought, although it was known, and stated, that one of the purchasers of the books were government officials acting on behalf of the the Services. They were bought by N.A.A.F.I. officials and distributed to the Forces with such success that repeat orders were placed with the publisher. A question in the House of Commons raised by Sir Richard Ackland (M.P. for Gravesend) as to how many copies of the books 'by the so-called Hank Janson" had been distributed by government representatives elicited the reply, from Nigel Birch, Parliamentary Secretary to the Ministry of Defence, that a small quantity had been purchased, but all unsold copies had been withdrawn. The *Daily Sketch* reported that in a survey of 150 boys at a nautical training college asked to name their favourite authors 35 gave Hank Janson.

In the wake of the Janson trial a number of other mushroom publishers were prosecuted successfully; they received a lot of press coverage because the titles under attack made good headlines: "Infants' Teacher Wrote 'Cutie Is A Corpse'" announced the *Daily Mirror* on July 28 1954, misquoting the Pete Costello title *My Cutie's A Corpse*, almost matched by the *Daily Sketch* on September 25th 1954 who led with "'Big Sin'

Pair Are Sent To Jail" after another case.

One of the first of the post-Janson trials was concerned with the magazines *Zest* and *Slick* and the novel *Caressed* by Henri Le Fontaine published by R.S. Gray Publications. In June 1954 the company, company directors Ralph Stokes and Leonard Thornton, printers G. Barclay Ltd. and company secretary Walter Blochert, and author Roy Hill were all found guilty at Clerkenwell Magistrates Court, with Stokes, Slater and Blochert all sentenced to three months imprisonment and crippling fines imposed on the companies. In this case, the magistrate, Mr. Frank Powell, said: "This sort of crime is far more dangerous than many other forms of what we commonly call crime, like stealing." Once again, evidence at the trial showed that the skids were already under the publishers: only 6,000 copies of the book had been printed and the book's total profit was under £150. The jail sentences were later quashed by the London Sessions Appeals Committee and the fines greatly reduced.

Another Clerkenwell Court case featured Edwin Self, three authors - George Bell, Ernest (Lisle) Willis and Albert Garrett - and printers G. Barclay (with Walter Blochert again in the dock), charged in July 1954 with publishing obscene libels in the form of five books. The five titles were *Collette Cherie* by Jean Paul Valois, *The Big Panic* by Bart Banarto, and three titles by Pete Costello, *My Cutie's A Corpse, Honey Don't Dare* and *Murder In Mink*. All five titles were found to be obscene, and Self and Bell jailed for nine months and six months respectively. The other defendants received fines between £10 and £100.

The hounding of the mushroom publishers continued; in one incredible case there was a total of 49 summonses against twelve defendants, for publishing 4 books, a witch-hunt run wild: Kaye Publications as publishers, directors Bernard and Alfred Kaye, printers Maxwell Love and Co., director Howard Love, printers A.J. Tull and Sons Ltd., directors Stanley and Eric Tull, wholesalers L. Miller and Sons, director Leonard Miller, authors Gordon Sowman and Derek Kirby, cover artist Leonard Gard and his agent Charles M. Hall (who said, when seen by police, "The trouble with you people is that you don't know art when you see it"). The Kaye brothers were accused of setting themselves up as "universal purveyors of pornography" by the soliciter for the Director of Public Prosecution.

As the case was heard, a number of the summonses were dismissed and the jury directed to find some of the defendants Not Guilty. However, the August 1954 trial ended with Bernard and Alfred Kaye sent to jail (nine months and six months respectively) and their publishing firm fined £200. The printers, their directors and the authors were also fined. The titles involved in the case were *The Big Sin* by Josh Wingrave, *Academie of Love* by Maurice Caval, *Shameless* by Andre

Latour and *Soho Street Girl* by Marty Ladwick, which the Jury were ordered to read at the end of the first day.

The many different cases in 1953 and 1954 brought to light the fact that courts were divided in their opinions on the merits of the Obscene Publications Act, with one judge saying "Edgar Wallace might be held to be obscene according to this definition. If any murder story is to be held to be obscene, I don't know where we are getting."

But what of the books mentioned in the Janson trial?

In all, five cases were brought, involving the books *The Image and the Search* by Walter Baxter (Heinemann), *September in Quinze* by Vivian Connell (Hutchinson), *The Man in Control* by Charles McGraw (Arthur Barker), *Julia* by Margot Bland (Werner Laurie) and *The Philanderer* by Stanley Kauffmann (Secker & Warburg). Of the five, two had already been tried in the Isle of Man; *Julia* and *The Philanderer* were seized at Boots circulating library and during the case, in September 1953, the High Bailiff had said that he was bound by the law: modern books were regarded with a different eye by the public now than they had been by their fathers, but the law had remained the same. He reluctantly found the books guilty, imposing a nominal fine of £1 on each of them.

Of the five cases, Werner Laurie and Margot Bland pleaded guilty and were fined £30 and 10 guineas costs; Arthur Barker and Herbert van Thal were acquited by a jury who retired for only thirteen minutes; the other three cases make for interesting comparisons.

The most celebrated of these cases was brought against Secker & Warburg who were charged with publishing *The Philanderer* by Stanley Kauffmann; the trial opened on July 29th 1954, prosecuted by Griffith-Jones, who had misquoted so much at the Janson trial. The Jury were sent home to read the book, with instructions to read the whole book and not to simply pick out the highlights.

The judge, Mr. Justice Stable made an much-quoted Summing Up of the case which was reprinted in the Penguin edition of the novel published in 1957. In part Stables said:

> Your verdict will have great bearing on where the line is drawn between liberty and that freedom to read and think as the spirit moves us, on the one hand, and, on the other, a license that is an affront to the society of which each of us is a member...Remember the charge is a charge that the tendency of the book is to corrupt and deprave. The charge is not that the book is either to shock or to disgust. That is not a criminal offence. Then you say: 'Well, corrupt or deprave whom?' and again the test: those whose minds are open to such immoral influences and into whose hands a publication of this sort may fall. What exactly does that

mean? Are we to take our literary standards as being the level of something that is suitable for a fourteen-year-old school girl? Or do we go even further back than that, and are we to be reduced to the sort of books that one reads as a child in the nursery? The answer to that is: Of course not...

The book does, with candour or, if you prefer it, crudity, deal with the realities of human love and intercourse. There is no getting away from that, and the Crown say: 'Well, that is sheer filth'. Is the act of sexual passion sheer filth? It may be an error of taste to write about it. It may be a matter in which some, perhaps old fashioned, people would prefer that reticence continued to be observed as it was yesterday. But is it sheer filth? That is a matter which you have to consider and ultimately to decide.

I do not suppose there is a decent man or woman in this court who does not agree wholeheartedly that pornogaphy, the filthy bawdy muck that is just filth for filth's sake, ought to be stamped out and suppressed. Such books are not literature. They have got no message; they have got no inspiration; they have got no thought. They have got nothing. They are just filth and ought to be stamped out. But in our desire for a healthy society, if we drive the criminal law too far, further than it ought to go, is there not a risk that there will be a revolt, a demand for a change in the law, and that the pendulum may swing too far the other way and allow to creep in things that at the moment we can exclude and keep out?

The jury found the book Not Guilty. The press saw it as a win for common sense and for applying the law to the then modern standards; but, of course, the law as it stood could easily be interpreted otherwise, as it was in the case against *September in Quinze*.

Hutchinson Ltd. and Mrs Katherine Webb were tried at the Old Baily before the Recorder, Gerard Dodson, and prosecutor Griffith-Jones. "A book which would not influence the mind of an Archbishop might influence the minds of a callow youth or girl just budding into womanhood," he said. "Sex is a thing, members of the jury, which you may think has to be protected and even sanctified, as indeed it is by the marriage service and not dragged in the mud." The jury found the book guilty and both defendents fined £500.

The third case, against *The Image and the Search*, came to court at the Old Bailey in October, the jurers having read the book and heard the prosecution (Griffith-Jones again) describe it as "pornography dressed up as a twelve-and-sixpenny novel". After retiring for three hours, the jury could not reach an agreement, and the situation remained the same after retiring again.

A second trial in November and December 1954 also resulted in a hung jury, and at a third formality trial, the jury returned a Not Guilty verdict when the prosecution offered no evidence.

* * * * * * *

The five cases highlighted the fear that things may have been taken too far, and certainly that the law as it stood was not adequate. No publisher wanted to risk prosecution and condemnation, but none wanted to see the British book industry stagnate as it may have done if a book could not include some of the fundemental basics of human life. One contemporary trade spokesman was reported as saying, "In view of the Old Bailey verdict, the Public Prosecutor has got to watch his step. He must not give the impression that he is forcing on the courts the kind of case that a High Court Judge has already thrown out. The wave of prosecutions may now die away."

Several obscenity cases were in fact dropped, and in Hull a destruction order against 1,642 publications seized at a wholesalers was refused, with the presiding magistrate of the case (Mr. G.W.H. Palmer) saying that the flamboyant nature of the covers was sufficient to indicate the nature of the reading matter, but that the court did not feel that those wishing to read such trash should be prevented by grandmotherly legislation from doing so.

The prosecution of novels was all but halted as a new target was found in American comicbooks. These had been the subject of an American campaign during the 1940s which culminated in the publication of *Seduction of the Innocent* by Fredric Wertham in the spring of 1954 and a Senate Subcommittee on Juvenile Delinquency investigating the corrupting influence of children's comics, particularly the E.C. school of horror comics. In October 1954 a Comics Code Authority was set up with a strict set of rules on what was and what was not allowed to be published. These comics were quite widely available in Britain at a time when import restrictions were being dismantled and British Reprint Editions were common. The outcry was beginning to grow in the UK throughout 1954: the nature of comics meant that they were far easier to prosecute. Whereas novels were often condemned on the implication of sex or torture that was not actually described, the visual image of a torture scene was beyond doubt. That comics were aimed at children was a second damning piece of evidence and the Horror Comics Bill was introduced in 1955 outlawing the E.C. type of sadistic terror comic (Horror Comics and the Horror Comics Bill are further discussed in Appendix One).

Tremendous arguments in literary circles and through the pages of newspapers and magazines eventually led publishers and authors to put forward a proposal for a new Obscene

Publications Act in early 1955 which would repeal the Obscene Publications Act of 1857 under which all the prosecutions had been brought. The Bill made certain provisions such as that the literary merit of the book should be considered, evidence of a book's corrupting influence should be given, its dominant effect on a person when read as a whole, and evidence as to the type of person who would be able to obtain copies should all be considered. The Draft Bill also defined maximum penalties: the highest fine as £100 and the maximum jail sentence as six months. The draft had been made by a committee of 17, set up by the Society of Authors with Sir Alan Herbert as its first Chairman (later taken over by Sir Gerald Barry), and amongst the luminaries who helped were author H.E.Bates, publisher W.A.R.Collins, Mr. Roy Jenkins, M.P., and the then Barrister Norman St. John Stevas.

The Obscene Publications Bill was made public in February 1955, and introduced to the House of Commons by Roy Jenkins on March 15, 1955 as a Private Member's Bill under the ten minute rule, and was given an unopposed first reading. However, it did not get much further, but continued pressure led the to the setting up of a Select Committee to discuss the matter, with evidence being given from all those concerned including authors, publishers, police, and the Director of Public Prosecutions. The Committee's report finally appeared in 1958, but no action taken on its recommendations. Roy Jenkins, again, introduced a Private Member's Bill in 1959, but, again, it failed to get a second reading. Sir Alan Herbert threatened to resign his seat, complaining that the fight for reforming the Obscene Publications Act was becoming a game of snakes and ladders.

Eventually the government acted, and the new Obscene Publications Act, 1959, became law on August 29.

Even this Act did not stop the many arguments as to what was considered obscene, as the cases of *Lady Chatterley's Lover* and *Fanny Hill* in the early 1960s proved. However, Lady Chatterley's Lover in particular saw a tremendous degree of cooperation between the publisher, Penguin Books, and the Director of Public Prosecution, Penguin delaying the general release of the book and 'publishing' only a few copies which could be tested via the courts. The result was a verdict of Not Guilty, and a fantastic amount of free publicity for Penguin.

Similarly the case of *Last Exit To Brooklyn* by Hubert Selby only led to higher sales for the book when the original verdict of Guilty was overturned at Appeal. The case was notable for the admission under oath of prosecution witness Sir Basil Blackwell that the book had depraved him. It also came to light that Blackwell had only read the book *after* he had been asked to appear against it.

* * * * * * *

The impact of the obscenity trials on the mushroom publishers was devastating. The salacious cover girls were enough to have the books swept up in their thousands in raids usually against nudist and men's magazines. The covers were very much the target and Mr. Palmer's remarks that their flamboyant nature was sufficiant to tell the type of the books they adorned is very telling.

Whilst accurate figures for how many paperbacks were destroyed are impossible to come by they must have run into hundreds of thousands. The five Hank Janson novels brought to trial had 112 seperate destruction order granted against them alone. The 193 prosecutions in 1953 had mostly been against newsvendors and book shops who stocked the books and this must have made them think twice about stocking similar titles. Certainly the prosecutions against the publishers invariably put them out of business or on the verge of bankruptcy. Of the publishers mentioned above only Edwin Self survived as a publishing imprint (publishing war fiction) and even that was superceeded by the Pedigree Books imprint within a couple of years. The changes brought about in the wake of the Janson and *The Philanderer* trials were too late to save the mushroom publishers. The damage had already been done.

Printed in England and Published by
EDWIN SELF & CO. LTD.,
42. GRAY'S INN ROAD, HOLBORN,
LONDON, W.C.1.

* * * * * * *

While prosecution and bankruptcy was to be the fate of some mushroom companies, others were still clinging on to dear publishing life.

The over-production of titles in 1953 was the kiss of death to most of the smaller companies such as Cooper Book Company whose publishing schedule had included gangsters, thrillers and westerns. A survey of those companies which had started in the immediate post-War years shows that only Scion, Curtis Warren, Hamilton/Panther, John Spencer, Modern Fiction, World Distributors/Fiction House and Brown Watson were publishing with anything like the regularity of other larger houses. Yet these seven paperback houses accounted for over 35 original titles a month alone many with a simultaneous hardcover library edition (and this figure rises to around 50 original novels a month when all the other smaller mushroom publishers are taken into account). The decline in sales was not solely the blame of the ever increasingly stiff competition from the more respectable reprint publishers.

1954 saw the closure of two of the most prolific of the mushroom publishers. In 1953 Curtis Warren and Scion Ltd. had published over 200 titles between them, all originals, but this incredible schedule (4 new books a week) was to work against them in the end.

Curtis Warren had revamped their line in 1953, expanding their novels to 160 pages apiece and redesigning the covers so that many of them featured a picture set into a coloured border. Apart from the ever prolific Western schedule, many of them written by the prolific John Jennison, Curtis reintroduced Brett Vane for a series of crime thrillers, written by a number of authors including Frederick Foden and Arthur Kent. Science fantasy tales written mostly by Dennis Hughes and foreign legion novels by Brian Holloway were also regulars on their list. Amongst the experiments was a historical series under the name Cecil Alexander, and a lost world novel, entitled *Southern Exploration* which was written by Holloway under the house name Adam Dale.

At 160 pages the books were generally longer than those of Curtis Warren's contemporaries, and the 1/6 pricetag had not changed since 1950 (2/- being the usual price of a paperback by 1954), and with simultaneous hardback editions for all titles it might seem that Curtis Warren was a highly successful company. 1954, however, was to be their last year. In July they produced the first issue of a new magazine, *Suspense Stories*, a 96 page pulp containing borderline horror stories, and the hardback line was discontinued. The page count of the novels remained 160 pages, but the books were now redesigned along American lines, slightly smaller and published as part of a newly instigated numbered series. The "Curtis Books" series started its numbering at about No.120 and lasted for some 30 novels by which time the company was in severe financial difficulty. The last few novels had shown a great deal of diversity, ranging from historical novels to a traditional English detective story *(Strictly Poison* by David Norris) and supposedly biographical African adventures *(With Allan in Africa* by R. Allan).

These were to be the last titles published by Curtis Warren, and at least one of the novels (*Challenge* by H.K. Bulmer) had actually been submitted to Hamiltons and was never paid for. In November 1954 the company went into liquidation, calling a meeting of creditors in London where some of the authors gathered to claim money owed to them. One author who was attending to lend support to a colleague did not realise that he had been owed money himself, having submitted a story which he believed had never been published (it had actually appeared in the second issue of *Suspense Stories* under a pen-name). At least one novel with a December 1954 copyright date had been quickly issued before the liquidation, but no more was to be heard from Curtis Warren.

Scion Ltd. had brought up a number of gangster bylines in 1952 and these were in regular use once the company had re-established itself after the 1952 gangster fine. The flow of original novels continued throughout 1953 and into 1954, with the regular gangster bylines of Karta, Vogel and Zore being most prolific. Vic Hanson wrote many of the later Duke Linton

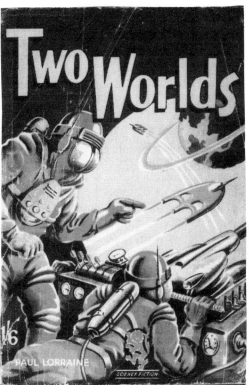

Across & Below: Days were numbered for the surviving "mushroom" publishers. Surprisingly perhaps, Curtis Warren were still in their number despite the quality of their offerings.

novels, and both Gray Usher (under his own name and the pen-name Pete Garroway) and Alistair Paterson (as Hans Lugar) kept up a steady supply of hard-boiled Private Eye tales. The western market had become highly overburdened, and Scion were producing far less when compared to their earlier output. They did, however, attract the talents of John Jennison from Curtis Warren who by that time were publishing less than the one-a-week Jennison was able to supply. For Scion Jennison took on the pen-names Pete Sandys and Doorn Sclanders for his action packed tales of the West.

Scion's most prolific writer was still John Russell Fearn, now writing as both Vargo Statten and Volsted Gridban. Ted Tubb was now producing novels under his own name, having taken the opportunity to dispense with the anonymity of house names, and the success of these science fiction lines prompted editor Alistair Paterson to issue a science fiction magazine, named after the most popular byline, the *Vargo Statten Science Fiction Magazine,* in January 1954. The magazine could have succeeded in attracting some excellent stories had the editor not requested that his authors write down to the anticipated juvenile audience. Brian Aldiss was one writer who found that his submissions were returned with this request and he, like others, did not bother to try again. The two main authors were, again, Fearn and Tubb, although the magazine did attract a number of efforts by fans who appeared here for the first time, including the first published story by Barrington J. Bayley.

Scion's line was supplemented in 1954 by romance tales by Eileen Wilmot and others, but the writing was on the wall for them as with many companies. In 1954 they were fined again for gangster obscenity, apparently for the publication of just one book, but this time the fine was sufficiently large to force the company to almost close down. Director A. Lou Benjamin left and a new company was formed under the name Henry Squire & Co. Ltd., with backing from Dragon Press who were reponsible for printing many of the paperbacks of the time. The new company, known as Scion Distributors Ltd., was temporarily based at 139 Borough High Street, London SE1, the offices of Reginald Carter who, at the time was still imprisoned after the court case involving Hank Janson.

When Carter was released and returned to his offices, Scion was sold to Dragon Press who quickly phased out the Scion name in favour of their own Dragon Books imprint. They continued to publish novels under various bylines, including the most popular gangster bylines Nat Karta and Duke Linton, although they concentrated primarily on romance novels, written by John Russell Fearn under the names Gene Bentley and Elizabeth Rutland; Fearn also wrote two excellent detective tales featuring his scientific detective, Dr. Carruthers, one as Nat Karta, the second reviving his Hugo Blayn pen-name, as well as taking over the editorship of the *Vargo Statten Science Fiction Magazine* which he soon retitled the *British Space Fiction Magazine*. John Jennison continued to supply westerns, notably the "Cactus" series under the name Doorn Sclanders, and Jack Trevor Story produced an excellent mystery in *Murder on My Mind*. Possibly the most collectable of all Dragon Books' titles is *Creature From the Black Lagoon* by Vargo Statten (Fearn), based on the classic horror film. The book appeared in both hardback and paperback, but the circumstances of its publication by such a small publisher means that few film buffs will know of its existance.

The two companies that had been created through the 1952 obscenity fine had mixed fortunes over the next couple of years. Milestone had achieved a heavy publishing schedule of 6-8 books per month under the editorship of Frank Rudman. Most of the writers were ex-Scion regulars, led by Dail Ambler and Donald Cresswell, and they could boast a new series of "Miss Otis" novels written by Ben Sarto (Frank Dubrez Fawcett) and a high proportion of romances, including tales by Denise Robins and Faith Baldwin. In 1954 the Milestone imprint was phased out in favour of the new Merit Books, and library hardcover editions were also published for many titles. The Merit Books imprint was often used on American reprints, and towards the end of their existance Merit published very little original fiction. Their last titles appeared in July 1955 and Merit Books vanished from the racks.

B.Z. Immanuel, the driving force behind Scion at their launch, had set up O.K. Fiction and Ken Publishing and a new paperback and magazine line was launched in May of 1953 under the Ken Publishing imprint. This was quickly dropped in favour of Gannet Press (Sales) Ltd. who were to publish a diverse line of fiction, some of which were amongst the most outrageously ridiculous tales to ever appear! Gannet attracted only a few first rate authors; Immanuel, as director of Scion, had signed up many talented authors, at least one of whom refused to work for him when Gannet was first set up. Immanuel was blamed for the poor payment record of Scion (who took up to three months to pay for novels) and the better conditions offered by the new Scion and Milestone's better rates meant that few authors were left to serve Gannet.

Some of the more prolific authors did contribute, Victor Norwood and Donald Cresswell amongst them, but in the main the novels were by unknown hands. It sounds likely that Gannet were the culprits behind one piece of mushroom publishing legend: the story is told of the publisher (unnamed) who brought a manuscript for £5 and published without even bothering to read it first. The quality of the Gannet product is such that there are a number of contenders as few seem to have had the benefit of a read-through, and certainly not selection by a critical editor. The production quality was low, and mistakes often occured: some books were misbound, with half-stories from different novels bound together under one or other title. In one case (although not from Gannet) a gangster and a western novel were mixed up, and the incredulous editor noted that there was not one complaint. "Perhaps no-one noticed," was his comment.

Gannet continued to publish through 1954, but increasing debts to printers meant that they were soon to be taken over by the Merseyside Press in Birkenhead, Liverpool. The Gannet imprint was retained for a while, but shortly after was replaced by Teal Publications.

1953 was the last full year of publishing for Raymond and Lilian Locker. The R & L Locker imprint had been phased out in favour of Archer Press and Harborough Publications, and the reprints of Paul Renin were still the main line. As well as publishing various other racy-romances, in particular a series of stories by Ernest McKeag under the name Roland Vane, Archer had also launched the gangster novels of Spike Morrelli, Gene Ross and Michael Storme. These three were taken over by Harborough and all notched up a strong following, probably based on the selling power of the exquisite covers by Reginald Heade. As early as 1952 Archer were re-selling numerous titles to American publishers, Leisure Library and Kayewin Publishing, and on the surface appeared to be weathering the over-production storm quite well.

This was a false view, as both Archer and Harborough abruptly ceased publishing in January 1954. No contemporary report has been found to explain this very sudden dissappearence which left a number of advertised titles in limbo, but an obscenity fine is not out of the question: at least one of the Gene Ross novels had already appeared in court and the increased activity of the Public Prosecutor around that time seems to point towards that conclusion.

For those few who survived the persecution of the Home Secretary there was one final test to overcome. In February 1956 there was a general printers strike which closed down many of the printing presses throughout Britain. A ban on output and overtime had begun on January 18 in support of a claim for a minimum wage of £12. At the time the London Master Printers' Association was one of an alliance of organisations that had some 730 member firms throughout the country with some 4,250 members. The Newspaper Society, engaged in a provincial dispute, had a membership of 495 firms, producing 1,000 weekly newspapers and 125 daily papers. 6,800 members of the London Typographical Society were idle. A court of enquiry was set up by the Minister of Labour, and many provincial printing firms returned to work, but the strike was continued in London and when the overtime ban was not lifted 8,000 members of the London Typographical Society and the Association of Correctors of the Press were summarily dismissed. 8,500 other workers were dismissed because the stoppages had left them with no work.

The dispute was eventually settled with the court of enquiry recommending a minimum wage of £10.15s.6d, but normal work was not resumed until March 27. By that time some 200 printing houses had been closed and at least 80 periodicals (including *TV Times, Amateur Gardening, The Scout* and *London Illustrated News)* had been forced to miss issues.

Two of the publishing houses mentioned above were by then run by printing firms, Dragon Books and Teal Publications (Gannet). The strike put an end to both firms publishing of paperbacks. Dragon sold all outstanding manuscripts to Brown Watson, and closed the *Vargo Statten Science Fiction Magazine* which was the last link to their predecessor, Scion.

The printers strike was the final nail in the coffin for the mushroom publishers. Their era was well and truly at an end.

Below: Two covers from The Fantasy Library series. The Human Bat lasted for two books only. The Fantasy/Gangster combination leading to a wild cover but presumably not sufficient sales.

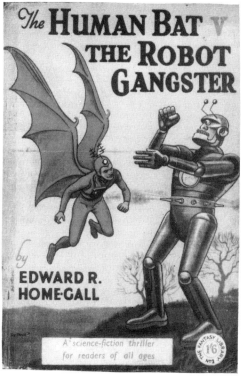

Below: In the mid '50s while Hamilton's Panther imprint moved on with the times, most of the "mushroom" publishers found it difficult to compete with the newer publishers (often printing *real* american fiction).

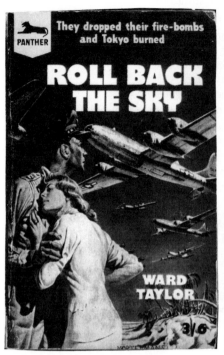

10

WHATEVER HAPPENED TO THE MUSHROOM PUBLISHERS?

Without flogging a dead horse or giving skeletons to vultures, I mention, briefly, that last year - the beginning of the silly sixties - was the most memorable in the history of the paperback industry.

Vic Briggs, feature in *Paperback News* (1961)

A publishing phenomenon the magnitude of the mushroom publishers, who were able to dominate the post-War decade with their original novels, does not vanish without leaving behind a legacy of some importance. The announcement of paper rationing in 1940 had struck the still waters of British publishing a punishing blow, and the tidalwave that resulted did not subside completely for seventeen years. But by 1957 the mushroom era could truly be said to be at an end. The prosecutions and subsequent bankrupcies had destroyed many of the original novel publishers; the printers strike had stopped production for many who remained and was a blow from which they could not survive; a new international copyright agreement that had been agreed in 1955 came into force on June 1 1957; the War Loan was paid off and import restrictions that had been in force to help the Sterling-Dollar balance were almost completely dismantled. This meant that American publishers who had been limited to non-fiction titles in the mid-fifties could now export fiction titles, and new lines were quickly established, with Thorpe and Porter achieving success with the import of Pocket Books; Corgi Books (Transworld Publishers Ltd.) were a subsidiary of the American group Curtis Publishing which owned Bantam Books and imports of Bantam titles were soon reaching Britain, as were Mentor and Signet books, the latter two via Frederick Muller Ltd.

In Britain the increasing number of books to be found on the market were also competing with other entertainments. On September 22, 1955 the Independent TV Services were launched in opposition to the British Broadcasting Company who countered admirably by killing Grace Archer in a fire; the influence of television began to affect cinema attendences, down from 1.4 million in 1950 to 1.1 milion in 1956, and vie with the novel and radio as the main sources of entertainment to be found in the home.

The survivors of the 1956 printers strike were few: Hamilton & Co/Panther, John Spencer, Brown Watson and World Distribu-tors were all to continue publishing, albeit in different circumstances to meet the new demands of publishing and the reading public. Others too, if only briefly in some cases. The mushroom publishers were, if nothing else, a tenacious bunch.

In February 1955 Hamilton & Co. had launched a new reprint line under their Panther Books imprint, taking hardcover non-fiction titles and issuing them in an attractive paperback format. These were mostly tales of adventure and travel, although the line included a great many books relating to the Second World War, now a decade in the past. The new reprint line was a great success, and the original novels were gradually

A Panther Book

phased out so that by 1956 only one or two fiction titles were
appearing for the first time. The popularity of Lauren Paine
meant that his original westerns under his own name and the
pen-name Mark Carrel continued to appear, whilst a few new
and reprint foreign legion novels were the last hang-overs from
the early days of Hamilton & Co. The Panther Books logo was
a familiar sight throughout the late 1950s, to be found on such
best-sellers as *The Teahouse of the August Moon* by Vern J.
Sneider (1955), *Anna and the King of Siam* by Margaret
Landon (1956) - the basis for the highly successful musical *The
King and* I - and *Away All Boats* by Kenneth Dodson (1957).
Panther were the publishers of Evan Hunter's *The Blackboard
Jungle* and scored a remarkable success with the novelisation of
the film *The Camp on Blood Island*. The works of Hans Habe
and Nicholas Monsarrat mingled with popular science fiction
writers Isaac Asimov and A.E. Van Vogt, the gangster novels
of James Hadley Chase (a perrenial best-seller for Panther) and
the novels of John O'Hara and Sinclair Lewis. Panther were at
the heart of agressive salesmanship when it came to bidding for
potential best-sellers, paying £5,000 for the rights to *The
Bramble Bush,* starting a trend in high-stake bidding which
would later see Corgi Books paying £15,000 for the rights to
Lolita by Vladimir Nabokov.

Panther was sold in the 1960's to the
Granada group which had grown up
from the conglomeration of companies
owned by Howard Samuel (which
included MacGibbon & Kee and Staples Press). When Samuel died in 1961
the group was sold to Sidney Bernstein
who also aquired Rupert Hart-Davis
and others. Panther soon followed, as
did another paperback firm, May-
flower, which had been launched in
1961. Panther was continued as an
imprint, although would later be
largely overtaken by Granada. The
imprint is now owned by Harper
Collins.

Corgi itself had a surprisingly unsuc-
cessful first decade despite its now
highly collectable line, and Alan
Cheek, who had been with the line
since its inception, resigned in 1961,
his position taken over by Sidney
Kramer who was sent from the USA to
replace him. It was Kramer who au-
thorised the payment for *Lolita,* and its
sales helped put Corgi on a sound
financial footing.

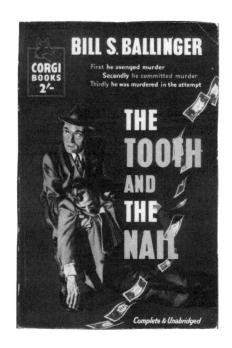

World Distributors also turned to the reprint market publishing a mixture of western, crime and war books under their new Viking Novels imprint from their new address of 36 Great Russell Street, scoring successes with the likes of *Look Down in Mercy* by Walter Baxter and *East of Eden* by John Steinbeck (both 1957). In 1957 Viking became WDL Books which in turn became Consul Books in 1961. Under editor John Watson (ex-director of Muir-Watson) Consul published many new and reprint novels ranging from original crime to biography (including the biographies of Cliff Richard and a second featuring the Shadows). Amongst many notable originals was the controversial *Lady Chatterley's Daughter* by Patricia Robins (1961), numerous TV adaptations which continue to be popular amongst collectors, The Avengers, The Naked City and Danger Man amongst them. Consul Books faded away in 1966, and World Distributors was later taken over by the First National Finance Corporation who had also taken over Ward Lock Ltd., and who later became the Pentos Group.

Whilst Pembertons of Manchester had vanished in favour of the World Distributors label, World's other allied company, Fiction House, continued to publish until 1959. The "Smashing Westerns" series reached 264 titles, having started their numbering in 1953 at No.151. World Distributors had developed an extensive range of childrens annuals in the 1950s, often based around television shows and these continued to bring the western to a new generation, albeit in a different format. The titles and stories were much the same as those published in the era when westerns were at their height although by the end of the decade westerns were beginning to lose popularity to a certain degree.

The original novel was still to be found. Apart from originals published by likes of Panther and Consul above, the true spirit of mushroom publishing could still be found in the publications of John Spencer. Spencers had launched two western lines, Blazing Western and Lariat Western in 1953 and 1954 respectively. These lines were still regularly publishing original novels as late as 1967, dominated from 1961 by pseudonymous writers under the house names Chuck Adams and Tex Bradley.

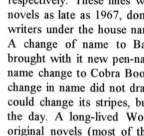

A change of name to Badger Books in the mid-fifties had brought with it new pen-names but little else, and another brief name change to Cobra Books in 1957 presumably proved that a change in name did not dramatically improve sales. The Badger could change its stripes, but it was still a badger at the end of the day. A long-lived World War Two series, mixing mostly original novels (most of them written by John Glasby) with a few reprints reached No.162 and other series included Crime, Romance, Spy and a number of non-fiction lines, True War and Science amongst them. Badger Books are these days remembered for the horror magazine series *Supernatural Stories* and the companion Supernatural and Science Fiction novel lines.

These were written with few exceptions by R. Lionel Fanthorpe whose prolificy has become legend amongst paperback collectors, although the lesser known Glasby was to be the most prolific of Badger's authors. John Spencer moved away from the fiction market around 1967, but continued as technical publishers for many years, occasionally re-issuing novels when the mood took them.

Brown Watson was the second publisher to continue publishing originals to any great degree. Their own output was supplemented by the acquisition of manuscripts from Fiction House in 1955 and Dragon Press in 1956, which led to the arrival of pseudonymous novels by John Russell Fearn amongst others. The prolific western house names Paul Daner and W.B. Glaston had replaced the earlier prolific gangster pen-names Rex Richards and Walter Standish, and Brown Watson were to continue publishing westerns throughout their history, scoring some remarkable successes. A move in 1956 to new premises prompted a change in name to Digit Books, and a new reprint policy that would bring Harold Robbins, Henry Miller and William Burroughs to the UK before they became famous. The Digit imprint published a great many originals, especially the War novels of Richard Bickers, David Bingley and MacGregor Urquhart under various pen-names, although by far their most represented author was Edgar Wallace who had 37 titles

Below: Digit Books brought US writers like William Burroughs (under his William Lee pseudonymn) & SF fan (and later publisher of DAW Books) Donald Wollheim to the UK.

The illustration of the rear cover of Junkie is shown below, now an expensive collectors item.

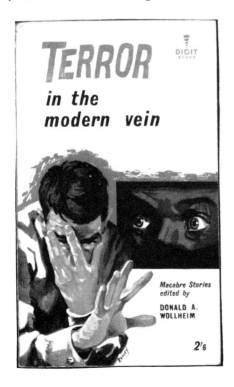

reprinted. A revival of the Brown Watson name in 1965 saw the end of Digit Books, although far from the end of this publisher. The Wagon Wheel series of pot-boiler westerns brought to the Brown Watson fold their most famous author, J.T. Edson. Starting in 1962, Edson proved to be their best-selling writer, and his rapid rise to fame soon secured him the position of Britain's most popular western writer. Edson's contract was later sold on to Corgi Books at around the time Brown Watson ceased to publish original novels, instead relying on reprints under the Sabre Books banner. The company was sold to a division of Warner Brothers Motion Pictures around 1971 who themselves sold it off to Peter Haddock Ltd. Thereafter they were known as Brown Watson (Leicester) Ltd., a title they retain to this day, although paperbacks have been lost in favour of a concentration on childrens books, particularly annuals and drawing books.

The closure of Archer Press and Harborough Publications in January 1954 were not to be the last heard of romance writer Paul Renin, for in 1955 Raymond and Lilian Locker reappeared as Verlock Press with more reprints. They had already experimented with a series of reprints under the names Trident Books and Trent Books, the former including the first reprinting of the now famous Jim Thomson, the latter reprinting a series of Ace Doubles from America. Rather confusingly they became Ace Books in 1957, although there was no connection with the American company. Ace Books was sold to Four Square Books in October 1959, then owned by the Godfrey Phillips tobacco company. Four Square, previously owned by Landsborough Publications - otherwise Gordon Landsborough, ex-editor of Hamilton & Co., and later founder of May Fair Books - was subsequently sold in 1960 to New American Library who renamed the company New English Library from September 1st 1961. Lest Paul Renin be forgotten, a further batch of reprints appeared in the early 1960s from Trident Books (an imprint of Verlock Press, which had been used briefly in the mid-fifties). The distributor for these novels was Award Publications, a latter-day venture for Ralph Stokes, the ex-publisher of Ace Cappelli and others, who was later to be managing director of Hamlyn Publications.

Edwin Self continued to publish novels after his release from jail in 1955, at first mostly war stories by Peter Baillie and Richard Bickers. In 1957 he formed the Pedigree Books imprint which brought many of the juvenile delinquency novels of Hal Ellson to Britain for the first time as well as reprints of such classics as Abraham Merritt's *Burn, Witch, Burn!*. The Pedigree imprint lasted only a few years, and no more was heard from Self.

The entrepreneurial spirit fostered in the post-War years could not be shown better than in the publications of Gerald Swan.

Swan had maintained his publishing house almost single-handedly since its inception in 1938, and books and magazines continued to flourish from his offices in Marylebone. Swan bowed to the inevitable decline of the paperbacks, but continued to publish his highly popular annuals for some years, as well as hardback novels by Elleston Trevor (Swan's own favourite of the many hundreds of authors he had published). In 1960 he produced a series of paperback-sized magazines using up stories he had purchased in the 1940s, but sold off his business in 1962. Swan himself retired and lived until 1986, but his policy of buying stories meant that tales he had purchased continued to appear into the 1970s, mostly in Deans' children's annuals. The rights to Swan's publications changed hands again as recently as 1984.

Some of the smaller publishers survived into the late 1950s and early 1960s, amongst them Paget Publications, who concentrated on the soft-core pornography magazine in the main. Modern Fiction continued to publish Ben Sarto novels and reprints of Ramon Lacroix until 1958, and continued to publish into the new decade, but were never to achieve anywhere near the success they had found ten years before.

Perhaps the most notable success story was that of B.Z. Immanuel. Ken Publishing returned briefly, but Scion's ex-director was soon to forget publishing in favour of employment agencies in the 1960s. The Court Agency established by his wife alongside his very earliest publishing ventures was to prove his fortune: in the early 1960s he founded the Conduit Bureau which showed a profit increase from £10,000 to £256,000 in five years. A succession of take-overs raised his turnover in leaps and bounds, and by 1969 he was estimated to have accrued a personal fortune of £8 million. He established a number of schools in France and England, later moving to Tel Aviv where he set up the Immanuel Charitable Foundation. He died in 1977 a very rich man.

The opposite could be said of another paperback entrepreneur, Reginald Carter. On his release from prison in 1955 Carter returned to his offices at 109 Great Russell Street and from there continued publishing as Alexander Moring. The latter had been founded by Moring and Walter Skeat in 1903, and taken over by Martin Secker and Graeme Hutchinson of the Richards Press Ltd. in 1951, who then sold it on to Carter.

Carter had found success and money with the Hank Janson novels and was not one to forget such success easily. The fear in 1955 was that a revival of Janson would result in imprisonment again, and the revival was therefore carefully planned. Carter still owned the rotary presses of Arc Press and acted as a printer for some time, although his insistant reminders to everybody that they were dealing with an ex-jailbird could not have inspired a great deal of business confidence. He also had Trade Union problems, warning customers who had been attracted by competitive rates that he could not guarentee uninterrupted production. Steve Frances recalled the situation thus:

For a time he printed a very responsible newspaper but then had to warn the proprietors to take their printing elsewhere. They did so, just a day before the Printer's Union brought the rotary press to a standstill. When the printshop burned down shortly afterwards it relieved Carter of a white elephant problem, and his insurance compensated for the material loss... Carter and I reaffirmed our gentleman's agreement. Everything I'd owned in Britain he'd had to sell or dispose of, even to my endowment policies, which were lapsed, to yield him immediate working cash...I began to write more Hank Jansons!

The threat of further prosecution was still a real fear, and both Frances and Carter took the threat seriously. Carter contacted a printer in France and a small edition of a new Hank Janson novel was printed and imported into the UK clearly labelled on all the packages. The customs took no action, and once again Hank Janson began to appear, selling widely throughout Britain. Frances was, at the time, living on an average working man's wage, but was happy to continue this arrangement, confident in the considerable investment he was making in Carter's company, and even artist Heade returned, although charging twice his previouse fee and not signing his work. But all was not well despite the success of the new line:

I made only brief trips to Britain and accepted Carter's business reports without question. Nevertheless, I became gradually aware that Carter had some new and odd friends, some of whom he had met in prison, and with whom he seemed to have private arrangements. He now talked incessantly about the 'handcuffs' with a strange relish, almost as though he delighted in flirting with lawlessness. He proposed various and surprising schemes which I rejected because they seemed unsound and probably illegal. Then I learned he was making the similar proposals to mutual business acquaintances. Some of them unwisely followed his advice and found themselves on the wrong side of the law, or insolvent.

During my brief visits I hadn't been able to extract from Carter more than a bare minimum. He hadn't liquid cash because all the money was locked up in paper and book stocks, he explained. But finally he had to admit that, contrary to our agreement, he'd invested in other businesses. When these businesses bore fruit, Carter promised, he'd settle up with me...

It became obvious that Carter would probably never be

able to comply with our gentleman's agreement. Instead of concentrating upon our Hank Janson breadwinner, he squandered our gains upon business disasters.

"Put it this way," said Carter. "Whatever you do they've got the handcuffs waiting. You might as well be hung for a sheep as a lamb. Scotland Yard was on the phone this morning. They want to see me this afternoon and they've warned me to bring my solicitor." He didn't seem disturbed. On the contrary he seemed to be looking forward to the visit and skating on thin ice.

The outcome of a series of disasterous investments lead eventually to the collapse of Alexander Moring, and after a brief period of publishing under the George Turton imprint, Carter sold the rights to Hank Janson to Roberts & Vinter Ltd. Alexander Moring Ltd. moved to 59-61 Union Street, London SE1, but folded after a short while. Carter himself continued to flirt with the law, and was involved some years later in a business scandal which was investigated by the Board of Trade.

GEORGE TURTON
PUBLISHERS LTD.

Robert & Vinter Ltd. continued to publish Janson until 1971, using a number of authors to pen the tales, notably Harold Kelly, William Newton and Victor Norwood, all of whom had been prolific writers for the mushroom publishers. The character of Janson changed dramatically, and in the last few years Janson appeared in a series of pornographic novels that made the novels deemed to be obscene in 1954 seem as tame as a nursery comic.

* * * * * * *

Hank Janson was the last of the 1950s gangster bylines to survive and whilst some companies still exist (Panther and Brown Watson amongst them) they no longer bear any resemblence or connection with their originators. When the name of Janson was sold in 1960 the paperback industry was thriving, with one trade journal estimating that some 70 million paperbacks were sold each year - a turnover of 10 million pounds - with over 200 new titles appearing each month. But these were mostly reprints of hardbacks, and the original paperback, although not dead (indeed it continues as a thriving part of the publishing industry to this day), was only a part of a larger canvas.

The mushroom publishers were essentially the product of the postwar decade; the conditions and motivations that helped them grow are never likely to reappear. They were a phenomenon that has surprisingly - or perhaps not surprisingly - never been studied at length before. This history has, I hope, re-addressed the balance a little and brought forward some of the names and figures who featured in the period of British publishing that could, in the words of Gordon Landsborough, easily have been dismissed as a writers fantasy.

APPENDIX ONE:

THE HORROR COMICS CAMPAIGN

The Horror Comics campaign ran alongside the persecution of British paperback during the early 1950s, eventually grabbing the headlines in late 1954 and culminating in the introduction of the Children and Young Persons (Harmful Publications) Bill in 1955, the government's response to many years of increasing concern at what were originally called "American comics" that had been flooding the country. The campaign later became more narrowed as "Horror Comics" came to the attention of the media, with questions raised in the Church and in the House of Commons. The campaign was accompanied by spirited correspondence in newspapers and groups such as the Comics Campaign Council were formed with an aim to stop the publication of comics that were deemed unsuitable for children.

Fredric Wertham's *Seduction of the Innocent* has historically been seen as the culmination of Wertham's campaign against what he saw as comics capable of corrupting the young. Violence, subliminal sexual messages, racism and outright obscenity were all to be found in comic books aimed at children, said Wertham, an American child psychologist who had long held the view that comics were the root cause of increasing juvenile delinquency amongst the youth of America. The results of Wertham's erratic and hysterical tirade against comics had wide-reaching results in the USA, effectively destroying the trade for crime and horror comics and leading to the foundation of the Comics Code Authority in 1954.

In Britain, *Seduction of the Innocent* was published on February 23 1955 by the Museum Press, only after the introduction of the Harmful Publications Bill to Parliament on February 11. Wertham's work was known in Britain and cited by a number of campaigners during the years of campaigning, but the attacks on Horror Comics came about independently in the UK.

The roots of the campaign date back to the immediate post-war years, but did not gather steam until 1952. Although not the first to voice unhappiness with "American comics", George Pumphrey, a headmaster at a junior school near Horsham, Sussex, was an early campaigner, having found comics in the possession of children at his school; he published his first article against them in 1948 in the pages of *Teacher's World and Schoolmistress* under the title "English or American?". Peter Mauger, a history teacher, was another outspoken critic of the American comics, having first discovered them on a train journey where he was astounded at the concentration - rarely seen in the classroom - of a young boy reading comics.

Pumphrey and Mauger were only two of many teachers and clergymen waking up to the 'threat' of comics. Many local campaigns were launched and newspapers began to pick up the threads of a witch-hunt: in 1949 the Reverend Marcus Morris - later famous for his co-creation and editing of *The Eagle* - voiced his fears in an article for the *Sunday Dispatch* entitled "'Comics' that bring Horror to the Nursery", saying "Morals of little girls in plaits and boys with marbles bulging in their pockets are being corrupted by a torrent of indecent coloured magazines that are flooding the bookstalls and newsagents." These papers were being read by "sons and daughters from seven to seventeen", hardly nursery age.

Morris put into words the worries of many individuals and groups. The growing campaign against comics charted by Martin Barker in his remarkable study of the horror comics, *A Haunt of Fears* (Pluto Press, 1984), is highly recommended. Some of the results of Barker's research and his conclusions, however, are worth repeating here. His research, for instance, showed that amongst the first groups to point the finger at American comics were the British Communist Party, of which Peter Mauger and others involved were members. The Communist Party was running an anti-American campaign under the agenda that many aspects British culture were being Americanised: the CP condemned all American culture, and Mauger in particular condemned American comics, in his speech on children's reading habits at the 1951 Cultural Conference and elsewhere.

The involvement of the Communist Party goes some way to explaining why the thrust of the campaign was for many years against "American comics"; as newspapers and other independent groups became more involved the whole campaign became more narrow in its attack, aimed almost solely at horror and crime comics, and the headlines switched from "American" to "Horror".

The campaign was actually aimed primarily at British black & white editions of American comic books, and British comics in the American format; import restrictions in the post-war years made bringing the real thing in almost impossible.

The growth in the trade of British reprint editions (BREs) had grown up soon after the beginning of the Second World War: the American comicbook was very popular in the UK and had been brought across, along with pulp and film magazines in bulk in the 1930s for sale at Woolworth's and on market stalls. With imports restricted and the major companies cutting down on their output due to the paper shortage, numerous 'pirate' publishers sprang up to take advantage, as they had with the paperback. Paper may have been in short supply, but children were not!

The BRE had come about because of the closing of a loophole during WW2: Midlands publishers Thorpe & Porter realised that the import ban did not extend to newspapers, and was importing Canadian Sunday papers, throwing away the paper and keeping the comic strip section. When the loophole was closed, the publisher imported the printing matrixes and printed his own editions. Thus a whole new industry arose, catering for the young fans of the American comic book and displaced GI's stationed in the UK. There were many publishers involved, producing countless titles, including a number of comics attacked by Wertham in *Seduction of the Innocent*; amongst the titles cited during the British horror campaign were BREs of *Black Magic* (Prize), *Crime SuspenStories* (EC), *Eerie* (Avon), *Ghostly Weird Tales* (Star), *Planet Comics* (Fiction House), *Startling Terror Tales* (Star), *Tales From the Crypt* (EC) and *Vault of Horror* (EC). Probably the two most prolific publishers were Streamline Publications, also known as United Anglo-American Book Co., who produced mostly war and western titles, some of which included their own self-censorship, with some panels removed and replaced with crudely drawn balloons; and L. Miller & Co., best known for reprints of Fawcett publications, including *Captain Marvel* which was to later become *Marvelman*. Leonard Miller's son, Arnold Miller, was head of Arnold Book Company, another prolific publisher of BREs which included the notorious *Haunt of Fear* of which we will hear more shortly.

At the end of the war import restrictions were maintained to help the sterling/ dollar balance of payment. The War Loan accepted by Britain in 1946 was not fully paid off until 1959, and all restrictions lifted; in November 1959, the American publisher of Batman and Superman, National (later known as DC), began exporting their titles to the UK.

The attack on "Horror Comics" came to a head in 1954, when a combination of circumstances finally forced the government into action.

It has always surprised me that the campaign took so long to produce results. Even France, where publishing has always been considered far less restricted, had bought in legislation against comics and children's literature in 1947. Canada banned Horror Comics in 1949, and Australia and New Zealand bought in new rules in 1954. Was Britain slow moving? As early as 1951 the Public Morality Council had drawn attention to the 'problem' in England, but no action was taken by the Home Office. Perhaps Maxwell-Fyfe's campaign against obscene literature overshadowed the Horror Comics campaign.

The campaign against books ground to a halt in 1954 as the number of convictions against publishers dropped. The defenders of books were asking for literary merit to be taken into account, and that the work as a whole had to be read and considered rather than a judgement be made on the titillating extracts read out in court. Books were bad news to prosecute.

Re-enter the comic. Where pornography and obscenity were subjective, as the difficulty in prosecuting books had proved, the Perversion of Our Children may have seemed a far easier target. In May 1953 a meeting of the National Council for the Defence of Children (later the Council for Children's Welfare) was called by Dr. Simon Yudkin, a consultant paediatrician at the Whittington Hospital, London; Yudkin had seen horror comics being passed from bed to bed by children in hospital felt that a more co-ordinated campaign by the numerous small groups would put greater pressure on the government. Out of the meeting came the Comics Campaign Council, chaired by Mr. A.H. Holloway, and with George Pumphrey as its chief publicist. Pumphrey's *Comics and Your Children* was published in 1954, selling over 3000 copies.

The campaign against comics was fuelled by numerous articles in the media: Kingsley Martin wrote a piece in the *New Statesman* (September 1954) entitled "Sadism for Kids", and on September 17 a letter from Pumphrey was published in the *Times Educational Supplement* in which he attacked the Arnold Book Company for publishing a comic entitled *Haunt of Fear* (it was, in fact, made up of EC reprints from *Haunt of Fear 23* and *Shock SuspenStories 14)*. Barker, who interviewed Pumphrey in 1981, quotes him as saying: "It is not too much to say that when I first saw it, I was delighted. I said to myself - this is it, they have gone too far, this is something the campaign can really use".

With the campaign against books behind them, other papers picked up Pumphrey's lead: *Picture Post, The Daily Worker* and *The Daily Dispatch* were just three of many papers to report on the publication of *Haunt of Fear;* the Ministry for Education (Special Services Branch) contacted Pumphrey to borrow the comic and the Institute for the Study and Treatment of Delinquency contacted many campaign bodies and M.P.s which led to a question in parliament. All this, as Barker points out, over one comic.

The acceleration of the campaign after September 1954 was to lead directly to action by the government. In the autumn of 1954 the Comics Campaign Council had a Bill drafted by lawyers which was presented to the then new home secretary, Lloyd George, who would later accept a deputation from the Church of England Education Council led by the Archbishop of Canterbury on November 12.

Another pivotal group involved during this period was the National Union of Teachers (NUT). There had been 14 motions submitted for debate about comics raised at their annual conference in 1952, but there was no great activity until the NUT opened a display of horror comics in London on November 11 1954 to create public awareness of them; it was widely attended by the public and the media, later moving to the House of Commons before touring the country.

The NUT had formed a committee, but a study of their records shows that they were fairly inactive until October 1954 when the exhibition of comics was mooted and put together very quickly. Barker implies that the sudden burst of activity was due to the fact that the NUT were just about to enter a wage negotiation, and needed to be seen as vital to the moral well-being of our nation's children.

The campaign, as seen by Barker, had narrowed its outlook, moving from specific allegations against crime and horror comics until towards the end the media seemed full of emotive but essentially meaningless phrases: "Drive Out the Horror Comics" and "Now Ban This Filth That Poisons Our Children" were just two of the headlines of the day, but there was little evidence outside of repetitive accusations to show exactly what was 'perverted', 'filthy' and 'degrading' about any particular title. However, 'public opinion' was outraged: the tabloids were full of anti-comic hysteria and Randolph Churchill was writing in his introduction to the British edition of *Seduction of the Innocent* that the course of action was for the Director of Public Prosecution to initiate actions against publishers who "enrich themselves at the expense of the minds of young children. If the magistrate or judge should prove to be so illiterate as to fail to punish the defendant, then will be the time to consider an alteration in the law."

There is good reason for him to write thus: to attack individual titles, which was the aim of many, would have required specific charges being brought. Under the laws of the time they would have had to be bought under the Obscene Publications Act then under review and which even the Home Secretary admitted had itself become perverted by judicial decisions: the word 'obscene' was already proving difficult to define and was open to so many interpretations, as the campaign against books had proven, and it was unlikely that a successful prosecution could be brought on horror or crime comics which, whilst violent, could hardly be accused of being sexually explicit, which was the thrust of the campaign against books. Only Fredric Wertham and his followers could see sex in every frame, even in the shadow of a man's shoulder blade.

Since the horror comics were not unlawful, the campaign thrust became to change the law and *make* them unlawful. This meant government legislation, which the government was slow to take. Churchill's blinkered attitude (only an illiterate judge would fail to punish the defendant?) and formulaic branding of horror comics as obscene contained the same ingredients as all pressure groups use to whip up support: generalise about their 'filthiness' (by late 1954 nobody dared deny that the horror comics were filthy, but nobody could pinpoint the exact nature of their filthiness other than to extract single frames or parts of frames which generally supported the idea that they were violent and unwholesome, as Wertham had); imply that their publication degraded the minds of children and turned them into monsters*; imply that they are published by shameless men who reap a vast profit from producing sordid material aimed at the defenceless minds of children and distributed by equally callous vendors (e.g. headlines such as "Still Cashing in on Muck"); imply that "all those men and women who want their children to grow up kindly, decent human beings are joining in" (and by implication that inaction would damn them to a future as unkindly, indecent human beings); ignore evidence to the contrary (a contemporary study by the Committee on Maladjusted Children chaired by Lord Underwood did not mention comics as being a cause for maladjustment or disturbance in children); isolate the argument about comics from other contemporary issues - e.g. the witch-hunting of publishers of 'obscene' books, the rise of Teddy Boys; and, lastly, never let a redeeming feature sway you from your argument (in most of the crime and horror comics under consideration there was always a morality in that the worst guys always came to the stickiest end, although this is probably the most subjective argument used in pro-comics campaigns)

The situation in late 1954 made it impossible for action *not* to be taken: the Home Secretary, Major Lloyd-George, had received a draft proposal from the Comics Campaign Council and the NUT exhibition and calls for action had whipped up the House. The result was the publication of the Children and Young Persons (Harmful Publications) Bill on 11 February. The Bill was introduced on February 22 and consisted of two proposals:

1. This Act applies to any book, magazine or other like work which consists of stories told in pictures (with or without the addition of written matter), being stories portraying: -

(a) the commission of crimes; or

(b) acts of violence and cruelty; or

(c) incidents of a repulsive or horrible nature;

in such a way that the work as a whole would tend to corrupt a child or young person into whose hands it might fall (whether by inciting or encouraging him to commit crimes or acts of violence or cruelty or in any other way whatsoever).

2. A person who prints, publishes, sells or lets on hire a work to which this Act applies, or has any such work in his possession for the purpose of selling it or letting it on hire, shall be guilty of an offence and liable, on summary conviction, to imprisonment for a term not exceeding four months or to a fine not exceeding one hundred pounds or to both.

The Bill was met with a lot of opposition, although a great deal of the debate was more concerned with clarifying the position of newspapers such as the *News of the World* and the *Empire News* which (according to M.P. Michael Foot) were pornographic and made vast sums of money for their publishers. There was also the argument that the Bill's aims were not clear, that it retained the Hicklin rule of "tendency to corrupt" which at the same time was under attack from the Herbert Committee Bill which hoped to clarify the problems with obscene publications, and that it was vague. A picture-spread about war in *Picture Post* could well fall into the bounds of the Bill.

However, the Bill was given a second reading and referred to a Committee where there would be an opportunity to amend. The Committee opened its discussions on 24 March, ending on March 29, and whilst numerous amendments were suggested, only two accepted: that all proceedings under the Bill were to be undertaken with the consent of the Attorney-General, and that the Bill was limited to a ten year duration. When the Bill reached the House of Lords there were further amendments which protected vendors who could prove that they had not read the contents of a work or had no reason to suspect that it was one which could be charged under the Act and that the new law limited its scope to publications "of a kind likely to fall into the hands of children or young persons". With these amendments it became the Children and Young Persons (Harmful Publications) Act 1955.

How many cases have been bought under the 1955 Act? To my knowledge only one. The Horror campaign had effectively destroyed the horror comics before the Act was passed. Speaking in February 1955, Sir Hugh Linstead, M.P., said that the two main firms that had been printing and publishing horror comics (Thorpe & Porter of Leicester and Cartoon Art Publications of Glasgow) had stopped publications of this sort and it was now virtually impossible to buy any horror comics. They had been hounded out of existence already.

The end of the Horror Comics era meant that no test cases

could be bought under the Act - no doubt the reason why the Act was renewed ten years later without discussion and is still in force. The one known case was against L. Miller & Co., who had produced so many BREs in the 1950s. Ironically, the new Miller comics were partly reprints from the 1950s horror and crime titles, and the firm was found guilty and fined £25. Perhaps that day in 1970 the campaigners had their final revenge...

*the case most often cited during the British campaign was that of Alan Poole who shot a policeman and was himself shot resisting arrest in 1952; Poole was reported as having a library of comics that ranged from the generally reported 50 to a social worker's estimate of 300. The truth was revealed in a parliamentary debate - Poole possessed one comic, a western.

SELECT BIBLIOGRAPHY

Atkinson, Frank Dictionary of Literary Pseudonyms, 3rd edition (Clive Bingley, 1982)

Barker, Martin A Haunt of Fears (Pluto Press, 1984)

Chevalier, Tracy Twentieth-Century Children's Writers, 3rd edition (St. James Press, 1989)

Chibnall, Steve Reginald Heade: England's Greatest Artist (Books Are Everything, 1991)

Contemporary Authors Vols 1-120 and New Revision Series Vols 1-20 (Gale Research Co., various dates)

Craig, Alec The Banned Books of England and Other Countries (Allen & Unwin, 1962)

Harbottle, Philip & Stephen Holland Vultures of the Void (Borgo Press, 1992)

Hoggart, Richard The Uses of Literacy (Chatto & Windus, 1957)

Holland, Steve The Trials of Hank Janson (Books Are Everything, 1991)

Hubin, Allen J. Crime Fiction 1749-1980 (Garland Publishing Inc., 1984)

Hubin, Allen J. Crime Fiction Supplement 1980-1985 (Garland Publishing Inc., 1987)

Leavis, Q.D. Fiction and the Reading Public (Chatto & Windus, 1932)

Lofts, W.O.G. and D.J.Adley The Men Behind Boys Fiction (Howard Baker, 1970)

Norrie, Ian Mumby's Publishing and Bookselling in the Twentieth Century (6th edition, Bell & Hyman, 1982)

Reilly, John M. Twentieth-Century Crime and Mystery Writers, 2nd edition (St. Martin's Press, 1985)

Rolph, C.H. The Trial of Lady Chatterley (Penguin, 1961)

St. John-Stevas, Norman Obscenity and the Law (Secker & Warburg, 1956)

Steinbrunner, Chris and Otto Penzler Encyclopedia of Mystery and Detection (Harcourt Brace Jovanovich, 1976)

Smith, Curtis C. Twentieth-Century Science Fiction Writers, 2nd edition (St. James Press, 1986)

Tuck, Donald H. The Encyclopedia of Science Fiction and Fantasy Through 1968, 3 Vols (Advent, 1974, 1978, 1982)

Vinson, James Twentieth-Century Romance and Gothic Writers (Gale, 1982)

Vinson, James Twentieth-Century Western Writers (Macmillan, 1982)

Several magazines (at the time of publication) carry articles and features on the "mushroom" publishers as well as on authors and artists from the period. Many of which are articles by Steve Holland These include:

Paperback, Pulp & Comic Collector (Zardoz Books, 20 Whitecroft, Dilton Marsh, Westbury, Wiltshire, England, BA134DJ)

Paperback Parade (Gryphon Publications, PO Box209, Brooklyn, New York, 11228-0209, USA)

Books Are Everything (RC & E Holland, 302 Martin Drive, Richmond, KY.40475)

Copies of each of the above publications can be obtained from Zardoz Books.

In addition various collectors and enthusiasts' events are organised on a regular basis. These are publicised in the above magazines. Further details of these and other related material available from Zardoz Books.

Currently also UK newsstand magazine:-

Book & Magazine Collector, 43-45 St Mary's Road, Ealing, London, W5 5RQ

also carries occasional articles on related material (several written by Steve Holland)

ABOUT THE AUTHOR

Stephen Holland was born at Broomfield, Essex, England on April 13th 1962 (a Friday!). He has been an avid reader for as long as he can remember and quickly built up a library of popular fiction ranging from boys' adventure and comics to '50s paperbacks (particularly SF & Crime).

His research into popular literature began at the age of twelve, firstly with the idea of putting together a magazine. This brought him in touch with fellow researchers Phil Harbottle and Mike Ashley. Since then Steve has seen his articles in print in numerous magazines (*After Image, Comic Cuts, Eagle Times, Fusion, Golden Fun, Paperback, Pulp & Comic Collector, Paperback Parade, Book & Magazine Collector, CADS, Million, Midweek, Books are Everything, Comic Journal* and many more).

He has written over a dozen paperback bibliographies for Dragonby Press (1984-1990), edited and produced the *Fantasy Fanzine Index* (1986) for the British Fantasy Society. As a tribute to one of his favourite artists he wrote *"The Mike Western Story"* in 1990 and together with David Ashford produced *"Thriller Picture Library: An Illustrated Guide"* (A&B Whitworth, 1991).

His forays into paperback culture gave rise to his book *"The Trials of Hank Janson"* (Books Are Everything, 1991). He also contributes annually to the *"Comic Book Price Guide For Great Britain"*. In 1992 after a long delay Borgo Press published his opus *"Vultures of the Void - A History of British Science Fiction Publishing, 1946-1956"*, written as a collaboration with co-author Philip Harbottle. Yet to appear from the same publisher is the companion volume *"British Science Fiction Paperbacks, 1949-1956: An Annotated Bibliography"*.

Current projects include a *"Price Guide to British Paperbacks"*, due out from Zeon in 1994.

Steve is currently editor and writer for the newsstand magazine *"Comic World" (winner of the 1993 CCG Special Award)*

By The Same Author

The Trials of Hank Janson (1991)

The Fleetway Companion (1992)

The Power Pack: An Index To Power Comics (1993)

With David Ashford

Thriller Comics Library: An Illustrated Guide (3 Vols, 1991-92)

The Comet Collectors Guide (1992)

Super Detective Library: An Illustrated Guide (1992)

The Sun Collectors Guide (1992)

Cowboy Comics Library: An Illustrated Guide (1993)

With Philip Harbottle

Vultures Of The Void: A History of British Science Fiction 1946-1956 (1992)

British Science Fiction Paperbacks, 1949-1956: An Annoted Bibliography (1993)

Below & Across: Prewar Cherry Tree & Hutchinsons paperbacks & 50s BREs of *Weird Tales*. Also British uncanny/weird magazine of late '50s *Phantom (over)*.

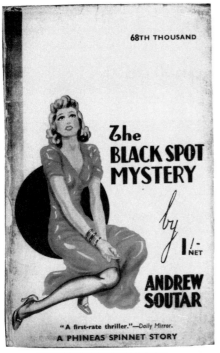

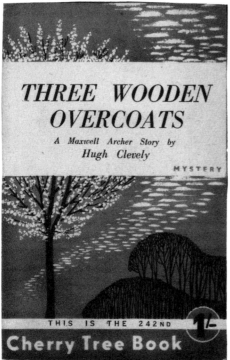

INDEX

THE
ARCHER PRESS LTD.

TRANSWORLD PUBLISHERS
LONDON

CURTIS   BOOKS
LONDON   ENGLAND

FICTION HOUSE, LTD.,
162A STRAND,
LONDON, W.C.2.

FUTURISTIC
SCIENCE STORIES

GAYWOOD PRESS LTD.,
36, GAYWOOD STREET, LONDON, S.E.1.

MARK GOULDEN LTD., LONDON
Distributed by
W. H. ALLEN

 SENTINEL PUBLICATIONS (LONDON) LIMITED

 A SMASHING WESTERN

 A SUNDOWN Book

 NOVA S-F NOVELS

 NEW WORLDS fiction of the future

 POCKETS

Published by
TEMPEST PUBLISHING COMPANY
BOLTON   LANCS.

Sole Distributors
W. HEAP (Booksellers) LTD., Baker Street, Rochdale

Printed by
CARTER, HALLS & CO., LTD.
COVENTRY

 TIT-BITS SCIENCE-FICTION LIBRARY

THE
DISSENTIZENS
BY
BRUNO G. CONDRAY

PUBLISHED BY
UNITED ANGLO-AMERICAN BOOK CO.,
LONDON

 WDL BOOKS

THE MUSHROOM JUNGLE

GET A **KANER** BOOK

MILESTONE PUBLICATIONS LTD.

98 GREAT RUSSELL STREET
LONDON, W.C.1

 MORING
WESTERNS

FREDERICK MULLER LTD
LONDON

Published by
MUIR-WATSON LTD.

A Panther Book

PENGUIN BOOKS LIMITED
HARMONDSWORTH MIDDLESEX ENGLAND

PHOENIX PRESS
Hamilton House, 45 Kennington Lane, London, S.E.11

Seductive
Dangerous
and Thrilling

Printed in England and Published by
EDWIN SELF & CO. LTD.,
44, GRAY'S INN ROAD, HOLBORN,
LONDON, W.C.1.

THE MUSHROOM JUNGLE